# COOPER

## AND THE

## Enchanted

## *M*etal

## Detector

# cooper

### AND THE Enchanted Metal Detector

ADAM OSTERWEIL

namelos

South Hampton, New Hampshire

First edition

Library of Congress Control Number: 2012938164

ISBN 978-1-60898-149-6 (hardcover : alk. paper)
ISBN 978-1-60898-150-2 (pbk. : alk. paper)
ISBN 978-1-60898-151-9 (ebk.)

## ACKNOWLEDGMENTS

I would like to thank Taylor Murphy, Raymond Ledda, Aly Dayton, Kaylee
Mendelman, Jake Talmage, Finn Wainwright, Luke Valentine, and Amy
Turner for read-testing this book during the draft stages, and for the
encouragement and support they gave me throughout the writing process.

namelos
www.namelos.com

*For Mom, Aunt Susan, Aunt Barbara,
and Cousin Lisa, who taught me that antiquing
adventures can open up a portal to the past.*

*For Dad, who showed me how to metal-detect
as soon as I could walk.*

# CHAPTER 1

## GARAGE SALE

Saturday 9 A.M. to 4 P.M.
11 Cemetery Road
(Just off Route 17, southeast of Elmira)
Books, toys, bric-a-brac, kayak,
furniture, linens, clothes, etc.

SOMETHING FOR EVERYONE

**No Early Birds**

My name is Cooper, and when I turned nine I started going to garage sales on my bike. I have a blue bicycle with a basket on the front. I named the bicycle Squeaky because the wheels make strange noises when they spin. It sounds like *Please don't oil me, Cooper. Please don't oil me, Cooper. Please don't oil me, Cooper.* After I pick up some speed, it's more like *PleasedontoilmeCooper, pleasedontoilmeCooper, pleasedontoilmeCooper.* The brakes groan whenever I press them—a long, complaining whine—because Squeaky knows I'm going to get off him soon. He doesn't want to be alone. Squeaky and I have been friends for a long time, and he's been bringing me to garage sales for almost two years already.

A long time ago I thought a *garage sale* meant that people were selling their garage. First they had to sell all the stuff inside of it, and then a truck would come and cart the garage away. Sometimes they're called *yard sales.* That really messed with my mind. I imagined a big yellow machine lifting the lawn away, all the way down to the lava at the center of the Earth. Later, I learned that those names mean that people are selling a lot of their old junk, and they just put it in their garage or on the lawn. That way strangers don't come into the house and get the rug dirty.

There are some secrets to reading a garage sale advertisement. *No Early Birds* means you shouldn't go there before the official starting time listed in the ad. There are hidden treasures at garage sales—stuff that's worth a lot of money that people sell for a quarter—but you have to find them before somebody else does. That's why customers try to sneak in early to get the best stuff. Mom taught me all about garage sales. But neither of us can figure out what *bric-a-brac* means.

I have a confession to make.

I'm an early bird.

It was a chilly summer morning when I pedaled Squeaky to the garage sale at 11 Cemetery Road. Rays of sunshine squeezed through the clouds and made speckles on the distant forests. I live in Upstate New York, on the side of a hill overlooking the Chemung River Valley. At the bottom of the valley lies the Chemung River, which wanders next to a highway called Route 17. The river is silent, but loud trucks roar down the highway all day long. They're heading to a town called Elmira. Mom once said that if I ever try to cross the highway by myself, she'll sprout wings and bring me home, and then I'll really be in trouble. Squeaky and I are stuck going to garage sales on our side of the valley.

The ad said not to arrive before 9 A.M., but we showed up at 8 A.M. We weren't the only early birds. A bunch of other people were already lined up on the sidewalk. I recognized the man at the front of the line right away. It was Mr. Shepherd. He runs the Elmira Museum. I went there on a school trip once. The inside of that place smells like a lonely shelf that hasn't been dusted for a thousand years, and wherever Mr. Shepherd goes, the smell follows.

The best way to get to know Mr. Shepherd is to imagine an ancient kingdom hidden away in a green valley. Deer nibble on grass, and rabbits hop through meadows filled with sunflowers. Scruffy people live in yellow huts surrounded by flocks of sheep. In the sunniest part of the valley there's a big castle with tall towers. On a castle balcony, Mr. Shepherd sits on a golden throne. He has one long eyebrow and a big shiny forehead that goes to the top of his noggin. He's only one head taller than most of the kingdom's children. He wears a furry jacket even when it's warm out. Around his neck dangles a purple amulet that has all the evil in the world jammed into it. When he rubs the amulet, the bunnies and deer stop nibbling and run over to the next valley. Clouds cover the sun, and it rains on the villagers. Lightning hits Mr. Shepherd's nose, creating little red craters there.

"Cooper, you still haven't oiled that bike?" he asked. I see him a lot at garage sales. Sometimes he gets inside before me and walks away with the hidden treasure. But the real reason I don't like him is that he wants to hurt Squeaky.

"No," I said, getting off my bike and letting it fall onto the grass.

"One day I'll oil it for you," he said. His furry jacket was open, and I could see the purple amulet glinting in the sunlight.

"Don't. Please."

I walked up to the house, which had a rough stone chimney and round windows surrounded by lumpy rocks. The garage was closed because the people inside were still setting up for the sale.

"How about getting in line like the rest of us," Mr. Shepherd said.

I knocked on a small oval door on the side of the garage. A lady with red hair opened it and said, "No early birds. Oh, hello, young man."

I scanned the inside of the garage, which was filled with tables of items for sale. Most of it was worthless junk—

plastic dolls with cut hair, tricycles, modern furniture, chipped plates, new games. I can usually spot the one hidden treasure in only a few seconds. Mom taught me how to do it in the days when we used to go to garage sales together. You need really quick eyes and total concentration.

My gaze jumped from a bunch of rusty golf clubs, to some fishing poles, to a table full of kitchen stuff. And there it was—the hidden treasure. A large, dented cup made of pewter, which is a gray metal that people long ago thought was pretty. The cup was from colonial times, before the United States was its own country. Mom told me there aren't many cups of this type left. Now it's a valuable antique.

"Hello, Earth to young man, can I help you?" The red-haired lady waved her hand in front of my eyes.

"Have you seen my lost kitten, Fluffy?" I stuck out my bottom lip and made a pouting face.

"Oh, you lost your cat? You poor thing."

"He only drinks milk from metal containers. Can I buy that metal cup from you?" Bigger pout.

The lady turned around and looked at the cup that I was pointing at. "Herb, bring that big cup over here."

A man came out of the shadows and handed the cup to the lady. She put it in my hands. There was a tag on it that said 25¢. I handed a quarter to the lady and wiped away a fake tear.

"Thanks, ma'am."

On my way back to Squeaky, I waved at Mr. Shepherd and held up the pewter cup. Everybody in line started mumbling and complaining.

"Cooper does it again," he said. "I'd like to see you pout like that when you're forty."

I placed the cup in the basket and pedaled toward home.

"What'd you get today?" Squeaky asked.

"Pewter cup. Probably from the seventeen hundreds."

"Sweet. Your mom will like that."

"I know. If this sells fast enough, it will pay the electricity bill."

# CHAPTER 2

Our house sits at the back of a dead-end street, the last home built at the top of the valley before it became too steep. On clear days we can see across the highway and the river, past big green farms, all the way to tree-covered mountains on the other side of the valley.

Our front yard is covered in gravel. Our backyard is mostly weeds. Beyond the weeds is a steep hill covered with two types of trees—the ones that stay green all year round, and the ones that shed their leaves for the winter. I know those woods are haunted because I hear banging, yelling, and drumbeats whenever the moon is full. I purposely don't cut the weeds so that whatever is back there won't come into our house. Tall weeds have lots of ticks in them.

There's one spot where the forest is so steep it's more like a cliff. Only small bushes can grow on it, and big chunks of dirt fall off and make piles at the bottom. At the top is a lumpy ridge. It looks like a big train that got stuck above our house as it rumbled through the mountains. There's a grassy clearing on top of the caboose. I call it Ghost Conductor's Bluff—that's where the leader of the ghosts stands when there's a full moon. His big shadow falls on our roof while me and Mom are sleeping. The Ghost Conductor looks down on the valley, deciding which houses all the other ghosts should haunt. But then he frowns because of the weeds and just tells everybody to go *Woo-woo* like ghosts do.

Mom runs an antique store out of an old, rotting barn next to our house. The roof is made of metal, and on rainy days it sounds like rocks are falling. Our store has no sign, and we don't advertise, but somehow everybody knows we're open for business. It's like a permanent garage sale, only we don't carry naked plastic dolls with cut hair and big Lego pieces covered in dried baby puke. We only carry the good stuff—antiques that I find at garage sales or that people bring here to sell to us. And the people who buy from us come from all over the place. I've counted twenty-two different types of license plates in our front yard, since I started keeping track.

We specialize in local antiques—pewter, clothing, jewelry, toys, books, tools, furniture, and anything else that's at least fifty years old. This valley dates back to the time of the Iroquois, the native people who lived here before Columbus sailed across the Atlantic, before colonists came here from Great Britain, before America became its own country. During the Revolutionary War some battle took place near here, and every summer I can hear cannons firing in the distance on its birthday. I know about it from the old yellow-and-blue signs on our side of the highway. The signs are mostly covered by tree branches, but Squeaky and I have read them. There are also big rocks on people's lawns that have green plaques nailed into them. Every one mentions the year 1779. Mom says there aren't too many better places to live if you like old things.

There's good stuff hidden away in attics and basements all over, and Mom has been showing me how to find it since I was born. My first antiquing memory is pushing a toy train in some basement. It turns out that train was from 1890 and made out of tin. Mom picked me up and whirled me through the air, telling what a good boy I was for finding it. We made a great team—she taught me everything she knew, and on weekends we would go to garage sales, basement sales, attic sales, antique shops, and flea markets (where there aren't really fleas, I finally learned). All I cared about was finding the thing at each place that would make her give me a big hug.

When Squeaky and I struggled onto our gravel lot, there was a yellow car with no roof parked in front of the house. Mom doesn't own a car anymore, so it's always easy to spot customers, even from far away. A man in a white suit was standing next to Mom. He held a toy truck that I had bought at a garage sale a few months earlier. Mom was looking at the ground. That meant she was thinking about lowering the price from what I wrote on the label. I've strictly forbidden any price dropping, even when the customer begs for it.

I quickly hopped off Squeaky, causing him to crash to the gravel. The pewter cup fell out of the basket and rolled onto the rocks.

"Ow," Squeaky said.

There wasn't time to pay attention to his feelings. I ran over to Mom, my heart pounding.

"He wants to pay twenty instead of twenty-five," she said.

I grabbed the truck out of the man's hand. "You can't afford twenty-five, mister? That's food for us for a week. That sure is a nice car you drive. Why don't you drive it back to…" I looked over at the car. "Pennsylvania."

The man stared into my eyes and rubbed his chin. Then he looked down at my ripped jeans. They have holes big enough for my knees to fit through. I like them that way because they keep me cool in the summer. My sneakers also have holes that my big toes poke through. That way if my pinkie toes ever try to escape and go *Wee wee wee* all the way home, the big toes can bust out and drag those little brats back.

The man looked at our house for a while, and then

at the barn. I didn't know what he was looking for. Finally he took out a fat wallet, opened it, put a folded-up bill in my palm, and closed my hand around it. Smiling, he gently plucked the truck out of Mom's hand.

"Spunky kid. Reminds me of myself when I was young." He walked away, his boots making crunching noises on the gravel.

The car roared to life and backed out of the yard. A cloud of dust choked my bicycle. Soon we were left with only the endless sounds of summer insects buzzing in the weeds.

"This is turning into a bad day," Squeaky said, coughing.

I looked down at my hand. In it was a fifty-dollar bill. Mom stared at me, waiting to see what I would say. She knew how much trouble she was in. I frowned at her, but I didn't say anything.

The best way to picture Mom is to imagine a rocky cliff riddled with caves next to a pounding ocean. It's night-time, and dark clouds cover the moon. The smell of sea-weed tickles your nose, and howling wind sends sea spray into your eyes. High up in a cavern lit by glowing crystals, in a pool of sparkling blue water, sits a mermaid with a long tail wrapped around a rock. She has yellow hair that casts a strange shadow on the wall. She never combs it, but somehow it could never be prettier. Her eyes glow like the water, and when she stares straight at a human, her perfect beauty makes them fall to their knees and lose the power of their legs. She's lonely in that cave, but the tide went out a long time ago and never came back, stranding her up there.

I frowned even more, trying to hold in a smile.

She drooped her head.

Then I wrapped my arms around her and gave her a big hug. I closed my eyes and inhaled the scent of pure

Mom—not some dumb soap with chemicals in it. She hasn't taken a bath in a week, and I don't force her to.

"How many times have I told you not to lower prices? It makes me so mad."

"It was only five dollars. I thought it might be okay."

"It's not." I took another deep breath and closed my eyes.

"Every antique shop haggles."

"I don't care. If everybody jumped in a lake, would you do that too?"

Mom pulled away from me and looked at me with a serious expression. She stared at my face for a long time. Then she burst out laughing—a loud shrieking that made the insects stop chattering for a moment. She fell back into her aluminum chair and laughed more. Her whole body was shaking.

"What's so funny?"

"Come over here, Cooper."

I walked over. She cupped my face in her hands really hard.

"What are you doing?" I said through puckered lips.

"You're so beautiful, I can hardly believe my eyes."

"Look who's talking."

I sat on her lap and leaned my head on her shoulder. We were quiet while branches scraped against the barn's metal roof. A tall line of pine trees comes up from the direction of the Chemung River, goes past the dark side of the barn, and connects to the steep mountain in the back. Thorny jungles of bushes and vines are jammed between the trunks. We live near the end of the mountain, so we should be able to see other valleys off to the side, but wilderness blocks the view. We can only see down into the Chemung River Valley. I know a secret way through the wall of trees, but I don't use it too often because I need to help Mom with customers.

Things aren't like they used to be. Mom sold the car a few years ago, and we don't go to garage sales together anymore. Something changed in her. For a long time I tried to get her to bike with me to garage sales, but some days I couldn't even make her get out of bed. So I started going to garage sales on my own. Mom kept teaching me about old things with her books, and our antique business stayed open. Then one day I found a huge pile of unpaid bills under her bed. Since then I've been in charge of pretty much everything. Dad's no help because he hasn't been around since I was little. Every once in a while a letter comes in the mail, with "Somewhere in Europe" as the return address. That way we don't figure out where he lives and force him to pay money to support me. But he's dumb to write that—the postmark is from an American city, and the letter has an American stamp on it. If he ever turns up here, I'm going to throw gravel at his car until he leaves, like I do to the bill collectors. Business isn't so good lately. People aren't buying antiques like they used to.

"I found something," I finally said.

"Is it going to make me smile?"

"Maybe."

I scrambled over to Squeaky, petted him to lift his spirits a little, and then snatched the pewter cup from the gravel. I ran back to Mom and handed it to her. She held the metal cup in one hand and put the other over her mouth. Then she shot to her feet and paced across the gravel—all the way into the barn and back out. She always does that.

Mom paced for a long time, and each time she came out into the sunlight I clamped my eyes shut like I was taking a picture of her. The image got stuck in my brain and then faded away. So I had to keep doing it.

One of my favorite things about Mom is that her sneakers have a big white strip across the bottom that disappears whenever she takes a step. The rubber is so bouncy that it squeezes into nothingness under the weight of her skinny body. When I'm done taking brain pictures, I watch her sneakers for a long time, wondering how rubber could just disappear like that. I always get disappointed that my rubber strips hardly squash down at all when I walk, but it would be dumb to get new sneakers just for that.

Mom finally stopped in the doorway of the barn. She turned the cup over and looked at the bottom, jamming it right into her face so that her eye was almost touching it. The little hairs on my arms tingled, like they always do when Mom examines my treasures. Then she closed her eyes. I don't know where she goes when she does that, but I imagine that she has the power to see the whole life of the antique—the person who made it, all the people who owned it, and the last person to use it.

"Peter Young, late eighteenth century," Mom said, opening her eyes. "You can see the mark on the bottom."

I ran over to her. She pointed to the letters "PY" stamped in a little circle on the bottom. That shows who made it.

"Is it good?"

"Cooper, you are a fearless treasure hunter." She sat down with the cup and searched every inch of it. I was waiting for my hug, but she was so interested in the pewter she forgot. I knew she would spend the rest of the day cleaning it, looking it up in pewter books, reading about how they were made, and then teaching me a whole bunch of new things about pewter. But when it comes to the price she'll make me pick it. I always have to write out the price labels and stick them on everything.

"I'm gonna pay the electricity bill. Are there any stamps left?"

"One."

"That one's no good, postage has gone up since then."

"Coop, can you take the spider out of the bathroom?"

I opened the ripped screen door and walked inside. It slammed behind me on broken hinges.

# CHAPTER 3

Our house is dark and smells like a wet cat. Only we don't have a cat and never did. I just made up the Fluffy story to get into garage sales early. I know the smell isn't coming from the blankets and sheets because I do the laundry all the time. It can't be the bathroom because I mop in there until it's spotless. So that leaves the yellow rug. Moppy says not to use her on the rug, so I have no idea how to clean it.

We have a kitchen with a window that looks out at the steep forest in the back. When you enter the house you walk right into it. There's also a couch next to a broken TV, and a small table in the middle. Off to the right of that main room is the bedroom where Mom sleeps. To the left is my bedroom and a door that leads to the bathroom. The smelly yellow rug covers the floor of the whole house, except the bathroom. Actually, I forgot one thing: there's another door on the right, and it leads to a closet with the washing machine and Moppy. So just to review—two doors on the right (closet and Mom's room), two doors on the left (bathroom and my room), kitchen and couch in the main room.

I walked into my room and sat down at the desk where I pay the bills. I only ever send cash because Mom doesn't have a bank account. I keep our money in a coffee tin. Koala, a stuffed bear I've had since I was a baby, lives in my room. He's gray. His eyes are closed, and he has no mouth below his plastic nose, just a lot of fur. I love him, but sometimes I can't understand what he's saying. I try to be nice because you can't blame somebody for not having a mouth.

"Hefflw, Coofer," Koala said. "Hof wut youf day?"

"Fine," I said impatiently. "Go to bed, I have to pay bills."

Then I felt guilty, so I leapt onto the bed and gave Koala a hug. We communicate mostly by squeezing. Then I got up carefully to avoid hitting my head on the bed above mine. I have a bunk bed because Mom and Dad originally wanted two kids. I keep a pillow and blanket up there clumped into the shape of a small body. I even know what my little brother's name should be: Tanner. Both of our names are jobs that people had in olden times. A cooper is somebody who makes barrels, and a tanner is somebody who makes leather.

Sometimes I imagine that Tanner and I are wrestling and having fun and banging into walls. The room smells like little-brother sweat, and his face turns red from giggling. We try to be quiet so Mom won't notice, but Tanner can't stop giggling. I cover him with a blanket. I put my palm over his mouth, but the laughter squeezes through my wet fingers. Mom yells, "Don't make me come down there!" Only I know Mom would never say anything like that. Also, our house is only one story.

I remembered that Mom asked me to get rid of a spider in the bathroom. I grabbed the electricity bill and ran in there. My usual way of getting rid of a spider is to let it crawl onto a piece of paper and then run outside to free the spider. We don't kill things because it could change the future. Mom told me all about it when I was little.

It's like this:

If I kill a spider, it will never get to have babies. If it was going to have 100 babies someday, then I would actually kill 101 spiders just by killing this one. But there's more—if each one of those 100 baby spiders was going to have 100 babies someday, then I've actually killed 10,001 spiders by killing this one, because I've killed the spider, its children, and its grandchildren. If you fast-forward a million years, I've killed trillions of spiders—maybe all the spiders on the planet, if this one spider was the ancestor of them all. And spiders help the world by eating flies, so maybe the whole Earth is overrun with flies, and humans don't exist anymore.

Mom reads too many books and thinks about things too much. Sometimes I wonder if that's why she won't leave home anymore. If she goes into Elmira, she might bump into a lady and cause her to fall down. If the ambulance bringing the lady to the hospital runs over a squirrel, that squirrel will never have kids, grandkids, and great-grandkids, all the way to the year One Million when there are no more squirrels anymore. Earth is just a big pile of nuts and nobody can breathe or move. The people use futuristic technology to find out why this happened, and they trace it back to Mom. They time-travel back here and yell at her. She doesn't need that.

I lie awake at night wondering if that's what's going through Mom's head. My goal is to get Mom to come with me to garage sales again. There's nothing better than finding a rare treasure hidden away in a dusty corner of somebody's attic and whispering excitedly about it, crouched over, trying not to bump our heads on the big wooden beam covered with spider webs and mouse droppings. Mom giggles, and I give her my scowl that tells her to be quiet before someone yells, "Don't make me come up there!" Then we climb down the ladder and enter the real world again.

I put the spider outside through the rip in the screen door and shooed it away from the house. Then I ran back to my room and jammed the fifty dollars into the envelope. My tongue licked the gross glue, and I spit a blob onto the rug to get rid of the taste. I went back to the front door and dropped the envelope on the floor until I could ask Jill for a new stamp. I was tired from getting up early, so I went back to my room, crawled into my bottom bunk, and took a nap while holding Koala.

This is where I slept for a while. Sleep. Sleep. Sleep.

When I woke up I leapt out of bed and looked out my window. Mom was leaning over a big hardcover book, her eyes closed. I ran outside and tiptoed past her, into the barn. It's really hard not to make noise while walking on gravel, especially when your sneakers only squash down a little.

The inside of our antique shop doesn't make sense. Everything is just lying around randomly on tables or the concrete floor. I know I should put the pottery together in one spot and do the same for the books, clothes, tools, and other stuff. But I never have time. I keep telling Mom to organize it, but she never does.

Sometimes I stand around in the gloom and look at the stuff, wondering if Mom's power is inside me too. What kid played with the metal soldiers speckled with orange paint, or the board game covered with farm animals? There's a bumpy metal washboard that people used before washing machines were invented. What was the last piece of clothing that was washed on it? Hanging from a hook on the wall is an old sword with a dull blade. Was it ever sharp, and did anyone get hurt with it?

Suppose a boy came home from a one-room schoolhouse in 1829. He ran inside and started playing with his metal toy soldiers. Then his little brother came in. They played the farm board game, but only if the little brother could be the iron pig. After dinner they were supposed to wash their dad's clothes on the washboard because he had gotten all sweaty from farming. But when they were getting out the washboard they found the old metal sword, and they played pirates instead. The next day their dad went out to farm in smelly clothes. The smell upset the chickens, and they began clucking wildly. Dad became frustrated and kept the boys home from school to tend the chickens. The kids missed a geography lesson at school, and they were a little less smart about the world.

Whatever happened with these antiques, it's over, and nothing can change it. The future is not done yet, and that's what makes it so scary to Mom. The worst part is that every little thing, like stepping on a spider, or even deciding what to eat, can cause one of those chain reactions that change the future in a big way. That's why she likes to live in the past, and I have to make all the big decisions—like what price to put on our antiques.

I grabbed a sticker from the back of the barn and wrote "$300" on it in permanent marker. Then I brought the sticker out to Mom and gently stuck it on the end of her nose. I sat in my little aluminum chair and smiled.

She woke up with a confused look on her face.

"I'm hungry," I said. "Mario's is having a special. Free garlic knots with a pizza."

"Did I miss any customers?" She closed the book.

I shook my head. "I'm hungry."

"No meat."

"I know, just plain and knots."

"Wait, your lesson." She opened the giant book and showed me a page full of pictures of pewter plates. "Point to the reproduction." A reproduction is a fake antique—a copy made to look like the real thing. Reproductions are hardly worth anything.

I pointed to a shiny plate.

"No, shiny or dull has nothing to do with it. Try again."

I pointed to a dented plate.

"No, look at this one. It has a line here that shows it was made by machine, not hand. Hand-made plates don't have a seam like this."

I giggled. It was so funny seeing her talk seriously about plates with a sticker on the end of her nose. She finally found it and pulled it off slowly.

"Brat!" She laughed and pulled me into her lap, tickling me until I begged her to stop. Then she saw a cut on my knee and got all serious again. "What's this?" She pushed away the torn fabric to show the whole cut.

"From the gravel."

"Show it to Jill when she gets home."

"What else should I do?"

"Put the sticker on the cup." She stuck it on the end of my nose.

"No, c'mon, what else?"

"Nothing else."

"About the highway?"

"If you cross that highway, I'll sprout wings and bring you back in my sharp claws."

"My teeth?" I grabbed my top lip and folded it up to my nose.

"Did you brush them today?"

I shook my head.

"Brush them, silly."

"And the garage sale ad?"

"Did you leave it on the table so I know where you went?"

I shook my head.

"Cooper, you have to do that tomorrow."

"What else?"

"Order the pizza, I guess."

I kissed Mom on the cheek and walked over to our neighbor's house. The nice lady there named Jill lets us use her phone because ours has been shut off for a long time. She's usually at work, but she told me where the key is hidden. It's inside a fake rock.

Whenever I go inside her house, I get jealous about how nice her carpet smells. I dropped down on my hands and knees and sniffed the white rug. My brain got filled with the scent of Jill's feet, rainbows, fairies, angels, and baby powder. Some of the carpet fibers got jammed in my nose and made me go into a sneezing fit. Through the screen door I could see Squeaky sleeping where I had left him on our gravel lot. Good thing he didn't see me—I'd never hear the end of it.

# CHAPTER 4

---

## GARAGE SALE
Sunday Only 9 A.M. to 4 P.M.
Iroquois artwork, beads, pottery, tools, crafts,
and more. Something for Everyone.
**No Early Birds**
29 Sullivan Crest Road, southeast of Elmira

---

The next morning I didn't want to get up for garage sales. My stomach felt like I had swallowed a bowling ball. Usually I can eat pizza for lunch, dinner, midnight snack, and breakfast the next morning, but I think the garlic knots made it heavier.

I rolled out of bed and trudged over to my old scale in the corner. I stepped onto it. Eighty pounds. Usually I can barely break seventy-five. Squeaky says it's good I'm small, for two reasons:

1. It hurts him less.

2. I can talk my way into garage sales easier.

There's an old broken mirror opposite the scale that's missing a lot of its reflection. Sometimes I stand on the scale and just stare at myself for a long time. My hair is down to my shoulders—I don't cut it because hair weighs a lot. I just wish it was yellow instead of black. I have hardly any muscles, even when I try. I can't pinch any flesh together anywhere, except where my muscles should be—and six ribs are showing, up from five last month. I have a zillion freckles. I'm always afraid they're going to start talking, and then I'll never have peace and quiet for the rest of my life. The only good thing is that my lips are really big. It's perfect for pouting. Sometimes I practice my lost-kitten face in the mirror, just so I don't embarrass myself when I'm out on the road.

"Mirror, tell me when I'm going to grow tall." Pout.

"Please, I'm old, and I've answered that question thousands of times. You humans are always so concerned with your looks. Nobody ever asks me how I'm feeling—which is bad, in case you care. And pouting won't do any good. You just look silly."

Of course, I get stuck with the grumpy mirror. We sold all the nice antique mirrors in our shop. They're always the first things to go, and the hardest to carry home.

"You're booful, Coofer," Koala said. "Mom saif so."

I quickly got dressed and kissed Koala and Tanner goodbye. Then I walked into the kitchen, grabbed a slice of pizza, and threw it on the table. I picked off the cheese and ate it first.

It was a misty morning. The whole valley was hidden inside one giant summer cloud. On days like this I imagine I've woken up in heaven. Squeaky brings me to the first garage sale, where there are a hundred people lined up outside. I smile at the nice lady by the garage door, and she lets me in early. Under a pile of books I find an original copy of the Declaration of Independence—the essay that the colonists wrote to tell Great Britain that we didn't want to be part of their country anymore. I blink my eyes to make sure it's real. The date says "July 4, 1776" in big letters. Fireworks go off inside my head when I see the price tag—25¢. I pay the lady and race back home, Squeaky begging me the whole time to tell him what I bought. Mom gives me a record-breaking hug. I sell it for a million dollars, and Mom and I retire to Florida and swim in blue water with brightly colored fish.

"We're here," Squeaky announced. "Wake up, Cooper."

I didn't even realize that Squeaky had driven me all the way to the garage sale listed in the ad. It was a tiny house covered completely with ivy, including the garage.

Mr. Shepherd was waiting at the curb. A few antique dealers from Elmira were lined up behind him, just like always.

"We couldn't see into the mist," Mr. Shepherd said. "But we could hear Cooper coming. This time, how about getting in line like the rest of us?" He wore thin blue gloves, bright red pants with a lion stitched into one leg, and sneakers with yellow sparkles in them. His furry jacket was closed, but I knew the evil purple amulet was there because of the silver chain around his neck. All of the above, plus his big shiny forehead, were covered in a clear plastic raincoat—so thin that it was almost invisible. It wasn't even raining out.

"Why?" I walked up a stone path and knocked on the door on the side of the garage.

"No early birds," a voice said from inside. The door creaked open, and a lady with tan skin appeared. Deep wrinkles covered her whole face, even her lips. A waterfall of pure white hair started on top of her head, dribbled down her shoulders, flowed past a necklace made out of shiny coins, tumbled past her waist, wrapped around her bathrobe twice, and then trickled all the way to her feet, where a stuffed turtle with huggy arms kept the hair clamped together. Then I followed the waterfall back up until my eyes found the valleys cut into her face. They looked familiar, like I was sitting on a satellite in outer space looking down at Upstate New York.

She stared at me for a long time without blinking or saying anything—gazing right into my eyes and making me feel lightheaded. I couldn't move my head or look away. Shadows danced on her dark pupils—within them I saw small figures and reflections of misty trees. I wondered if she was having a summer daydream too.

"Oh, hello, Little Butterfly," the lady finally said.

"Have you seen my lost cat, Fluffy?" Pout. I scanned the inside of her garage for hidden treasures—there were lots of paintings, paintbrushes, easels, sculptures, a computer, and other stuff that wouldn't be good for our antique shop. Then in the corner, hanging on the wall, I spotted a very old blanket with symbols stitched into it—from left to right there was a square, a rectangle, a tree, a rectangle, and then another square. The blanket was oddly shaped. It looked sort of like this:

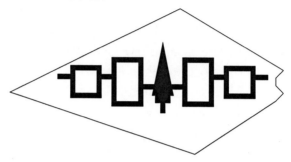

"Yes, I did find a cat, as a matter of fact," the lady said. "I gave her some milk. Poor thing."

"Huh?"

"Your cat's not allergic to milk, is she?"

"No, but she's probably cold. I should really wrap her up in a blanket when I find her."

"Fluffy would probably like that eighteenth-century hand-stitched Iroquois deerskin, wouldn't she?" She pointed to the blanket on the wall.

"I can't speak for sure about Fluffy, but it would be a helpful addition to the equation."

The lady laughed. "Oh, Little Butterfly, you haven't changed at all."

"You know me?"

"Like I know the sun, the moon, the stars, and the rain. Like I know the rustle of leaves in the forest." She stared at me with those big black marbles again, but I didn't see any images in them this time. The melody of her voice made my spine tingle, and the little hairs on my neck stood up.

"About that blanket . . ."

"It's a quarter. Do you have that kind of cash?"

"I think I can manage." I dug a quarter out of my pocket and gave it to her.

"A New York quarter. How perfect." The lady squeezed through piles of stuff, mumbling to herself, until she reached the far end of the garage. She carefully took down the blanket, folded it neatly, and made her way back over to me. She placed the blanket in my hands.

"Thanks, ma'am."

"You're very welcome, Little Butterfly."

I walked back toward Squeaky holding the blanket carefully in my arms. While Mr. Shepherd and everybody else scowled at me, I gently stuffed the antique blanket into the basket and got ready to pedal away.

"Little Butterfly, you forgot to ask which way Fluffy went." The lady stood on the concrete stoop and waved at me.

"Oh, which way did he go?"

"Back toward your house."

"Okay, thanks."

"Little Butterfly, will you do me a favor before you leave?"

"Okay."

"Will you take this old junk and put it in that garbage pail?"

I put Squeaky down on the pavement, blanket and all, and walked back to the lady. She handed me a strange-looking device that had a white plastic disc connected by a long pole to an electronic box. There was an armrest and a little TV display. It didn't look much like old junk, but I lugged it toward the garbage pail on the side of the house.

That's when I heard a noise coming from the white plastic disc. It sounded like crying.

# CHAPTER 5

"What are you?" I asked.

"A metal detector," the machine replied. The white plastic disc had deep scratches on the bottom in the shape of a mouth, a nose, and two eyes. The mouth was at an angle and slightly open, the eyes were different sizes, and the nose was flattened. It looked like a face that had been squashed like a pancake. I decided not to put it in the garbage pail until I asked more questions.

"Why are you crying?"

"Would *you* like to be thrown away?" It bent its plastic neck and looked up at me with sad eyes.

"I guess I could take you home even though you're not an antique."

"I'm Decto," the metal detector said.

"I'm Cooper."

The lady smiled and shut the door. When I got back to my bike with the metal detector, Mr. Shepherd was folding the blanket, which had fallen out of the basket. He gave me trouble, just like always.

"Cooper, this is a rare Iroquois artifact—it belongs in the Elmira Museum." He stomped his foot and held the blanket tightly against his crinkly raincoat.

"If you don't put the blanket back, my metal detector will bite you." Decto stared at me with wide eyes.

"I'll pay you ten dollars for it."

"Come to our antique shop tomorrow, but it will be more."

"I'm a good customer, Cooper. Have you seen the

museum lately? Many of the items are from your store." He gently put the blanket into the basket.

"You should be a braver early bird. Try it." I turned Decto's face so that he wasn't looking at me anymore.

"Will you sell the blanket for twenty dollars?"

"There's better stuff in there." I pointed at the ivy-covered garage.

"Really? What? Iroquois jewelry? Clothing?"

"Go see."

Mr. Shepherd stomped his foot again, tore off the clear plastic raincoat, and unzipped his furry jacket. He rubbed the purple amulet around his neck. I looked up in the sky, but there were no lightning bolts or other signs of pure evil.

"Why not?" He walked confidently up to the door and knocked on it. The metal detector lady opened it. Her wrinkled lips were shaped into a frown.

"No early birds."

"Thank you for helping my nephew locate his lost kitten. Is that an original frame on that oil painting?" Mr. Shepherd pointed inside.

"If that's your nephew, then I'm Minnie Mouse. I'll be open in half an hour." She slammed the door. Mr. Shepherd drooped his head.

I put Decto on the handlebars and hopped on Squeaky. While I pedaled away, Mr. Shepherd was trudging back to the line of people at the curb. The sun was starting to break through the mist, and my knees didn't feel so chilly. It was hard to balance on the bike with so much stuff. It didn't help that I was laughing almost the whole way home.

"Decto, it would be helpful if next time you backed me up."

"I've never bitten anyone before."

"You didn't really have to bite. Just growl or something."

"I'll try." Decto's neck suddenly got really long and

rammed into my foot. He hissed at me. My heart started pounding, and I swerved Squeaky. Me, Squeaky, and Decto screamed as we raced toward an old tree at the curb. I slammed on the brakes just in time, leaving a black line in the road.

"Not now, you kooky metal detector! Next time there's an enemy."

"It burns! It burns!" Squeaky said.

I put Decto's pole back in place, gently petted Squeaky, and struggled back onto the road. When we weren't in danger of wiping out, I decided to make conversation with Decto.

"What are you for?"

"I find metal underground, like lost coins and jewelry. My face scans the ground, and whenever I smell metal down there, the electronic box beeps. Then a human digs it up."

"Wow, you could really come in handy. Garage sales are only on the weekend. I could use you during the week to dig up valuable stuff. This area is really old."

"I eat twelve double-A batteries, and I go to bed at ten."

"You two are getting a little heavy," Squeaky complained.

"I think we're gonna be good friends," I said to Decto. "Like me and Squeaky." I patted Squeaky, and he squeaked in return.

I pulled into our gravel lot, where Mom was sitting in her usual spot. I let Squeaky crash to the ground, but I promised to make it up to him sometime. I placed the metal detector by the front door and then ran over to her with the blanket. She went through her whole routine again, examining the blanket, mumbling, pacing in and out of the barn, me taking mind pictures, the hair on my arms tingling. It never gets old.

Mom spent a long time with her eyes closed, which

meant that this blanket was really old and had a lot of history to it. Then I did something that I'd never done before—I didn't wait for my hug. I just ran to the front door, picked up the metal detector, and struggled inside with it, banging it against the broken screen door a few times. I stepped over the envelope and ran into my room. I plunked the metal detector on the floor. It was time for a full examination.

The white plastic disc was about the size of a dinner plate but as thick as three plates. It had a lot of dirt and scratches on the bottom, besides the deeper grooves that looked like a face. A gray wire came out of the disc, spiraled around the long pole, and plugged into a black box with the words TREASURE SEEKER 5000XS written on its side. The box was covered with buttons and knobs and had a little TV screen sticking up. Underneath there was a foam handle for holding the metal detector. At the far end of the metal detector there was a little armrest made out of curved plastic. I stuck my arm in there and wrapped my fingers around the foam handle. It was pretty comfortable, except I'm not that strong, so I still needed my other hand to help lift the whole thing up.

"That tickles," Decto said.

"I've never had any electronic toys. I'm going to try you." I pressed the ON button. There was a little musical sound, and the TV screen came to life. Strange beeps and bloops came out of it, and a bunch of numbers flashed on the screen. The numbers kept changing.

"There is metal in the floor," Decto said. "It's better to use me outside."

"Whuf thaf?" Koala asked.

"A metal detector. I'll tell you all about it tonight. We're going outside."

I was so excited about looking for lost treasure that I kicked open the screen door. Maybe I did it too hard. The bottom hinge fell off, and the door swung at a strange angle. Mom must have thought I was fighting off aliens or something because she opened her eyes and broke out of her trance. I did feel pretty special bursting out of the house with my new hi-tech gadget. Not to mention that the broken door could mean my legs are getting stronger.

I carried Decto over to a patch of moss on the side of the house. When I hit the power button this time, a low hum came from the electronic box. A zero appeared on the little screen. I put my arm in the plastic holder and held the foam handle so that the plastic disc was hovering over the ground like a miniature UFO.

"Put my face right up against the ground," Decto said. "A short beam comes out that senses metal. The closer I am to the ground, the deeper the beam can go."

I moved the plastic disc so that it touched the moss. Decto's face scraped against the ground. He started sniffing the moss like a hound.

"Now move my face left and right in a big arc."

"In a big what?"

"A big curve."

"Oh, I thought you meant one of those things that holds two of every animal."

I moved the white disc left and right, holding on tight with both hands. It was easy to keep the disc against the ground because Decto is so heavy. Near a small purple flower the electronic box started beeping. Mom walked over to investigate.

"Where did you get that?"

"A lady was throwing it out."

The number 227 appeared on the little screen. I grabbed a stick and poked at the ground a little to the left of the purple flower. It just went through the gooey moss. I picked up Decto and double-checked the spot. The beeping got louder a little to the right of the purple flower. I poked again, and my stick hit something hard. I quickly dug away the dirt with my fingers, getting my nails all grimy. Soon I saw something shiny and red. My heart pounded.

I cleared away some more dirt and saw fancy writing—swirly letters like the kind on the Declaration of Independence. Only this writing said "Coca-Cola." I pulled the object out of the ground. It was a bottle cap—my very first find with a metal detector.

"I wonder who dropped this," I said.

I rubbed the bottle cap on my shirt and cleaned out the dirt. Small letters on the inside read, "Sorry, you are not a winner. Please try again."

"There's never a dull moment with you around," Mom said.

"It's my first find. I'm going to keep it."

# CHAPTER 6

"What used to be on this spot exactly, where our house is?"
I asked Mom.

"This land has been in our family for hundreds of
years," she said. "Since colonial times. It used to be much
bigger, but your great-grandfather sold off most of it during
the Great Depression. Now we just have this small section.
The barn belonged to the old house at the end of the block,
near the cemetery."

My mind was spinning—I wanted to find every buried
secret that was waiting to come up. I looked over at the tall
weeds in the backyard, the ones that guarded us from whatever haunts the steep forest. They would have to go. After
I cut them down, our house wouldn't have any protection
during the next full moon. I didn't want to think about that.

Garage sales are fun, but even the old stuff there has
been touched by people for hundreds of years. A buried
thing hasn't been touched since it was dropped. Like when
I held the bottle cap, I was shaking hands with its original
owner. Who was it? Mom, when she was a little kid, sitting
against the house on a hot summer day? Was she disappointed that she didn't win a prize? I imagined Mom getting angry at her soda and throwing the bottle cap against
the barn. It bounced off and landed next to the purple flower's great-great-great-great-grandflower.

I picked up Decto and began scanning the rest of the
moss patch. The plastic disc kept bumping into Mom's
sneaker.

"Mom, move back."

This time I heard a low beep, and the number 150 appeared on the little screen. I decided that I needed a shovel before I could do any more metal-detecting. The old cast-iron shovel in our antique shop would be worth keeping if it was going to help dig up old treasures. I ran to get it and then went back to Decto and Mom. The ground was hard and full of rocks, but I leaned on the shovel with all my weight. A big scoop of dirt came out and landed on Mom's sneaker. I went over the hole again with the metal detector to see if I was digging in the right spot.

I was off by a lot. Mom got bored and went back to her aluminum chair. Then I dug a new hole out of the side of the old one, this time in the correct spot. I dug for a long time, and every time I scanned the hole with the metal detector, there was another low beep. After a while I was up to my elbow in the hole.

Finally when I swung Decto over the hole there was no beep at all, but he beeped when I ran him over the mound of dirt next to it. I had dug the object out! I quickly spread the dirt around, searching for whatever it was. And then I found it—a round ball that looked like a big marble. It was heavy and squashed on one side.

My heart sank. Metal-detecting was harder than I thought. All that work for a squashed little ball of metal.

"What is this, Decto?" I shoved it in his face.

"Hmm, I've found some of those before, but I forgot what they are."

I spent the next few hours searching the rest of the little moss-covered patch. By the time I was done I had found twelve of those little balls. Some of them were dented and strangely shaped, but others were perfectly round. I piled them all up near the bottle cap.

The weird thing about metal-detecting was that after each hole, all I wanted to do was dig another hole. It didn't really matter what I found. It's very cool to hold something that nobody's seen for a long time, even if it's a little heavy marble that can't even roll.

"Where should we go next, Decto?"

Decto grunted and spit some dirt out.

"It's all gravel in the front and weeds in the back," I said.

"Cut down a small patch of weeds," Decto suggested. "That way I can take a little nap." He made a snoring noise and closed his eyes.

For the rest of the day I used an antique clipper to cut down weeds that were taller than me. My stomach rumbled. Bugs danced on my face. Sweat dripped off the end of my nose. Crickets hopped everywhere. Whenever I saw a tick, I jumped around and swatted myself until it was gone. Some flying bugs got disturbed and escaped into the steep forest. They sing a long song that goes on forever, because by the time one bug stops, another has started up. There's no peace and quiet in the summer.

Come to think of it, the forest is never quiet. In the winter, when the whole valley is frosty and the birds have gone away, the trees drop things that clunk on the forest floor—sticks and pinecones and nuts. At night I can hear them from my bedroom. The forest can't even go a hundred seconds without dropping a new thing. I've counted. Sometimes the stuff rolls down the hillside toward our house. I've never figured out if it's the naked trees or the green ones that drop stuff, though.

It took until dusk to clear a small chunk of the backyard. A pile of cricket-free, melody-free, tick-filled weeds sat behind the barn. My hands were shaking from holding the heavy clippers. I flopped on my back and looked up at the top of our peak, where birds spiraled around Ghost Conductor's Bluff. Sweat dripped into my mouth, reminding me of the salty flavor of food. My tongue wanted more, so I licked my lips, thinking about the cool breeze that must be blowing up there. It's one of the world's secret spots, right in my backyard—my own private mountain peak that nobody knows about except me, Mom, and the forest creatures.

If only it wasn't so haunted.

I leaned back and stared at the towering pines that march beside our barn and connect to the steep forest. Our land would be better if that wall of trees didn't block our view of the other valleys on that side. The Chemung River Valley is pretty, and it feels safe to be cornered by giant pines and a steep forest, but the rest of the Earth seems so far away. I closed my eyes and hoped something good was buried in our little hidden backyard.

Soon the wind began howling, and black clouds appeared on the far side of the valley. Thunderstorms around here are tricky. It can be clear over our peak, but above the distant mountain lightning flashes silently every few seconds, as if the humans are battling giant robots that are heading this way. It's not long before we're overrun and big booming footsteps shake the windows.

The rain got me to my feet.

I slammed the barn doors shut and clamped the rusty lock in place. I shooed Mom inside and bolted the front door. The wind moaned and blew the aluminum chairs across the gravel lot. Squeaky is too heavy to blow around, but I knew I was going to hear it from him about how I brought Decto inside but not him. He gets jealous about the littlest things.

# CHAPTER 7

Thunderstorms are nice because me and Mom are trapped in our cozy little house. Nobody goes anywhere during a thunderstorm, even people who aren't afraid to go out in the world—so it's almost like we're a normal family for a little while. But it would have been better if we had sold an antique so that I could have ordered food just before the storm hit. That pizza didn't last long, and my coffee tin only had change left in it and a Canadian dollar. I should have cracked open the electricity bill and used that money—usually they give you plenty of warning before they shut off the power. One time I didn't pay the bill for six months before they put a yellow sticker on the front door.

After I ate crackers and drank water to fill my stomach, I went into my room and waited for Mom to come in for bedtime stories. My clothes were covered in grass clippings, bugs, and dirt, so I threw them in the corner and put on my pajamas. I hopped into bed and waited for Mom.

Soon I heard coughing from the floor. Decto was wheezing. "Usually I get cleaned. I ate dirt, and your sweat was dripping on me all day." He spit out some brown specks.

"Decto, I'm so tired. I can't move. Can Koala do it?" I picked up Koala and put him on the floor. My arms were still shaking from those heavy clippers, so I could barely lift him.

"Whuf?" Koala seemed too frightened to walk closer to the metal detector. Lightning crashed nearby and lit up the room.

"This is the scene I get to reflect in my twilight years," Mirror said. "As if anybody cares."

I must have dozed off. When I cracked open my eyes, Mom's face was hovering over me. A soft glow came from the tiny lamp on my desk. I pretended that I had stumbled into her mermaid's cavern and collapsed after looking at her beautiful face. My shaking hand could barely reach up to squeeze her soft hair.

"Why do you humans always come to my cave?" she said, holding my hand.

"Because you're a beautiful mermaid, duh. Everybody's talking about you."

"Don't they know—"

"Talk louder so Tanner can hear the story," I interrupted, pointing to the top bunk.

"Don't you humans know that once you enter my cave, you won't be able to leave. You'll be lying helplessly on the ground, slowly transforming into a mermaid."

"Can boys be mermaids?"

"Yes, there are merboys."

"Will I become one?"

"Yes, but I'm not sure how."

"I know," I said. "When a boy falls to the ground, if the mermaid beats him in a staring contest, then he becomes a merboy."

Mom put her face right up to mine. I opened my eyes wide and stared back. We were locked in a battle for a long time, and my eyes started feeling tingly. The power drained from my legs as they transformed into a tail. I opened my eyes really wide.

Mom stuck out her tongue a little and quickly pulled it back. I giggled and blinked.

"Now you're a merboy," she said.

"You cheated!"

"A mermaid can win any way she wants. There are no rules in the cave."

"Some people have to escape."

"Nobody escapes."

"Then how does everybody know you're here?"

"Oh, a smart boy has shown up. What's out there for you, anyway?"

"The king is doing mean things, and we're going to sneak into the castle and take his purple amulet."

"I suppose I could let you go, but first I have a question that only a human boy could answer."

"What?"

"Why are you covered in dirt and grass?" She rubbed something off my face.

"I was working all day."

"Don't you think you should take a bath?"

"Too tired."

"Cooper, you're filthy. You smell like weeds. You're covered in sweat."

"So, you haven't taken a bath in a week."

"Fine, but don't complain to me when you're all itchy tomorrow."

"No, keep going," I said, squeezing her hand. "About the bath."

"You're covered in germs."

"What else?" I smiled.

"You're going to track dirt all over the house."

"What's going to happen if I don't listen to you?"

"I'll be mad."

"How mad?"

"I'll take your metal detector."

"If you do, I'll slam my door and yell."

"I might start with something smaller, actually."

"No, Mom, stick with the metal detector. You were doing good. Now what are you going to do when I yell?"

"Cover my ears?" She looked confused.

I giggled. "I'm going to take a bath." I kissed Mom on the cheek and walked out of the room.

After my bath I cuddled with Koala while thunder rumbled in the distance. My whole bed was covered with dirt and grass, getting me filthy again. Mom's lucky I'm so responsible—if little Tanner was actually here, he'd take advantage of her. He wouldn't ever go to bed or take a bath.

I stared up at the top bunk, which had thick wooden planks holding up Tanner's mattress. I wondered if his small body would make the beams sag a little. Would his snoring be really loud? Would he admire me like a little brother is supposed to? Or complain that there was no food in the house and his stomach hurt? Maybe I wouldn't be smart enough to take care of a little brother. My last thought before dozing off was about how cutting down the weeds would make it easier for the ghosts to come into our house and scare him.

# CHAPTER 8

The next morning I decided that if nobody bought anything by noon, I would tear open the electricity bill and order groceries. They deliver if you spend at least fifty dollars. If I just got thirty boxes of spaghetti, some bread, juice, and tomato sauce, then we would be prepared for an emergency. There are people in the world who have underground bunkers packed with food in case the Earth gets split in two by a meteor and the nearest grocery store ends up on the other half. I wasn't prepared for a thunderstorm. Dumb, Cooper, dumb.

First, I went into the kitchen and emptied the bucket that catches water dripping from the ceiling. It had overflowed and made a big wet spot on the rug. Second, I went outside and fetched the aluminum chairs from the street. I put them back where Mom likes to sit, just beyond the shade of the towering pines. Third, I picked up the green garbage pail that belongs to Jill and put it near her garage. Fourth, I fixed the gravel by the house where water running off the roof had pushed away a long line of rocks. Dirt from the ravine splashed all the way to Squeaky. Fifth, I unlocked the shed and examined the antiques inside. Last, I apologized to Squeaky.

"You like him more than me," Squeaky said as I gently brushed off dirt with my hands.

"He's just new."

"But he finds treasure. You'll always like that more."

"So do you. Don't you remember all the mornings we came back with garage sale stuff? Like that metal bank where you press a button and a monkey dove through a hoop and put a penny in a barrel. We played with that forever on the side of the road before coming home."

"I couldn't press the button."

"I pressed it for you, and you laughed each time."

"Cooper, I wish I was human."

"Yeah, Squeaky. That would be cool." I gently patted him.

The little pile of marbles was in the same place I had left it—on the side of the house, right next to the old cast-iron shovel and clippers. They don't make things like they used to.

When I looked at the backyard, I realized that it was going to take longer than I thought to clear the weeds. I had only done a small spot, and the whole place was covered in dewy spider webs. The crickets that had lost a home chirped even louder from other parts of the yard. I felt guilty because eventually most of the yard would be cut down, and all the crickets would have to find a new home.

I clipped weeds all morning and kicked big bundles of stalks onto the pile behind the barn. During the breaks I looked up at Ghost Conductor's Bluff and wondered if there was any way I could climb up there. Then I could take over as leader of this land and wake the big lumpy train that got stuck there ages ago. Its crumbly wheels would slowly turn as it chugged off the end of the mountain, into the sky, and over to the bigger mountain that's hidden behind the wall of pine trees. That way the ghosts would bother somebody else for a while.

When the sun came over the trees and burned the back of my neck, I struggled to finish the last part of a big square that was five times as long as me. It went close to the steep forest, but I left just enough weeds to protect us.

That's when a car pulled onto the gravel. Perfect timing—we were out of money, so this customer *had* to buy something. I dropped the heavy clippers and ran around to the front of the house. Mr. Shepherd was getting out of his green pickup truck. He wore baggy pants that had one orange leg and one blue leg. They were tied onto him with a golden belt.

"How are you folks today?"

"My feet ache," Mom said from her chair.

"Well, that's interesting. How are you folks today?"

I can always tell when Mr. Shepherd is nervous because he repeats whatever he just said. While he bumbled around, I fetched the Iroquois blanket from inside the barn, ran back outside, and threw it at him. He made a funny noise and caught it like he was snatching a falling puppy.

"It's one hundred dollars."

Mr. Shepherd immediately stopped caring about how any folks were doing today and pulled a magnifying glass out of a hidden pocket in his furry jacket. He shut one eye and jammed the other into the lens. He examined every inch of the blanket while me and Mom watched. I'll say one good thing about Mr. Shepherd—his concentration is amazing. A nuclear sunbeam could blast through the magnifying glass and set his sparkly sneakers on fire, and he wouldn't blink his giant eye until the flames got close to the blanket.

What upsets me the most about Mr. Shepherd is that his sneakers don't squash down when he walks. You can tell a lot about a person by that little strip of rubber. On Mom's sneakers the strip just disappears. Poof, gone, abracadabra! But Mr. Shepherd's twinkling yellow sneakers don't flatten at all—they're like solid bricks stomping around.

You can also tell a lot about a person by how much they sweat in the blazing sun. I melt like an ice cream cone, which makes up for my sneakers squishing only a little. Mom sweats a medium amount, adding a pinch of sweetness to her smell by the evening. Mr. Shepherd doesn't sweat at all, even in a furry jacket. And after all that non-sweating, *he's* the one who stinks like a thousand years' worth of dust.

Mr. Shepherd finally pulled the magnifying glass away from his big eye and put it back in his jacket. Then he pulled out a little electronic device and starting pressing his finger against the glass screen. The gadget beeped and flashed lots of words and pictures. I don't like those little things because they hiss at me, and who wants a little know-it-all freak sitting in your pocket?

"Cooper, the museum is on a limited budget. I know you don't like to go down in price, but would you take fifty dollars?"

Mom stared at me like she was trying to win another contest.

My stomach rumbled. I really wanted to eat something, and fifty dollars would buy a lot of food without me having to open up the electricity bill. But I couldn't do it. I never go down in price. I stared at the bottoms of Mom's sneakers and said, "It's a hundred dollars. You know it's worth way more." My legs were shaking, and I felt dizzy.

Mr. Shepherd pulled out a red wallet and gave me five crisp twenty-dollar bills. I couldn't believe it. There they were in my hand. I could buy food for two weeks, pay the water bill, and give Jill the twenty dollars I owed her for Mom's medicine. (She's studying to become a doctor and is the second-prettiest woman ever.) I really wanted to shout and dance around, but I couldn't do that in front of Mr. Shepherd.

I couldn't help it—I smiled.

"So the boy does know how to smile," he said. "Did you find anything with your metal detector?"

He was starting to get all conversational, but I wasn't going to let him get too close to me just because he gave me a hundred bucks. "A pile of marbles and a bottle cap. I have to go make a call."

"That's strange. Marbles aren't made of metal."

"These are."

"Where are they? Wait, one minute." He walked over to his pickup truck and gently placed the Iroquois blanket on the front seat. Then he walked back over to me. I led him over to the pile of marbles on the side of the house by the moss patch. He knelt down and pulled a smaller magnifying glass out of another hidden pocket. He held one of the marbles between two fingers and examined it for a long time.

"Cooper, do you know what these are? They're musket balls. A pile of musket balls from the Revolutionary War. Do you have any idea of the importance of this find?"

I stared at the craters in Mr. Shepherd's nose and didn't say anything. The sun was trying to make me sneeze, and I fought off a couple of half-sneezes until I finally gave up and launched myself backwards with the biggest kachooey of my life. Then I shivered as the truth seeped into my body.

Those ghosts in the woods were there for a reason.

# CHAPTER 9

"Cooper, how much do you know about the Revolutionary War?"

"The colonies didn't want to be part of Great Britain anymore because the king was making them pay too many taxes. They wanted to be their own country. That's what they wrote in the Declaration of Independence."

"That's right. The war lasted from 1775 to 1783. There were battles all up and down the colonies, out at sea, and even in other countries. But one particular battle was fought right on this side of the valley."

"I thought it was up where that cannon fire comes from every year. You mean all those signs down by the highway are leading to my house?" I couldn't believe that after teaching me about antiques my whole life, Mom never mentioned that there was a Revolutionary War battle in our yard. Then again, she won't kill spiders, and she won't even *talk* about something that has to do with killing.

"The Battle of Newtown took place on this hillside in August of 1779. Did you learn about that battle in school?"

"Maybe." I was too ashamed to tell Mr. Shepherd that I don't do very well in school. My mind wanders away, and by the time it comes back the teacher is too far into the lesson.

"The British and their allies were hidden below that ridge—" He pointed to the imaginary train bursting off the top of the steep forest. "The colonists were marching along the river, lined up neatly in rows. Can you imagine over four thousand soldiers carrying long brass muskets that fired lead balls like the ones you found? The guns fired only one shot at a time, and they had to be hand-loaded by pushing the musket ball and gunpowder down the barrel with a ramrod. Soldiers could fire three shots a minute if they were good at it."

"Was it a big battle?"

"It had nearly one-quarter of George Washington's army in it. But they were all walking into an ambush. About a mile north of here, at the highest point of this mountain, there's a state park commemorating the battle."

"Then why aren't the musket balls buried in the park?"

"The battle took place over five square miles, much of it outside the boundaries of the state park. This land was already under private ownership, so it wasn't included in the park. The exact hotspots of the fighting have never been excavated. Most of them have probably been paved over by roads, spoiled by houses, or plowed through by farms. Cooper, your yard is part of a historic landmark. It really needs to be dug up by archaeologists. These finds need to be mapped, catalogued, and placed in a museum."

"Are musket balls worth anything?"

"Cooper, you can't sell anything you find. They need to be studied—for the sake of history. The museum—"

"You never stop talking about that museum. It's my yard, and I can do what I want."

Mr. Shepherd got down on his knees and put his arms on my shoulders. "Cooper, don't you want other kids to look at these items and learn about the Revolutionary War—to know how bravely people fought for your freedom? Don't you ever daydream that you were part of it all, back in simpler times, carrying your musket into battle?"

"You shouldn't kill people. When you kill one person, you kill a billion."

"That's very smart. Who taught you that?"

I motioned with my head to Mom. My hair got caught in my mouth, and I had to spit it out.

"Then maybe you could have been the drummer boy. Back in those days a young boy would lead the troops into battle. He wouldn't carry a weapon, just a drum. His drumbeats kept the soldiers marching at the correct pace."

"Mr. Shepherd, I'm really hungry." I held my stomach.

"Stop by the Historical Society sometime. It's on the second floor of the Elmira Museum. There's so much I can tell you about this battle." He handed me a business card and walked back to his truck.

"Mr. Shepherd, my musket balls!" I ran after him.

"Oh, silly me." He handed me the musket balls.

I counted twelve of them before I stopped frowning.

"Cooper, I want you to write down the exact spots where you find each item. Can you do that for me?" He pulled a piece of paper from his back seat, put it on a clipboard, and then attached a pen with the words ELMIRA HISTORICAL SOCIETY written down the side of it. He placed the clipboard in my hand. The paper had a grid of little boxes printed on it.

"Why was it called the Battle of Newtown? We're near Elmira."

"There used to be an Iroquois village called Newtown not far from here, near where the highway is today. Back in those days the highway was just a well-worn trail that passed by the village." He got into his truck and slammed the door.

For some reason I didn't walk away. I just stood there staring at him—through his face, back to colonial times, when this whole area was forests, rivers, and trails. Trucks didn't barrel down the highway disturbing the peace and quiet, and from inside the morning fog boomed the sound of drumbeats. Wearing tattered pants and carrying a drum,

I marched in front of a huge army, my face covered in dirt and sweat. We passed a small Iroquois village. A lady with black eyes, a wrinkled face, and white hair down to her feet looked up from the blanket she was making and saw me passing. She stared at me curiously. I tried to focus on drumming, but gazing into her eyes I became hypnotized. Within her pupils I saw the reflection of people marching beside misty trees. They journeyed across the whites of her eyes and disappeared above her nose.

I came back to reality when a hand patted me on the cheek.

"I know the sight of a kid hooked on history," Mr. Shepherd said. His furry coat tickled my chin. "I was one myself."

The truck roared to life. As he drove away, I wondered if that coat was made from real fur.

# CHAPTER 10

"I think you could also have been the fifer," Mom said.

Mr. Shepherd's truck disappeared around the corner at the bottom of our steep street. I saw it again for a moment between two trees before it went away for good.

"The what?" I turned around.

"The drummer boy would march front and center, but the fifer boy would march off to the side of the troops."

I couldn't believe that Mom was talking about battle—it made me feel uncomfortable. "Mom, I'm going to Jill's and getting a food delivery." I pulled the pile of twenties out of my pocket and blew the bits of grass and dirt off them.

"Don't you even want to know what a fifer is?"

"Fine, what's a fifer?"

"A fifer is a person who plays a fife—a high-pitched flute. In the old days the fifer would play musical notes to give information to the soldiers, like what time of day it was or when to load their weapons or fire. Fifes are so high-pitched that their sound can be heard miles away, even over the battle sounds."

I looked at Mom and wondered how she knew all this stuff. Then I remembered that she's read every book about every object in existence. There's a loft in our antique barn that has zillions of books about every *thing* in history. Whenever I find a book at a garage sale about stuff—furniture, clothing, dolls, instruments, pewter, or whatever—I buy it so that Mom will have something to read while waiting for customers. I try not to buy any books about weapons or anything like that.

"Why did they pick boys to be drummers and fifers?"

"They were too young to hold those heavy weapons."

I couldn't listen to Mom talk about war stuff anymore. It was like the time she tried to talk about boy/girl stuff at bedtime, and I had to change the subject six times. Anyway, my stomach was rumbling again. I headed into Jill's house to make the food call.

Spaghetti, sauce, bread, lots of fruits and veggies, cheese, double-frosted chocolate cake, and fruit punch. It came out to a little more than fifty bucks. After ordering, I put the twenty dollars I owed Jill on the refrigerator under the magnet shaped like a hamburger. Then I plopped down on the beautiful white carpet and spread my arms and legs out like I was making a snow angel. The fluffy rug always feels good, besides smelling so wonderful. I wondered if I would ever get the courage to ask Jill how she cleans it.

Then I had an idea. *Tanner* could be the fifer.

We could be a team, drumming and fifing during the Revolutionary War. I imagined us going to George Washington's house to sign up. He writes our name on a list with a big pen made from a feather. "It will be dangerous," George Washington says. "People you don't know will be trying to hurt you, but you will never hurt them." Tanner tries out his fife, but the sound comes out wrong, like he's spitting into it.

We make a good team, always traveling together and practicing our instruments. By the time we march into the Battle of Newtown in 1779, Tanner is so good at using his fife that he can play an entire song without missing a note. When we march past the native village by the river, Tanner is with me, and he stops fifing when the lady with the long white hair gazes into his eyes. While drumming, I want to ask him about what he saw on her pupils, but there's no time because musket fire comes from enemy soldiers hidden in the steep forest. Then a horrible fear makes the drumsticks feel heavy—I might never get the chance to talk to him about it. But I don't miss a drumbeat.

When I came out of my daydream I noticed that there were little green and brown specks all over Jill's carpet. I shot to my feet. Dumb, Cooper, dumb. My clothes were covered with weed juice, pine needles, and dirt from my backyard. On my hands and knees I desperately picked up every last speck and shoved them all in my pocket. Then I used spit to rub out as much of the green color as I could. By the time I was done, there were a few dark spots left, but it didn't look so bad.

When I got outside, a man and a woman were browsing inside our antique barn. A big rusty car was parked on the gravel. Things were suddenly good—we had food on the way, customers in the barn, Tanner and I had jobs, I paid back Jill, there was leftover money, and it was time to metal-detect the backyard, where part of an important Revolutionary War battle had taken place. Sometimes on summer days the birds chirp just for me.

I ran inside our house to get Decto. As I came back out, a second car pulled into the gravel lot. It always feels good when there are customers around. Our home seems different when voices echo around the barn. I always want the people to stay in there. Some days I try to sell random things to people as they're walking back to their car, and if I'm really lucky they will go all the way back into the barn to take another look. Mom once said that I could sell winter coats in a desert. I smiled at her and walked into the backyard with my metal detector.

"Okay, Decto, now I know there's going to be good stuff here. Do your thing."

I swung the white disc back and forth over the ground. It felt good to have the soft foam handle in my grip again.

The constant hum of the metal detector was relaxing.

"I'll try, Cooper. I'm still not feeling too well."

I swung the detector back and forth as I walked slowly over the big patch that I had cleared. My arms were shaking a little, and Decto's head kept bumping into roots and weed stumps. In the middle of the clearing Decto started beeping. It was such a faint beep that I could barely hear it. The number 330 appeared on the little screen.

"What is it, Decto? I haven't seen that number before."

"So dizzy," Decto said.

"Oh, Decto, what's wrong?" I patted his white disc.

"Don't worry, just dig, dig, dig. I always gets excited when there's something very deep."

I dug into the soft dirt and made a little hole. Before I went any deeper, I swung Decto's face over the hole to make sure I was digging in the exact spot. This time, I had gotten it right on the first try. I dug and dug and dug. Car doors slammed in the front of the house, and voices chattered, but all I cared about was unearthing the treasure. I kept scanning the big dirt pile to see if the metal item had come out yet. After a long time, I didn't hear a beep when I swung the detector over the hole. The treasure was free and sitting in the pile of dirt!

My fingers squeezed and sifted the dirt, making littler piles that I checked with Decto one by one. I finally narrowed it down to one tiny pile. I stuck my fingers into it and felt something hard. My heart pounding, I grabbed the object and brought it out into the sunlight—it was a small brown disc about the size of a quarter. I wiped away the dirt with my thumb and saw a very light number 4 written on the front, surrounded by a sloppy circle of raised bumps. On the back was a tiny lump in the middle. Whatever this was, the last time a human had touched it was 1779.

I fell backwards onto the dirt, clutching the disc in my hands. I looked up at the blue sky and suddenly realized the entire forest above me was chattering with summer sounds—I was so lost in digging that I had forgotten about the real world.

"Decto, what is this? We found something good." I sat up and jammed it under his face.

"I don't know, Cooper. You should show it to Mr. Shepherd."

"Yeah, I can't wait to see the look on his face. C'mon, give me a high five. I know it's good, whatever it is." I put the brown disc in my pocket and raised my hand.

"A high what?"

"High five, slap my hand." I waved my hand.

"I don't have five of anything." He twisted his neck around and put his white plastic face with droopy eyes against my hand so that I was petting him. He closed his eyes and made a sighing noise. "Cooper, I need to rest in the shade."

"Just one more hole, Decto. I promise." I picked him up and started running around swinging the machine crazily. There were some weird chirps and bleeps, and then the constant hum disappeared for a bit. I jiggled Decto, and the hum came back. I wasn't getting any good signals, so I ran to a new spot closer to the house. When I swung the detector back and forth, a loud beep came out of the electronic box and the number 1000 appeared on the display. A burst of energy raced through my body.

"Decto, we found something!"

When I moved the detector to the left and right, the beep continued for a long time. Usually it's just a quick beep. Whatever this was, it was huge.

"Decto, how deep can you go?"

He didn't make a sound.

"Decto?" The screen was blank. I hit the power button, but nothing happened. I gently placed him down and wiped some dirt and grime off his face. His eyes looked asleep. I jiggled him and pressed the power button over and over again, but he stayed quiet. I picked Decto up and took him around the front of the house.

"We sold the Shirley Temple doll," Mom said. She showed me a pile of money.

"Mom, I have to go somewhere. Back to where I got the blanket. The address is on the counter. It's not far. A nice lady lives there."

"Did you find anything good?"

"Maybe. I'll show you later. When the food delivery comes, put the stuff in the refrigerator. Don't stick your finger in the chocolate cake, and when the delivery person asks how you are, just say 'Good,' not 'My feet ache.'" I handed her the food money. Actually, she had another two hundred from the Shirley Temple doll, so I just took all the money and left her with enough for the groceries and a tip. I didn't want her sitting outside alone with all that cash. I ran inside and put the rest in my coffee tin. On the way out I kicked the screen door open, almost sending it into outer space.

"Slow down," Mom said, grabbing my hand as I was running across the gravel. She pulled me toward her. "You are always running around doing a million things. You're going to wear yourself out."

"Mom, I'm fine." I tried to wriggle free.

"You're out of breath. Take a deep breath."

"There. I did."

"Now drink, you're dehydrated." She put a cup up to my mouth. I took a drink. A stream of refreshment swam through my arms and legs. I drank the whole glass with my eyes closed while breathing through my nose. Mom got some more water while I sat on the gravel, and I drank that too. We sat for a while, leaning against each other in the shade of the house while the strength came back into my body.

"Mom, we're in the money now. I can get the phone back up."

Mom made a noise that sounded like she was agreeing.

"I'll go to the dentist with Jill if you want."

She didn't say anything.

"Mom?"

Her body was shaking. It took me a few seconds to figure out what was going on. At first I thought the noise she made next was laughing, but then I realized it was crying.

# CHAPTER 11

"Mom, c'mon, you need to go inside." I pulled Mom up with all my might while tears streamed down her face. I opened the screen door with my big toe and helped her inside. I led her into the bedroom and onto the bed, and then I took off her sneakers.

I hopped into the bed and put my arm around her while she let out the rest of the crying. Eventually it turned into faint whimpering. When we're in the money again after a long slump, Mom gets enough strength back to be miserable. I think it's like when I get an A on a test instead of the really low grades I normally get—I suddenly know what it's like to be one of those students who have their papers up on the bulletin board. Then I'm unhappy about my grades, and I want to change everything. Only I never do.

A car pulled into the driveway. Soon there was a knock on the screen door. It was the food delivery. I hopped out of bed and ran to the front door.

"How are you doing today?" the woman asked.

"Good, how are you?" I gave her the money and a tip.

"Good." She handed me the bags.

I ran into the kitchen and put a bunch of random food on a plate—fruits, vegetables, a handful of cake, a chunk of bread—and brought it into Mom's room. We ate from the plate quietly until everything was gone. I was so groggy after eating that I put my head on Mom's pillow and closed my eyes.

Mom's voice caught me as I was falling asleep. "You don't have to stay. Go take care of your metal detector."

"I'm staying." I held her tightly.

"I don't know why I was blessed with such a beautiful son and you were cursed with such an awful mother."

Whenever Mom says things like that, I tell her stories from the past. The first one I told was about career day in second grade, when everybody's parents came in to talk about what they do for a job. Mom brought in a whole bunch of antique toys and taught all the kids what it was like to play in the old days. The kids were so excited that they asked a lot of questions, and there wasn't enough time for the next parent to give a talk—and that was Jimmy Egan's dad, who's a fireman.

Then there was the time me and Mom were in some building in Elmira, and I needed to use the restroom. When we got to the bathrooms, there were two doors—one with a picture of a stick figure, and the other with a picture of a stick figure wearing a dress. There weren't any words, so I thought the dress meant that you had to be wearing really baggy shorts. I went in that one. Mom was wearing jeans, and she went through the other door so I wouldn't be embarrassed.

I got interrupted by honking from outside. A car pulled onto the gravel. I rolled out of bed and trudged out of the house. I could barely keep my eyes open.

"Excuse me, young man, do you mind if we look through your antique store?"

"We're closed. Come back tomorrow."

"Can't we just take a peek? We'll be out of state by tomorrow."

"We're closed."

"The barn's right there, I can almost see inside from here."

"Get out."

"Is your mother home?"

I picked up some gravel and walked toward them. "Go away, don't you see?"

They got in their car pretty quickly after that. I thought I heard the words "Crazy kid" as they were pulling away. I closed the barn and put the lock on it.

When I got back to Mom she was fast asleep. My spot was still warm, but I noticed that it was covered with dirt, pine needles, weed clippings, chocolate frosting, and bits of bread. I hopped into the bed anyway and pulled up the ratty blanket to cover Mom.

The next morning I stared at Mom for a while, waiting for the sun to come up a little more. She was breathing softly, and when I leaned close there were two separate nostril breaths tickling my cheek. Her warmth flowed through the air and made me stop shivering. My hand reached over to the plate and felt around for some scraps of chocolate cake. I put my head on the pillow and imagined that we were floating on a raft in the middle of the ocean.

A little later I woke up and looked around. The sun was far enough up. I kissed Mom on the cheek, leaving a little chocolate mark. I jumped out of bed and ran to the bathroom. Then I grabbed Decto, quietly opened the screen door, and told Squeaky to take me to the metal detector lady's house. Sometimes when Mom is sad she sleeps until the barn's shadow is poking into the backyard. I wanted to get home before that.

The chilly morning air woke up my lungs as Squeaky whizzed down the road. Decto sat on the handlebars. He was still quiet. No matter how hard I concentrated, I couldn't get a peep out of him. Mom and Decto—both sick on the same day. It made my insides feel weak.

Spider webs drenched in morning mist looked like little white blankets on the passing lawns. I imagined they were a disease spreading across our side of the valley, one that wouldn't go away until everybody was feeling better. Through the trees I could see the highway and the Chemung River. There were no trucks roaring by to wake everybody up, only some crows high up in the sky making prehistoric noises. I pedaled like crazy and kept my face close to the handlebars. Squeaky zigzagged around a bunch of turns.

A few minutes later I came to the lady's house. I knocked on the door of the ivy-covered garage, then realized that was dumb because she wasn't having a garage sale anymore. I walked down a stone path choked with weeds and came to a red door. I knocked softly. After a long time the door creaked open and the lady appeared. Her long white hair twisted around her nightgown like a flesh-eating alien vine. The stuffed huggy turtle was jammed in her right slipper.

I stepped backwards.

The little lines around her lips changed shape when she recognized me. "Little Butterfly, you've returned!"

"Do you know how to fix Decto?" I held out the metal detector.

"Oh, no! He broke already? Come in."

She led me into a big room that had a tall ceiling with windows in it. You could see the sky from inside. The floor had a brown furry rug that didn't smell. The whole room was filled with shiny sculptures standing on white squares—some smaller ones were on the wall. The lady placed Decto next to a big green chair and disappeared into another room.

I took off my sneakers and walked over to a sculpture. It was a tree with a long trunk and thick branches covered with green leaves. When I got closer I noticed that it was made out of lots of little metal things—slivers of green bottle caps, cut pennies, crushed cans, nails, paper clips, and lots of other little metal scraps. There were thousands of shiny bits all piled on top of each other. When I stepped back, the sculpture looked like a perfect tree again. When

I moved close, it looked like little pieces of metal jumbled together. It was amazing how it changed.

The whole place looked like a museum. I saw a giant butterfly sitting on a flower, a face bursting out of the wall, a big fire with flames leaping out of it, the planet Earth with all the continents, a person walking in a stream, a group of people sitting in front of a long building, a windmill, deer nibbling grass. On the wall was the same symbol I had seen on the Iroquois blanket, a tree surrounded by two squares and two rectangles—only this design was made completely out of coins with buffaloes on them.

In the far corner a brown bird stood on a rock, its shiny beak pointed toward the ceiling. I snuck close, like I was fooling it into showing me what it was really made of. The beak was made from aluminum foil, and its wings were made from hundreds of keys fanned out on top of each other. Then I hopped back and imagined the bird coming to life, stretching its stiff metal wings and soaring through the ceiling window, sending little bits of glass tinkling down. I tiptoed forward and stared into the eyes of the bird, which were made from shiny silver balls.

"I can already tell that you like them," the lady said.

I jumped back from the bird and stood up straight, facing her. "Sorry."

"It's all right, Little Butterfly. They want you to look at them." She knelt down and put a wet glob of paper towel to my face. She wiped my skin while muttering to herself. For a long time she cleaned me. I tightened my lips together and closed my eyes. It hurt when the towel pressed in really hard, but I didn't stop her because it would have been rude. "There, that's better," she finally said.

The lady went over to her green chair and put the dirty towel on a small round table. When she sat down, her long mane of hair scrunched up behind her and looked uncomfortable. She picked up her glasses and put them on with shaky hands. A beam of sunlight shone through the ceiling window and lit up her face. Bones at the top of her cheek pushed the skin out and made her face look strong. I imagined that she could have been a princess once, locked away in a tall tower with only one small window.

"*Metal detector lady, let down your hair,*" *a man said, standing at the bottom of the tower next to a gurgling stream.* "*I want to climb up.*"

"*No, I am waiting for my Little Butterfly. When he arrives, he will flutter up here.*"

"I'm Jan. Shall we take a look at your metal detector now?" She leaned down and picked up Decto.

"Did you make all those sculptures?"

"I did, Little Butterfly." She pushed on the cord connected to Decto's white disc. It snapped in, and Decto's eyes opened wide in shock. Then she picked up the dirty paper towel and wiped Decto all over so that he giggled. "There, it should work now. You have to take good care of your possessions." She wrapped Decto in a small blanket and handed him back to me.

"But you were going to throw him out. You said he was old junk."

"I wasn't going to throw him out. I just wanted to see if you would."

"I don't get it."

"There are some things in this world that are beyond our understanding, Little Butterfly."

Even though she was speaking in riddles, the lady's voice made my spine tingle, and the tiny hairs on my back felt prickly. I didn't even know I had tiny hairs there.

"How come you call me that?" I just wanted her to keep talking.

"Take a seat and I'll tell you a story."

# CHAPTER 12

I sat down on the soft rug and rested Decto next to me. He was snoring inside his blanket. Jan picked up a plate of brownies from the small round table and held it out to me. They looked delicious, but I never eat without Mom around.

"No, thanks."

Jan put down the plate and began her story.

"Little Butterfly, you probably already noticed my heritage. I am of Iroquois descent, Onondaga tribe, turtle clan. The Iroquois have lived in this region for a thousand years. The original name of my people's strong nation is Haudenosaunee. That word means They Are Building a Long House. They built houses that many families lived in. Did you learn about these things in school?"

I shrugged. I didn't want to explain about school to her either.

The fuzzy hairs on my arms stood up as she spoke, and I stared into them deeply, imagining that they were rows of corn stretching into the distance. A big group of people walked out of the cornfield and started building the world's biggest house. It started at the top of the valley, zigzagged down the hillside, went over the Chemung River as a big curved bridge, and then continued across the valley and up the mountain on the other side. It took a thousand years to build, and everybody lived inside of it as one big family. There were bathrooms at both ends, so whichever side of the valley your room was on, you would use the bathroom on that end of the house. If you lived in the room exactly in the middle, over the river, you had a choice.

I imagined walking through the house to the bathroom, passing everybody on the way.

*"Hi, Cooper, how are you today?"*

*"Coop, great to see you!"*

*"Hey, my man, how is Cooper today?"*

I give everybody a high five and tell them how I really am, instead of just saying "Good." After all, we're one big family and we actually care about the answer.

When I stopped thinking, I remembered that I was in Jan's house. She was nestled in the green chair, pulling on the side of a bottle cap. A little rectangle popped off that she put on the small round table.

"Sorry."

"Don't apologize, Little Butterfly. Now I know when your eyes glaze over, you've found something you like. You admire the People of the Longhouse, don't you?"

I nodded.

"That's the power of the Iroquois people," she continued. "People are instantly swept away by the majesty of their culture. And I've only just begun to talk about them." She pointed to that strange design on the wall.

I told her about my imaginary house.

"Longhouses weren't quite that big, and there was no indoor plumbing back then." She pointed to one of the sculptures I had glanced at earlier that showed people sitting in front of a long building. I was so curious that I got up and walked over to it without even asking her permission.

The house was long, but not as super-long as I expected. The building didn't have any windows, and it was only one story. There was a door on each end. The roof was curved and had two holes in it. The sides were held up by a lot of skinny poles, and the whole thing was covered by rough tree bark. I snuck up close to see what the sculpture was made out of. The tree bark was made from brass buttons that were all chewed up and mangled. The poles were made from squashed metal pens. The people were made from thousands of colorful squares, like the piece she took off the bottle cap. It must have taken her a long time to make. I stepped back and looked at the perfect longhouse.

"You make everything so nice. It looks real."

"Little Butterfly, I want you to remember your daydream about the longhouse that stretched across the world. It will become part of the story later."

I hopped back over to Jan and sat on the soft carpet. "That was a good story."

She laughed. "Don't you want to hear the rest of it?"

I shrugged. "I just want you to keep talking."

"We'll get back to the Iroquois sometime, but the next part of the story is about Xavier. Isn't that a wonderful name? X-A-V-I-E-R. Ages ago when I was in France studying art history, I met the most wonderful man. He had never seen anyone of Iroquois descent before, and he swept me off my feet. The first thing he said to me was, 'An eternity will go by, and there will be no more beautiful woman than you. My name is Xavier.' Imagine that in a French accent—it was so romantic. And what was he like? He had a mop of black hair down to his shoulders, bright red lips, and green eyes that shone like emeralds. Anybody who looked into them was instantly envious of those who had his attention. Does that description sound familiar?"

I shrugged.

Jan picked up a mirror from the small round table and dusted it off. That little table sure had room for a lot. She held the mirror so that I could see my face. My black hair was tangled and creeping all over my shoulders. The light from the ceiling windows made my eyes glow bright green. I had never really noticed how bright my eyes were in sunlight.

"I have black hair that touches my shoulders, and green eyes."

"The story continues, Little Butterfly. It was love at first sight for Xavier and me, but over time we learned that the two of us were as compatible as waves and a sandy beach. He painted with oil, and I made sculptures. We loved traveling and searching the world for lost treasures. We married in the jungles of South America and hunted for Spanish gold off the coast of Brazil on our honeymoon. Over the years we searched for Roman coins in the moors of England, dove for shipwrecks off the coast of Florida, and backpacked through Greece looking for hidden ruins. For fifty years we had spectacular adventures—and Xavier never ran out of energy or love for me. I used to call him My Butterfly Who Flapped His Wings and Never Stopped Flapping."

Jan became silent. The little hairs on my back settled down and didn't tickle me anymore.

"Why the sad face, Little Butterfly?"

"Can you tell me more about Xavier?"

"There's always more to tell. Did you know that Xavier considered every piece of metal he dug out of the ground to be a treasure? We were healing the Earth by removing alien objects, cleaning it and making it more like the perfect, pure world it once was. Our basement is full from floor to ceiling with bits of metal, half of them unidentifiable."

"And that's what you make sculptures from?"

"Very good, Little Butterfly. Xavier has touched every little metallic scrap on every sculpture—I cry when a customer buys one, and hope that it will have a good home. You see, when Xavier was about to pass on, he told me not to worry, because even death could not keep us apart. He said that he would come back for me, somehow. When you showed up the morning of the garage sale, I stared into your emerald eyes and saw the reflection of a beautiful woman. It was hazy, and I couldn't tell if it was my lost youth or the object of your own affection—someone whose presence lurks behind your every thought. You flit around with boundless energy trying to please her. Right away I suspected that you were Xavier—reborn, with all of his sweet gentleness, sensitivity, and uncontrollable imagination. And somehow you found me, even though you have a brand-new life now and no memory of the distant past."

My body started shivering when she stopped talking that time. I held myself to try and warm up.

"Little Butterfly, I won't be able to talk forever. Xavier had a favorite metal detector, and that day I decided to test out my theory by having you hold it. I had no intention of throwing it out. I just wanted to see what would happen. When you two hit it off so well, so quickly, I knew for sure that his spirit was inside you. I'm old, and you have your new life now, but somehow I think our kindred spirits still have one adventure left. What do you think of my story, Little Butterfly?"

Sadness washed through me when she stopped talking. I tilted myself over until I crashed against the rug, my face tickled by the fluffy strands. I stared sideways at the million little lines in her face—each one was a soft thread that had the memory of some great adventure inside of it. Together they wove together the most thrilling story ever told. Now I could come visit her whenever I wanted and listen to her voice tell me parts of it. She gazed at me with her dark eyes and strong face.

I smiled.

Then I sat up. Mom. She might have woken up while I wasn't there. I shot to my feet and picked up Decto.

"What's wrong?"

"Mom is sick."

"Go to her, Little Butterfly. You're lucky to have such a perfect mother, who raised you so well."

"You know her?"

"In some ways."

"Wait, you know metal. Do you know what this is?" I reached into my pocket and grabbed the little metal disc I had dug up. I handed it to her.

"It's a button," she said right away. "It once belonged to a piece of clothing. You can see the spot on the back where the shank was once connected. That's the part where the thread would tie on." She pointed to the little bump in the center.

"Why is there a four on the other side?"

"I don't know, but I'm sure Mr. Shepherd will know the answer to that."

"Okay."

I picked up Decto and left the house. I can't remember if I closed the door or not. Squeaky was quiet the whole ride home, so I could think about everything Jan had told me about the Iroquois people and Xavier.

# CHAPTER 13

When I got home, there were no cars on the gravel and the barn was locked. Our mailbox at the curb had thrown up, scattering little pieces of mail around the street. It does that a lot because it's tilted down and the door is loose.

"Sorry, old chap, that is just so rude of me," Mr. Maybox said. That's what I've been calling him since I was little.

"It's okay." I put Decto on the ground, still wrapped in his blanket. Then I gently lowered Squeaky's kickstand and balanced him on it. I ran around and collected the mail. One envelope was red. The water bill. I hadn't paid that in a long time. As I tore it open, I remembered that the electricity bill was still on the yellow rug inside, getting more crumpled each time I stepped on it.

I don't like reading bills that are angry. This one said that the water bill was overdue by a year, they had tried to call us, and if we didn't pay within a month the water would be shut off. We owed almost a hundred dollars. I drooped my head and shoved it in my pocket. There went a lot of the new money.

Sometimes I imagine that I own this whole valley, and nobody would dare send me a bill for water. They'd know that my dungeon was filled with people who tried to cheat me—like the guy who charged me for breathing air and the one who sent me a bill for sunlight. I've heard of a place called Cooperstown somewhere in New York. It sounds nice. Everybody would treat me with respect there. I wouldn't have to worry about too many people asking for my autograph because the Baseball Hall of Fame is also there. It would be perfect.

I went inside and peeked into Mom's bedroom. She was still asleep. I carefully closed her door. After grabbing Mr. Shepherd's clipboard with the boxy paper, a handful of bread, some vegetables, and cheese, I sat with my back against Mom's door. There's a worn spot on the rug that I fit into perfectly, and an old stain on the door from my hair.

While I was munching I got down to some serious work. I drew a picture of our whole property—the house, barn, gravel lot, backyard, the long line of trees that marches past the barn and blocks our view of the valleys on that side, and a little bit of the steep forest and Ghost Conductor's Bluff. Then I made a dot where each treasure was buried—twelve musket balls, the button with the 4 on it, and the mysterious long thing that made Decto sick.

A picture was starting to form on the map—of an awful thing that happened here. I threw down the pencil and the clipboard. A little voice inside my head (who I usually call Stephen) said I shouldn't dig anymore. I was waking up spirits that didn't want to be disturbed. The ghosts were going to be very angry at me during the next full moon.

I reached up and turned the knob on Mom's door. Then I tilted over until it opened enough for me to see her sleeping. My weight on the doorknob made the hinges groan. Mom's peaceful beauty made that little voice inside my head go away. If there was something super-valuable under our yard, I was going to find it and sell it, and then she'd never have to worry about money again.

I closed her door, wiped the crumbs off me, and went outside. I opened the barn for business even though I was going to be in the backyard. My hearing is pretty good, so it's easy to tell when a car pulls onto the gravel. If the rocks pop really loud, that means it's a big car.

I took Decto's blanket off and carried him into the backyard. When I turned him on, his eyes opened wide, and he had a determined look on his face. He sniffed the ground crazily and pulled me along.

"I feel so alive!"

"Decto, I promise to treat you better now. I'll clean you, I'll swing you gently, and you can sleep in my bed with me and Koala."

"Beep, beep, beeeeeeeep!" Decto screamed.

I swung the metal detector over the spot that he signaled, but I didn't hear anything the second time.

"Just kidding," Decto said, laughing.

"Oh, now you're going to be a brat?" Then I noticed that a knob labeled SENSITIVITY was turned all the way up. Jan must have moved it when she was fixing Decto. I turned it down so he wouldn't give fake signals anymore, just the normal hum. I really needed Decto's instruction manual— there were other knobs labeled DISCRIMINATION, MODE, IRON MASK, HEADPHONE VOLUME, DISPLAY, and PROGRAM. Maybe adjusting those things would make Decto find more treasure.

"Time to dig up the mystery object." I waved Decto over the spot near the house where that really long thing was buried. I carved a rectangle on the ground that marked its outline—as long as my whole body!

I turned Decto off and put him gently on the ground. Then I grabbed the antique shovel and got to work. I hoped the object wasn't too deep. Dig, dig, scoop, scrape, cut tiny plant roots, dig more, rest, dig like crazy, drink water.

That's how it went for a few hours until my shovel finally clunked against something metal. I put my arm in the hole up to my elbow. My fingernail scraped something hard. It didn't budge. The whole thing was hopeless. I would have to dig a ravine as long as me and as deep as my arm to get the mysterious object out. With both hands I shoved the mound of dirt into the hole and wrote "Really big mystery" on the map.

I turned Decto back on and searched for a regular signal. I went over the whole rest of the ground in the big square clearing. Not one good beep out of the metal detector. Then I had an idea. That sensitivity button made the metal detector beep even though there was nothing under the ground. Maybe some of the other buttons could make it beep also—only this time there really would be something down there. I turned the knob labeled DISCRIMINATION a little to the left.

As soon as I swung Decto, the metal detector beeped and the number 75 appeared on the little TV screen. That was the lowest number so far. I dug a hole—in the exact right spot—and went through my usual way of digging, then checking to see if the thing was still in the hole. It took only a couple of minutes before I had the treasure in my hand—a rusty blob that made my fingers turn brown. It didn't look like much of anything.

I decided to go over the whole square again with the new knob setting. That way I wouldn't have to cut any more weeds down. I even turned the sensitivity up a little, as far as it would go before it started giving fake signals.

"Look who's getting good at metal-detecting," Decto said.

"I have to, Decto. This is how me and Mom are going to get rich. C'mon, sniff me something good."

"I'll try."

I dug up a lot of things while the barn's shadow struggled to poke into the backyard—a rusty circle with a hole in it, a long piece of metal covered with brown blobs, a thin green triangle that was folded over, a jumble of twisted metal, and a heavy rectangle that had a fancy curved design around the outside. I marked each thing down on the boxy paper. I liked finding stuff and spending time with Decto out in the warm sun, but I was getting worried that we wouldn't find anything worth selling.

Popping sounds came from the front yard. A customer. Loud pops—it had to be a truck or something. Truck people are good because they usually buy big things like furniture. I turned Decto off, gently placed him on the ground, and ran to the front. A horn started honking. It was Mr. Turner's brown pickup truck with big holes in the side. Mr. Turner has four little boys, and they were all standing in the back of the truck next to a piece of furniture. Two of them didn't have shirts on.

"Get Cooper!"

"Bang bang, I got you!" One boy made his finger into the shape of a gun and pointed at me.

"Run!" All the boys jumped out of the truck and ran around the front yard, throwing gravel at each other. Squeaky got knocked over.

"Derek is it!"

"Guys, be quiet. My mom is sleeping."

Mr. Turner is so old-fashioned that he wears a thick hat, even in the summer. He took it off, uncovering a lumpy, spotted head that had a few strands of really long hair swirled around on it. He has a long nose with big nostrils. There are patches of fuzz on his face. Mr. Turner is a nice guy—he sweats so much that his clothes get soaked in big patches under his arms. Also, his sneakers are permanently squashed down. The strip of rubber is gone for good—I'm not sure what that means, but it can't be bad.

"How's business, Coop?"

"Good. Can you get them to be quiet?" One of the boys was opening and closing Mr. Maybox's jaw and making him speak. Another boy was throwing gravel in his mouth.

"Quiet, critters!" Mr. Turner yelled. The boys stopped playing and looked at him. Then they started screaming and running around again. I was afraid that Mom was going to wake up.

"Guys, stop. My mom is sleeping."

"Now, don't fib, business ain't good for nobody." Mr. Turner smiled. He has the longest teeth I've ever seen. They look like vampire fangs.

"We sold a couple of things, but it's been mostly bad. Hold on a second." I ran inside and grabbed the rest of the chocolate cake from the refrigerator. When I got back outside, I put it on the gravel next to the truck.

"Cake!"

"Cooper's the best!" One of them hugged me before kneeling down on scraped, scabby knees. The four boys quietly scooped up chunks of cake.

"They love you, Coop. That's why we picked you for this Queen Anne." He pointed at the piece of furniture in the truck. It was a child's desk from colonial times. The legs were bent strangely, making it look like a four-legged animal. "We're hurtin', Coop. Fifty dollars would help." He drooped his head and clutched his hat with both hands.

"I don't know. We just got a water bill in a red envelope."

"They say a month, Coop, but it'll be a good six months before they shut it off."

The boys were digging away at the cake. Chocolate frosting covered their hands and faces.

"Forty dollars, Coop."

"Hold on." I felt bad for Mr. Turner and those kids. I went inside and got fifty dollars out of my coffee tin. Then I crumpled up four paper towels from the kitchen and wet them under the sink. I ran outside and gave the money to Mr. Turner.

"I forgot, Coop don't haggle. Susan wishes you were our fifth—did I ever tell you that?"

Mr. Turner lifted the desk out of the truck. I'm always amazed at how strong he is, for such a skinny beanstalk. He carried it over to the barn.

"I win!" one boy said. He held up his frosted hands. The cake was completely gone.

"Line up and don't move, you're all under arrest," I said. The boys stood up and looked at me worriedly.

"Says who?"

"Sheriff Cooper. Now here's your punishment." One by one I used the wet paper towels to wipe their mouths. I pushed down hard until all the chocolate was gone.

I don't know what I did wrong because after that they all jumped on me and wouldn't let go. I tromped around slowly, like a big monster with puny humans gripping my arms and legs. I helped Mr. Turner put the kids into the back of the truck one at a time.

After they left, I fixed the gravel, closed Mr. Maybox's mouth, and wheeled poor Squeaky over to the barn so that he could sleep inside on his kickstand.

"I must be dreaming."

"No, Squeaky, I'm treating all my friends better from now on."

I patted the Queen Anne—it had a little inkwell on top for dipping a feather pen into. Usually pieces of old furniture have ghosts that travel with them, but this was a child's desk so I knew the newcomer wouldn't be any trouble.

# CHAPTER 14

When I went inside to check on Mom, she was sitting up in bed reading a book about antique furniture. That means she already knew about the desk—she must have been awake the whole time Mr. Turner and the boys were here. I kicked some loose books back under the bed and climbed up next to her. I jammed my nose against her arm, breathing deeply. She scooped me into an uncomfortable hug, but it was good enough.

Maybe an hour went by like that, and then she said the worst thing. "Cooper, I need new sneakers."

My heart sank. "Most of the money's gone already."

"I've been off my feet and they don't ache."

"Just go barefoot for a while. Your sneakers will get better."

"You don't even go barefoot anymore on the gravel."

When I was little it was hard to get me to wear anything on my feet. I would run around barefoot on the gravel and hot pavement.

"Fine, let's go to the shoe store." I pulled her arm.

"Just tell Jill. She knows my size." Then she said another horrible thing. "I think I need to take a bath."

My heart sank deeper. Mom was changing everything—her new sneakers weren't going to squish down, and she was going to smell like some dumb soap while tromping around. I jammed my nose back into her arm—the smell is like a mixture of cherries, honey, gasoline, girl sweat, pinecones, new-car smell, and Cheerios. Sometimes guys pull up to our house and stand close to her. I can tell by the way they look at her that they don't want to buy any antiques—they just want to inhale her pretty smell. That's when I *accidentally* toss gravel one at a time onto the hoods of their sports cars. They're gone pretty quick after that.

"Cooper, stop." She pushed my nose away from her skin.

"Fine, I'll run the bath in a little while."

"Did Mr. Turner say whether Susan's arm is better?"

"No."

"You should ask next time. It would be polite."

"What did you dream about?"

"I don't remember."

"The metal detector is fixed. I found a bunch of weird things. There's one thing that's too big to dig up. Jan is nice to me. She's Iroquois."

"You're out conquering the world, and look at me."

"Actually, everybody's been saying that you're the perfect mom."

"Oh, everybody has, huh?"

"Yep."

"And if everybody jumped in a lake, would you do that too?"

"If it was summer and the lake was clean." I grinned.

Mom tried to tickle me, but I rolled out of bed and dashed into the bathroom to run the bath. There are two rubber duckies in our bathtub—one for me, and one for Tanner. Mine is all dirty and beaten up, and Tanner's is perfect. Jill gave them to us. Jill once told me that a big ship in the ocean carrying thousands of rubber duckies tipped over, and all the duckies fell out. The poor little things are floating all over the world now, scattered in different directions. Sometimes they wash up on beaches. It must be lonely waddling over big mounds of waves in the stormy sea, so far from a child's home. They want to be squeezed, but there's nobody there to care. I squeeze Tanner's duck all the time, just so it won't feel left out.

That night I tucked Decto into my bed and plopped down next to him. I don't think Koala was too happy about having company. The moon was almost full, and the moonlight reflected off the gravel and made my room glow. An owl called out from deep inside the steep forest, like it was asking me who was this strange new beast in my bed. I knew there weren't going to be bedtime stories because I'd already tucked in clean-smelling Mom and fed her. Mom once taught me this thing called a super tuck-in where you shake the person up and down and left and right until they're dizzy. I don't think she's as enthusiastic about it when I use it on her.

"Decto, do you think metal-detecting is fun?"

"Well, I . . . think so."

"We're only finding weird things. Where's the treasure?"

"Have patience."

"Decto, do you really think I'm Xavier in a new body?" I pulled up the covers so that only his clean white disc was showing.

"I don't think so, Cooper. I think Jan just misses him. There are probably a lot of people with black hair down to their shoulders and green eyes."

"Do you miss him?"

"Yes, he was a good master. We found a lot of treasures together—one day Jan will show you. He used to take me to McDonald's, and I would get my very own large fries. It made me feel human."

"Why does she need me to be him? Can't she just imagine him?"

"When you miss somebody that much, sometimes imagination isn't enough. You know that."

"What do you mean, Decto?"

"My circuits have detected a pain deep inside you."

"They have?"

"A sadness in the furthest corner of your heart."

"Oh."

"If you feel like talking about it, or just thinking it to me, I'm a good listener."

"Decto, you're not human, you wouldn't understand."

"Maybe, but I'm just sayin'. I'm going to bed."

"No, wait. Don't give up. Make me tell."

"How?"

"Be strict."

"I don't know, Cooper. I'm really tired."

"Try."

"Fine, Cooper. I order you to tell." Decto yawned, showing me the electronic insides of his white disc.

"What will you do if I don't?"

"I don't know—I'm no good at this."

"Say 'I'll drain my batteries.'"

"I don't think that's possible."

"Say 'I'll give you the silent treatment. No more beeps.'"

Decto went silent.

"Decto?" I shook him.

When I was two and a half years old, Mom had a baby named Tanner. He was chubby and pink—there are some pictures in an old shoebox, but we never look at them. When I was four, Tanner decided that he didn't want to be my little brother anymore. In the middle of the night he just went up to heaven. He didn't even say goodbye. Nobody ever told me why. I only have one memory of Tanner. We were in the tub together, and there was an echo of him laughing. The memory only lasts a second.

Dad stayed for a while, but one day he couldn't stand

our unhappy house anymore. He just took off and never came back. After that, Mom turned into Robo-Mom. For the next few years she did everything to make my life perfect. That's when we went antiquing together and played hide-and-seek in other people's basements. For my birthday she would make cupcakes for practically the whole school. She would give me super tuck-ins, and we'd have sleepovers and roast marshmallows. She slept in the other bunk, but back then our beds were apart and on opposite sides of the room. Tanner's bed used to turn into a crib.

As I got older, I could do more things on my own. I could dress myself, ride my bike, make my own breakfast, open the barn door, do my own homework, wash the laundry, and lots of other stuff. Mom started drifting away—like water from our leaky roof got into Robo-Mom's electronics and started doing damage. I didn't know what was happening until it was too late. One day I jumped out of bed at dawn and got dressed for antiquing, but Mom wouldn't get up. She looked pale, like she had just seen one of the ghosts.

It was all my fault. If I had known what was going to happen, I would have pretended not to know how to dress myself or ride my bike or make breakfast or do laundry or clean the house or run the antique store. Then Mom would still be Robo-Mom. But it's too late. Now I don't do any homework at all, and I throw all the mail from school into the deepest corner of the backyard.

Everybody thinks I'm a good person, but I'm not. I liked having Mom all to myself for the perfect years. I didn't miss Tanner until I was older. Now I would trade away any body part to get him back. Sometimes I stay up all night wondering what it would be like to have a little brother. That's probably how my imagination got out of control. I don't know how many people imagine things they can actually touch.

Sometimes I lie awake trying to figure out what Mom

is thinking. I don't know why she hides away in the ancient past so much, with all those antiques. She's so afraid of doing *anything* because of what might happen next—like that whole thing about stepping on a spider and destroying the future. But it's not like that for me. Here's an example:

STEP 1: Cooper rides his bike to be an early bird.

STEP 2: He gets a metal detector.

STEP 3: He makes friends with Decto.

STEP 4: There's also a nice new friend for him named Jan, who's Iroquois.

STEP 5: Cooper now has something to do during the week, since garage sales are only on the weekend.

STEP 6: He searches for treasure and finds twelve musket balls.

STEP 7: Mr. Shepherd tells Cooper that part of a Revolutionary War battle—the Battle of Newtown—happened right in his yard.

STEP 8: Cooper finds a button with the number 4 on it.

STEP 9: Cooper finds out that Jan really likes him because he reminds her of her husband, Xavier.

STEP 10: Decto finds a bunch of strange things, including a super-long mystery object that doesn't want to come up.

See, if I never did step 1, then 2 through 10 would never have happened. They're all connected. I petted Decto while he was sleeping, remembering how boring it was without him (sorry, Koala). I don't understand why Mom doesn't like those chain reactions too much. The only thing I can think of is that she thinks step 10 is Tanner going up to heaven, and step 1 is something she did. There's no way that I can ever ask her about something like that, though.

# CHAPTER 15

The next day I woke up with detector face. A big curved line cut across my cheek, with a flattened area inside of it. Don't get me started on what Mirror said to me when I stood on the scale and looked at him. My hair was sticking in every direction. My eyelashes were clumpy. I didn't get much sleep from all that thinking. I was a grump-and-a-half. When I don't get enough snooze, you'd better step back.

That's when Mr. Shepherd pulled onto the gravel in his green pickup truck. Good timing. I needed somebody to explode at, and Mr. Shepherd was the perfect volunteer—after he told me what that button with the 4 on it really was, of course.

I tromped outside.

"Hi, Cooper, how are you folks today?" He wore purple pants with little feathery things sticking off them. He also had a purple shirt on under his furry coat. Everything matched his evil amulet.

"Bad." The barn's shadow was already getting close to the house. I held the screen door so that it didn't bang.

"Maybe this will cheer you up." He pulled a bag with a big curvy M on it out of his truck. I recognized it right away. McDonald's. He held out the bag.

"I can't eat hamburgers."

"Actually, I knew that. I only got French fries and a milkshake. They cook the fries in vegetable oil now."

"I shouldn't eat without Mom."

"That's why I got her a bag too." He pulled another bag out of his truck.

I grabbed both bags and checked to make sure they had the same things. The sweet and salty smell of French fries made my brain do cartwheels, but my mouth barely smiled at Mr. Shepherd. I went inside and put one bag in my room. Then I delivered the other bag to Mom. She was still asleep, so I placed it on the empty plate next to her bed. Out of the corner of my eye I saw Decto's face for a moment—staring at me all the way from my doorway. His neck was bent at a strange angle, like he was peeking out. When I turned to look at him, his face was gone.

There was a faint gulping noise and some munching.

I ran out of Mom's room and into mine. Decto was on the floor, and there was a big rip in the side of the McDonald's bag. The milkshake had spilled, and the French fries were gone!

"Decto, you ate my fries!"

His eyes opened wide, and he started coughing and struggling to breathe. He was choking! A few seconds later an empty red carton with a yellow M on it came flying out of his mouth and landed at my feet.

"Sorry, old chap, that was just so rude of me," he said in Mr. Maybox's voice.

"Decto, you didn't even share!"

"I can't control myself when I'm near those things."

I was so mad at Decto. First he forced me to think about a big secret that kept me up all night and made me feel worse. And he squashed my face from hogging the bed. Then he ate all my fries with no manners at all. I didn't yell, though. My explosion wasn't ready to come out yet.

"Were they good?" Mr. Shepherd asked when I came back out.

"Not really." I didn't feel like explaining.

"Well, Cooper. You know I'm dying to find out what you dug up."

Frowning, I reached into my pocket and handed him the button with the 4 on it. Mr. Shepherd forgot about me and looked at the button under his magnifying glass for a long time while I stared at the reflection of the sun on his big forehead. After a few minutes his nose got redder, and the little craters there seemed to grow deeper. He took a cloth out of his pocket and patted the drops of sweat on his head.

Mr. Shepherd was obviously trying to get on my good side. McDonald's. Sweat. I looked down at his sneakers—same old bricks. Not good enough.

"Well?" I crossed my arms.

"This confirms it. Battle of Newtown. 1779. This is a button from a soldier's uniform—on the American side. Below the four is a very faint letter P. This probably meant Fourth Pennsylvania Regiment. The man who lost this was from there. Aren't you going to ask if I want to buy it?"

"Do you want to buy it?"

"No, Cooper, the Historical Society is on a limited budget. But it belongs in the museum."

"Oh." I could tell he was starting to get mad.

"What else did you find?"

It didn't look like Mr. Shepherd was leaving any time soon, and he did have a lot of stuff in that truck, so I decided to ask an important question. "Mr. Shepherd, do you have a really big shovel?"

"You know I do." He reached into the back of his truck and pulled out a long shovel. He handed it to me. My shoulders felt a sharp pain, and my arms dropped low. The shovel fell on the ground. "Looks like you might need some help with that."

"Go in the back. I'll get Decto."

Decto was burping the whole way around the house. Leave it to me to get the only metal detector in the universe that eats McDonald's French fries.

"I'm sorry, Cooper." Burp.

"I don't care anymore. We're digging up that big thing."

Before showing him where to dig, I pointed out the pile of random stuff I dug up. Mr. Shepherd spent a long time examining all of it.

"Brass belt buckle, missing the iron tang." He placed the heavy rectangle to the side. "This looks like an iron artillery spike." He placed the long metal thing covered with rust blobs next to the belt buckle. "An iron pair of eyeglasses, squashed." He placed the twisted mess of metal next to the buckle. "I'm not sure yet what these other fragments are."

"I have to change the map," I said, handing him the clipboard.

"Stupid rusty long thing. Dumb heavy rectangle. Twisted mess of brown garbage," he read from my map. "You did well, Cooper. By the time we're done, this map may have a story to tell us. It's already shaping up."

I tried not to think about it.

As soon as I showed Mr. Shepherd where the big thing was buried, he put on white gloves and a white shower cap. He placed a doctor's mask over his mouth, with a strap that tied all the way around his head. Then he slammed the shovel into the ground and stepped on the metal part. I sat down with Decto and watched.

"Is it wrong to dig here?"

"Yes, Cooper, I already told you. This should be done by professional archaeologists over many years. But since you're going to do it anyway, we should salvage what we can."

He dropped the shovel and took off his furry coat. I frowned at him.

"It's polyester." He threw it next to me. "I've never seen a boy with so many facial expressions." He dug for a long time while I stared at him.

"What do you think is down there?" I finally asked.

"A time machine." The dirt pile next to him grew bigger. Big veins on the side of his forehead appeared each time he lifted a scoop out of the ground.

"Huh?"

"My father once told me that there are three real time machines in the world. Do you want to know what they are?"

"I guess."

"One of them is the sky. At night when you look up at the stars, you are looking into the past. Stars are distant suns that are so far away it takes a long time for the light to travel here, sometimes millions of years. When a telescope captures that light, it shows you what the star looked like when the light first left on its journey. It's kind of like if you yelled something and your voice took a year to travel to Europe. The people hearing it there would know what you sounded like a year ago. There are some stars whose light began its journey when dinosaurs roamed the Earth, and it's just getting here now to show us what the star looked like in prehistoric times."

Mr. Shepherd was sweating really hard. He had already carved out a big ravine and was making it deeper.

"What's the second time machine?"

"The arts—literature, paintings, photography, all that good stuff. When you read a story written hundreds of years ago, you're seeing the world through the eyes of the author. Every sight, smell, sound, voice, setting—all are unique to that time period. The characters spoke, dressed, thought, and acted in a way that fit their society. It can hypnotize you into thinking you are actually there—experiencing life as those people did. It's the same when you stare at an old photograph or painting. They take you back to a moment in time that will never exist again, even throughout all of eternity."

Mr. Shepherd removed a big rock from the hole and threw it in the dirt pile.

"Is the third one the Earth?"

"Very smart. There are buried secrets waiting to be discovered in every dark corner of this planet. It's our job to piece them together and listen to the story they have to tell us about the remote past. Lost civilizations, ancient battles, forgotten inventions, mysterious traditions—they're all down there. After my dad finished explaining about the three time machines, he told me to choose the one that would eventually become my job. He knew I was hooked on history at a very young age."

"You picked the Earth?"

"Actually, I picked all three. I have a big telescope on top of my house, a library full of old books and paintings, and, well, here I am digging up your yard."

I smiled. "What else did your dad say?"

"My dad still says a lot of things. He lives in California and calls me all the time."

"Should I go over the hole with Decto?"

"Whatever you want, Cooper. It took me an hour to get you to smile. I don't want to lose that."

I stuck Decto's head down into the ravine. A strange noise came out of the electronic box, and the number 1000 appeared on the little TV screen.

"We're close," Mr. Shepherd said. "That noise means the circuits are overloaded." He took a white pencil-like thing out of his pocket and poked it into the dirt. It hit something hard. He poked all along the ravine, and it hit something each time.

Just then a popping sound came from the gravel out front. A customer had pulled up.

# CHAPTER 16

"Wait for me," I said. "Don't dig it up without me."

I ran around to the front. A man and woman wanted to peek into our antique store, so I unlocked the barn for them. The lady had a cane and took a long time to go inside.

As they were browsing, I kept saying, "Do you want to buy anything?" to the couple. The man laughed each time I said it. Every minute I ran out and peeked around the side of the barn to see if Mr. Shepherd was digging. He was sitting on the ground holding Decto and cleaning sweat off his forehead.

"These are real antiques," the lady said. "Half the so-called antique stores around here just have collectibles."

"What's the difference?"

"Collectibles are purposely made so that people will collect them. Antiques are old things that nobody knew would be valuable someday."

"Oh. Do you want to buy any of our antiques?"

"Yes, we will buy something, if you stop asking."

I ran outside to peek again. Mr. Shepherd was leaning over the big hole. I tilted my head up so that the sun hit my eye at an angle. Then I sneezed so loud that it made Mr. Shepherd back away from the hole. I just wanted him to know I was watching.

The lady wanted to buy the child's desk that Mr. Turner just sold to me. I didn't want to sell it, so I made up some really high price. I needed that desk for a little while longer. The couple continued walking around, picking up everything and whispering to each other.

"Do you want to buy anythi— I mean, how are you folks today?" I stuttered.

"Bit too warm for me," the lady said. "And Frank's got allergies."

They finally bought the dull sword for seventy dollars. They paid me in one-dollar bills, so my pocket was stuffed. I waved to them and smiled as they pulled away. Once they were gone I sprinted back to Mr. Shepherd.

"Ready to solve this mystery?" he said.

"Yep."

Mr. Shepherd scraped away the last of the dirt in the ravine. My heart was beating fast. When he was done, I looked into the hole. It was a long rusty thing.

"Don't look so disappointed. Do you know what this is?"

"No."

"It's an iron cannon. Just the barrel—it's missing the wheels."

"How much is it wor—"

Before I could finish my question, Mr. Shepherd fell backwards and started moving his arms and legs all at the same time, like a beetle that was stuck on its back and trying to right itself. There was a big smile on his face.

"I bet it belongs in the museum," I said.

"Cooper, I have to tell you how significant this find is. We have no surviving cannons from the Sullivan-Clinton Campaign. The Americans abandoned their heaviest artillery at the end of this battle. They must have buried this one instead of sending it back to their fort."

I had no idea what he was talking about. My dreams of finding buried treasure were pretty much ruined. I put my hand on the wad of bills bulging out of my pocket. Soon it would be time to go to garage sales again. At least those bring in some real cash. I hadn't even looked at the newspaper to plan my next antiquing mission. Decto stared at me with a worried face.

"Is it worth anything?" I asked Mr. Shepherd.

"It's priceless, Cooper. Don't you want to know the whole story of the battle now? This iron spike might have been part of the ammunition pile. It looks unspent." He picked up the blob-covered iron spike I had found.

"The cannon fired spikes?"

"Spikes, grape shot, six-pound cannonballs, you name it. Artillery played an important role in this battle. Now sit down and listen to the whole story—"

"No, Mr. Shepherd, I don't want to hear it. That looks like it would hurt. Isn't there anything else about the drummer or the fifer?"

"Cooper, if you're going to get in a time machine, you have to put your emotions aside. You are just looking for the truth. The truth doesn't change whether you're happy or sad about it. The strategy the Americans used with their cannons—"

I covered my ears and started humming. No way I was spending another whole night without sleep. Mom was right not to talk about this stuff. Mr. Shepherd's mouth kept moving for a while as he brushed dirt off the cannon. When I uncovered my ears, I heard the word "Iroquois."

"Wait, what about the Iroquois?"

"There were many Iroquois warriors on the British side during this battle. The British and Iroquois were hidden behind breastworks below that ridgeline up there. Breastworks are made from logs and concealed with shrubs and tree branches." He pointed up the steep hill toward Ghost Conductor's Bluff. "They were planning to ambush the Americans as they marched along the Chemung River."

"Why were the Iroquois there? I thought it was Americans against British."

He stopped digging around the side of the cannon and turned to me. "Cooper, I know you don't like talking about these things, but you need to know this. George Washington sent that big army up here to destroy the Iroquois civilization."

I fell to my knees. A burst of energy shot through my body. A big lump made it hard for me to swallow, and my arms started shaking again. I wished that I had kept my ears covered for just a little while longer. I pictured me and Tanner marching next to the American army toward that Iroquois village sitting on the bank of the river. Newtown. I was playing the drums, and Tanner was playing the fife.

I suddenly knew why that Iroquois lady didn't smile at us when we passed her—we were going there to destroy her town. The image inside her pupils wasn't just a reflection of a war between the Americans and the British. It was about her people too. I went and signed up my little brother without even asking if he really wanted to go! He just followed me, and it was too late to turn back.

"If you're lying, I'll never speak to you again."

"Cooper, let me tell the whole story. From the beginning."

"No, we don't talk about things like that. Mom wouldn't want you to, and she'll be mad."

"Your whole property is filled with the remnants of a battle. So you're just going to sell the things and ignore the whole story? Don't you even want to know why George Washington sent the army here? Who won the battle? What strategies were used? What effect it had on the Revolutionary War? It's right under your yard, Cooper." He pointed to the cannon.

"I'll have nightmares. You should go away. I'm not feeling good."

"How about you go inside and take a nap, and I'll work on this cannon?"

"No."

"Cooper, be honest. You don't think about fighting off ninjas while you're stuck at school? They burst through the window, and it's up to you to defend the class."

"No, that's dumb."

"Aliens? Giant robots?"

"What's the difference?"

"Ah, aliens and giant robots. It's okay, all boys have thoughts like that."

Mr. Shepherd was starting to sound like Mom that time she talked about boy/girl stuff. I pretty much knew what he was going to say next: *Pretty soon you're going to go through a change, Cooper. You're going to stop thinking about battling giant robots and start thinking about firing big cannons filled with sharp spikes at people on hills. Such thoughts are okay, Cooper.*

"Actually, I throw rocks at cars. Is that violent enough?"

"That's a good example, too."

"Cars pollute."

"So you're perfect. Is that what you're saying? Did it ever occur to you that some parts of those sneakers you're wearing are made of leather? Do you know where leather comes from?"

"Tanners make it." I stuck out my tongue at him.

"Yes, once they have a dead cow's skin."

I walked away from Mr. Shepherd toward the front of the house, trying to hold back the tears that bubbled deep down inside. I didn't care if he insulted me, but Tanner is forbidden territory. Mr. Shepherd followed me. I picked up a handful of gravel and aimed it at his truck. The headlights scowled at me.

"I'll do it."

"Go ahead."

I threw the rocks softly and they plunked all over the

truck—some bounced off and some landed in the storage area in the back. Then I picked up some more rocks and I threw those too, a little harder. Once I got started I couldn't stop. I kept throwing rocks until I could barely see through my tears. I was really pitching them fast at the end. Finally I stopped because my arms were shaking. I looked down at my torn sneakers. I had never thought about how tanners made leather. Jill always buys our shoes for us off the discount rack—we give her money. She didn't know.

"Mr. Shepherd, will you please go?"

Mom appeared by the screen door. She opened it and walked outside wearing her nightgown. "What game are you two playing?"

"We found a cannon in the backyard. It got us both a little excited."

"Mr. Shepherd!"

"It's okay, Cooper. I've heard of cannons before," Mom said.

"So now you're going to take his side?"

"Mr. Shepherd has been a good customer here for a long time."

"Customers leave sometime!"

"I said some stupid things. I'm sorry."

"That's funny, and yet you're still here."

"Cooper, ask me a question."

"What?"

"When I was young and I made my sister mad because I got excited about something, I would always make it up to her by letting her ask me any question, and I would have to give a truthful answer. Go ahead."

"Why won't you leave?"

"Because I'm waiting for you to ask me a good question. Try again."

"Will you leave after that?"

"Yes."

"Fine. Why do you dress so weird?"

"Ever since I was a little kid my skin has been allergic to just about everything—pollen, dust, ragweed, you name it. I break out in hives. So I have to keep covered up year-round. It made me sad that I couldn't swim in pools like the other kids, or jump in a lake. To cheer me up, my parents used to buy me silly clothing. My sister dressed me up like a big doll. As I got older, I didn't want to give up shopping for the strangest clothes ever made. My sister and I still go to flea markets together, and she still dresses me up. This amulet is special too." He put his hand on the purple amulet.

I ran behind the truck and peeked out.

"My wife gave it to me on our honeymoon. It has spirals of diamonds and sapphires embedded in it—permanently embracing, like two people in love."

Mr. Shepherd's phone rang.

He babbled into it while I frowned at him. His flea market/sister story reminded me of when me and Mom used to go to garage sales together. I walked over to Mom and led her back inside. Then I closed and locked the door.

I don't know why I didn't think of that sooner.

# CHAPTER 17

I flopped down on the ratty orange couch next to the broken TV. Old springs pushed into my ribs, and I bounced up and down while creaks and groans came from under the cushions. The pile of dollar bills dug into my leg.

"You're a grump-and-a-half today," Mom said.

"No sleep." I pushed my hair over my eyes to block out the light, but there was a little opening so I could peek out.

"I'm making your favorite." She washed a pot under the sink and dried it with her nightgown.

"Spaghetti and blob?"

"Still a grump?"

"Down to a grump-and-a-quarter." I smiled, but it was hidden away under my hair.

Spaghetti and blob is a big pile of thick pasta with a giant ball of cheese on top. Hidden inside the ball are little bits of different vegetables. At the top is a hole filled with tomato sauce. It looks like a volcano, and you never know what you're going to get with each bite. It melts down into yummy ooze the longer it takes to eat.

I peeked at Mom. Sometimes, after she's been in bed for a long time, she turns back into Robo-Mom. It's like she was taking all that sleep time to remember how to do it. My coffee can full of money was on the table in the center of the room. The water and electric bills were next to it. My smile got so big it started pulling hair into my mouth.

The first time Robo-Mom returned, about a year ago, I nearly choked on happy tears. Everything was going to be like it was before. A few days after that I took the coffee can back into my room. Mom didn't even notice.

"Mr. Shepherd seemed excited," Mom said.

"He's going crazy about the Battle of Newtown."

"You should find out all you can about it."

"Why?"

"So you can tell me."

"But you hate that stuff."

"I think we should know what happened in our own neighborhood. Jill will want to know, too."

"But Mr. Shepherd said George Washington ordered men to destroy the whole Iroquois civilization."

"Then you should become Detective Cooper. Find out if they really did that. I think when school starts, you'll have a good report to write."

School. Mom didn't have a clue what was going on there. But if Jill needed to know stuff, I could teach her. I reached down and rubbed my hand on the yellow rug, then wiped off the slime on the side of the couch. Maybe in return she could teach me how to clean the rug.

I felt Mom's hand on my shoulder. My eyes opened.

"Go take a bath. Dinner will be ready when you get out. And throw your clothes in the wash."

"Too tired."

"Cooper. Bath. Now." She pointed to the bathroom.

I pushed my hair away so she could see my smile that time. She remembered. When she says it like that, she doesn't have to worry about what will happen next. I'll just listen for no reason. Falling off the couch, I grabbed her legs. She pulled me over to the bathroom. The dollar bills fell out of my pocket on the way.

"You are such a drag," she said.

"Very funny." I crawled into the bathroom.

"What's all this?" Mom reached down and picked up a few bills.

"Some lady bought that dull sword. She liked our shop."

"Tomorrow we should take the bus into town and get new sneakers for both of us. And jeans." She picked up the rest of the cash.

"Really?" I shot to my feet. Mom has *never* said that since she sold the car.

I closed the bathroom door and took the best bath of my life. I washed my hair twice to get all the slime and bugs out. I put both rubber ducks down and watched them swim around my feet. If they swam too close to the rust-colored stains on the side of the tub, I kicked them away so they didn't get some kind of infection.

After spaghetti and blob (the best ever), I plopped down on the couch and watched Mom clean up. I could tell by the quick way she was moving that her mind wasn't sad. When I was little, I was always amazed by how fast she was. I could never get too far when she chased me, and she would catch any ball I threw at her—even the ones that were way off. When I asked her to play with me, she never said no. Not once. Ever. I finally stopped asking. I would just say, "Mom, it's time to play."

I turned on the old TV with my foot to see if it worked. We only get one channel, and it's really fuzzy, and that's only if I kick it enough times.

"Ow. Ow. Ow. Ow. Ow. Fine, I'll show you something," TV said.

Mom and I watch a show together about people who bring antiques to a big building, and smart people say how much they're worth and tell a lot of history about them. After Mom cleaned up, I rested my head on her lap and we watched together. She moved her fingers gently through my hair.

That's the last thing I remember before waking up in my bed, under the covers. The moonlight streamed through the window and made my room super bright. I heard hundreds of footsteps in the distance, and whispering coming from the steep forest.

There was a full moon.

The ghosts were out.

I grabbed Koala and squashed him against my chest. That's when I realized I had left Decto out in the backyard. So much for treating him better. He was probably scared and lonely back there. I didn't even remember closing the barn.

The bed above me moved, and the covers flopped around up there. Tanner climbed down the ladder and floated next to my bed, glowing like the moon. He looks just like me, only smaller. His nickname is Mini-Cooper.

"Hi," he said.

"Hi." I cleared a space at the edge of the bed and patted it. Tanner climbed up. I put my arm around him and covered us both. My hand squished into him a little bit, but it didn't go all the way through. His body felt cold.

"I still can't go through things," Tanner said.

"Good."

"The teachers get mad. They say I should know by now."

"If you learn that, I won't be able to hug you anymore."

"I can float really good and turn into sparkly things." He sniffled and wiped his nose on my pillow.

"Cool."

"Why'd you sign us up for the Revolutionary War? I don't know if I can play the fife. I don't have any breath."

"I'm not sure. I wasn't thinking. I'm going to learn more about it."

"Find out by the next full moon."

"I got you a friend," I said.

"Who?"

"He's sitting in an old Queen Anne–style desk in the barn. You should go play with him."

"Will I be able to find my way back?"

"The barn's right next to the house."

"But the Earth rotates under me really fast. I get lost, remember?"

"The moonlight shines on the gravel and makes a bright beam that points to your bed. You can see it from miles away."

"But if I go on the other side of that wall of trees, I can't see the gravel."

"Don't play there, play down in our valley."

"Will you still be awake when I get back?"

"Yes, I have to go rescue a metal detector."

"Okay."

"Don't scare anyone. It's not nice."

"Okay."

Tanner turned into a bunch of sparkly things that floated into the air and made shadows dance on the walls. The sparkles turned into a long wispy snake and slithered toward the window. Mirror didn't reflect it. Soon the sparkles squeezed through a crack in the glass and disappeared.

I hopped out of bed and ran over to the window. Tanner's face appeared, really big. It made me fall backwards.

"Wasn't that cool?" he said.

"I just said not to scare anyone." My heart was pounding.

"Sorry."

"Never mind, go play."

Barefoot, I tiptoed out of my room. The moonlight bounced off the steep forest and came in through the kitchen window, lighting up a zillion dust specks in the air. The front door creaked as I snuck out into the night. The giant moon hovered over the valley like it was sitting on top of the biggest plate of spaghetti and blob in the universe. It smiled at me, but that didn't make me feel any less afraid. Sharp rocks dug into my skin. The barn was closed and locked. Through a crack in the side, two sparkling wisps came out and twirled around each other, giggling. They flew off into the valley.

I took really big, slow steps toward the weeds in the backyard. The night crickets chirped, along with a lot of weirder insects. One made a sound like water dripping into a pan, and another sounded like an alarm clock going off. The moonlight made everything look snow-covered—the house, barn, steep forest, and square clearing. It took a long time to get to the spot where Decto was sitting. When I finally made it, he didn't look so good. His teeth were chattering, and he turned his head sharply each time the smallest noise came from the forest. A family of deer scattered into the weeds when my foot crunched something. I took baby steps so I wouldn't fall into the ravine with the cannon.

"I'm . . . I'm sorry I ate the fries." Chatter.

"Decto, I didn't leave you out here on purpose."

I picked him up and rubbed his long neck. Just when I was about to head back, something froze me in place. Down in the valley ghostly soldiers were walking in a long line next to the Chemung River. Some pushed big cannons on wagon wheels. Most held long muskets. Their footsteps fell in a perfect rhythm, making the ground shake slightly. Generals on ghostly horses led them. Tanner played the fife, and the new ghost filled in for me on the drum. I didn't have time to tell Tanner that they were walking into an ambush!

Farther up the river, a village of longhouses surrounded by tall corn was filled with the sounds of men, women, and children shouting. They ran off into the forest, leaving the town empty, except for that lady with the long white hair. She didn't budge.

Up on top of the steep hill, the Ghost Conductor stood on the small clearing at the peak and peered out. Below him, glowing soldiers hid behind breastworks that curved around the front of the mountain. They waited silently, watching, as if at any moment the Ghost Conductor would command them to fire their weapons.

Then everything froze. The ghostly soldiers stopped marching, the fife and drums went silent. The Iroquois villagers didn't flee anymore. The conductor and his hidden army stopped waiting.

I ran as fast as I could back to the house, my feet sinking into sharp, painful rocks. At any moment everything might come back to life—I didn't know what was going to happen next, or even why it was happening. The screen door banged against the house, swaying back and forth on one hinge.

Slam the door. Put my back up against it.

Safe.

I brought the shivering Decto into my room and buried him under the covers with me. A few hours later, when the moon was setting, Tanner crawled into bed with me, too. It was me, Koala, Decto, and Tanner, all snug in my bed.

We made it through another full moon, together.

# CHAPTER 18

When I woke up the next morning something was tugging on Decto. My arms were wrapped tightly around him, so we both got pulled toward the edge of the bed. I opened my eyes and saw Mom trying to take him.

"No," I muttered groggily, yanking him back.

"Cooper, you can't sleep with a metal detector. Your face is all dented."

"Mom, I've got this room under control."

"There's a spoiled milkshake oozing into the carpet." She pulled harder, and I almost fell off the bed.

"Don't go Robo on Decto. You don't understand. He's really alive." I yanked him back and Mom lost her grip.

"You're in another one of your fantasy worlds. I get worried when you talk to things." She grabbed Decto again and pulled super-hard, but I held on in a tug-of-war.

"Well, don't worry then."

Mom cheated by using grownup strength, and Decto went flying out of my hands. His head hit against the top bunk. There was a loud cracking noise when the pole with the twisted wire broke. Decto's head hung down limply, and his tongue dangled out of his mouth. A burst of shock electrified my body.

"Mom, look what you did!" I leapt out of bed and grabbed Decto back. Mom let go on purpose. She put her hands up to her mouth.

"We had some great adventures, didn't we?" Decto sputtered. "Sorry . . . about . . . the fries." His eyes closed. My palms got sweaty and my eyes got watery.

"Mom, you killed him!"

I walked out of the room holding Decto against my chest. Tears flowed down my cheeks, and I took tiny breaths that sounded like hiccups. Barefoot and in my pajamas, I walked outside and tried to open the lock on the barn. It took me a lot of tries while Decto's loose head banged against my arm. Squeaky was very surprised to see us like this.

I don't even remember biking down the roads.

When I got to Jan's house I banged on the door until my hand hurt. My nose was running and mixing with salty tears. As the door creaked open, I took a deep breath.

"Little Butterfly!" Jan knelt down and held me by the arms. My body was shaking. She led me inside and took Decto from my tight grip. She had to pull each finger off to free him.

"Decto died," I said, letting my breath out.

"Little Butterfly, he's not dead. It's just a flesh wound. Come with me." She led me down creaky stairs into a cold basement. A gargantuan mound of metal junk filled the room and reached to the ceiling. Glass cabinets lined the walls. In one corner there was a table full of metal-detecting equipment, and some other metal detectors hung from the wall.

"Psst, kid, you don't need dat old detector. I'll find what you'z looking for," a fancy-looking metal detector said.

Jan put Decto down on the table and unplugged the wire from his head. Then she unwrapped the wire from the pole. She pulled a brand-new detector pole out of a drawer under the table. I walked over to the glass cabinets because I couldn't watch—it was too scary. At least there was hope, so the tears stopped and my breathing went back to normal.

The cabinets were filled with coins of all different shapes, sizes, and colors sitting on fuzzy black platforms. One brown coin was about the size of a quarter. It showed a lady's head with curly hair looking to the left. She had a headband covered with the word LIBERTY. The little paper card read, "United States Half Cent – 1809."

Another brown coin was even bigger than a quarter. It had a picture of that same lady's head on it, but this time she was looking to the right. Instead of a headband she had a big ribbon flowing off the back of her hair. The card read, "United States Large Penny – 1794." I wondered who that famous lady was, and why she changed the stuff in her hair so much.

One cabinet had only a single coin lit up by its own spotlight. It was a silver circle with the letters "VI" at the top. The rest of the coin was blank. The label said, "New England Sixpence – 1652." I wondered why they left this coin blank instead of putting that lady's head on it. Maybe she wasn't born yet. It was also weird that the boring coin with almost nothing on it was made from shiny silver, while the beautiful lady got the dull brown coin. Maybe that's why she kept turning to the right and the left—she was on the lookout for that dumb coin maker.

Some cabinets had coins from other countries. A lot of coins were really thick, or had holes in the middle and mysterious writing on them. Some had pictures of birds and trees. There were big ones and tiny ones, square ones and oval ones. Many were pretty colors like blue, red, green, yellow, and white. I eventually came to a cabinet labeled SPANISH TREASURE. It was filled with piles of silver and gold coins and maps with big X's on them. One big silver coin sat off to the side. It had a picture of a man on it looking to the right. He had long curly hair tied with a ribbon. A crown of leaves sat on his head. The words CAROLUS IIII DEI GRATIA surrounded his head. The little card read, "Spanish silver Eight-Real coin of King Charles IV of Spain, 1806. Often referred to as a *piece of eight.*"

Before I was done looking at all the cabinets, Jan appeared next to me with Decto wrapped in a blanket. He was sleeping peacefully. I hugged her.

"Little Butterfly, you must learn to take better care of this." She handed me the blanket and Decto.

"I will. I'm sorry."

"So now you've seen our treasures."

"Which is your favorite coin?"

Jan led me over to a small cabinet with a bunch of shiny silver coins in it. She pointed to one that showed a chubby man looking to the left. His head was surrounded by the words LOUIS XVIII ROI DE FRANCE. The man had long curly hair that was tied up with a ribbon. The little card read, "5 Francs of Louis 18th. 1816, non-military bust type."

"We found this in Xavier's hometown outside of Paris. It is our oldest French silver coin."

"Why did everybody wear ribbons in their hair back then?"

"It was the style of the times." Jan opened a small drawer under the display case and took out a small blue ribbon. She squeezed together my hair and tied the ribbon around it. It made a heavy ponytail that rested against my neck. My cheeks were less ticklish, and right away I could hear better.

"Now everybody's going to want me to be on a coin."

"Or me." She lifted up her super-long hair and swung it quickly so it wrapped around her body like a snake.

We giggled, and I suddenly became embarrassed that I was in my pajamas.

"Xavier and I were coin shooters. That's why these cabinets have only coins in them."

I stopped laughing and looked at the ground.

"Oh, don't worry, Little Butterfly, coin shooting just means that we specialized in lost money. We collected only coins. If we found jewelry or historic items, we donated them to museums."

"Mr. Shepherd said that George Washington sent an army up here to destroy the Iroquois civilization."

"Now why did he say something like that to such a sensitive boy?" She put a finger under my chin and tilted my head up.

"It's okay. I want to know everything now."

"Then let's go upstairs. You can listen to my voice again for a while."

# CHAPTER 19

I stretched out on the fluffy rug and let the soft strands tickle my face. Jan settled into her chair and picked up a steaming mug from the small round table. She took a few sips and then began to speak softly. The story she told went like this:

"According to Iroquois legend, a young boy held up the blue sky and protected the Earth. He invented all the good things on the planet—vegetables and trees, rivers, animals, and humans. The young boy was known as Creator. So busy was he holding up the sky that he needed many lesser spirits to dart around the planet and make sure all beings were happy.

"There was another boy that looked just like Creator—a twin. However, this boy was pure evil. He created all the bad things on Earth, such as poisonous plants, monstrous animals, hateful feelings, foul weather, and everything else that makes life on Earth challenging. The evil boy was known as Flint. Like the good boy, the evil one commanded a host of lesser spirits that went around the planet carrying out his commands.

"The Iroquois did not have a written language, but they created strings of shells called wampum to record important information. The patterns of white and purple shells often held records of family trees. One belt in particular told of a woman, extremely old and frail, who once lived in this area. She was the direct descendant of the first woman on Earth. Her name was Ji-Gon-Sa-Seh, or Mother of Nations. It is said that gazing into her eyes, one could feel the power of Creator, the good twin, stir within the body.

"For hundreds of years the Iroquois people dwelt in the forests near the fabled home of Ji-Gon-Sa-Seh. They split into many different tribes, and each tribe divided into family clans. They gathered and ate all the good things that Creator gave them—wild berries, fruits, nuts, roots, and mushrooms. Drinks were made from sassafras, birchbark, spicewood, and hemlock twigs. They grew corn, beans, and squash, and celebrated many thanksgivings each year that followed the harvests. In rivers and streams they fished and dug mussels. Men hunted deer, moose, beaver, and elk while boys practiced with toy bows and arrows and tomahawks.

"Women were the most powerful members of Iroquois society—the Clan Mother ruled over all, and children belonged only to their mother's clan. No decision—from appointment of clan chiefs to resolution of quarrels—was made without consent of the Clan Mother. There were no jails or police in Iroquois society. A Clan Mother taught all her children to follow the ancient traditions.

"The Iroquois lived in villages that contained many longhouses. The towns were surrounded by a wooden wall and sat close to water. Little Butterfly, you may remember your daydream about a longhouse that stretched across an entire valley. You weren't far wrong. You see, an unfortunate rule created by the evil twin stated that after the Iroquois people divided into different tribes, all tribes were at war with the others until friendships were made. That meant the Iroquois were in a constant state of war. On any day a group of warriors might head out to prove themselves in battle. They did not have to listen to commanders—creativity on the battlefield was encouraged.

"Constant warfare became tiresome, so some ambitious tribes decided to form a friendship. Five tribes—the Mohawk, Onondaga, Seneca, Oneida, and Cayuga—joined together in an alliance called the League of the Iroquois.

Their flag has five symbols on it, each representing one of the tribes."

"Like on that blanket, and there on the wall." I had to stop her for a minute, because with the sound of her voice making my spine vibrate as I lay on the soft rug, I thought I might melt. Goose bumps covered my whole body.

"Very good, Little Butterfly. The five nations were called Ganonsyoni, which means Lodge Extended Lengthwise. They thought of themselves as living in one giant longhouse that stretched across the heart of New York. The Mohawks guarded the eastern door. The Seneca were keepers of the western door. The Onondaga were called the fire keepers and watched the hearths in the center. That's why they are symbolized by a tree in the center of the flag. The tree is surrounded by two rectangles and two squares—the little and big brother tribes that joined them and sat opposite the fire from each other. Later, a sixth tribe, the Tuscarora, were invited into the alliance, though their symbol was not added to the flag.

"The Six Nations of the Iroquois became very powerful and ruled over the whole region. They swallowed or destroyed all those who stood against them. Clan Mothers decided which prisoners would be adopted to replace lost warriors and which would be punished. By the time the Europeans came to the area, the League had already ruled for a hundred years or more. As the French settled in the north and the English in the east, the League began trading with them. Europeans replaced their stone tools with metal ones—knives, axes, hoes, needles, kettles, muskets, rifles. The Iroquois began to rely on them and slowly abandoned their old ways.

"Little Butterfly, it was those British colonies to the east that soon brought so much sadness to the League of the Iroquois."

Jan began singing a song in a beautiful language, but after a minute I had to stop her. My body was starting to shake and shiver.

"Maybe you want to hear the rest later," Jan said.

"No, it's okay. It's just the singing—that's too much. But I want to hear more of the story now."

"As you wish, Little Butterfly. In the late seventeenth century the Iroquois put themselves under the protection of the British—a friendship they hoped would preserve their land. They thought of the British and their colonies as one people. When the colonists broke away from Great Britain during the Revolutionary War, the League of the Iroquois did not see any reason to join one side or the other. But the British gave great gifts to the Iroquois and asked their warriors to join them in the war against the colonists. They told the Iroquois that the colonists would steal away their land if they won the war. It was as if the once-united English had split into the good twin and the evil twin—only the Iroquois did not know which was which. For a long time the Iroquois remained neutral, but eventually the pressure was too great.

"So the Six Nations of the Iroquois divided—four on the British side, two on the American side. The Onondaga, Mohawk, Seneca, and Cayuga joined with the British. The Oneida and Tuscarora joined the Americans. The Revolutionary War had also caused a civil war among the Iroquois. Creator, so busy holding up the sky to protect Earth, did not see the evil twin and his minion spirits spreading war and sadness among their people once again. Men who once dwelt in the same giant longhouse were now enemies on the battlefield. In the years to come, terrible fighting would kill many and make their longhouses feel empty.

"The British devised a master plan. They wanted to split the colonies in two by sending armies down from

Canada to join with armies coming up the Hudson River from New York City. The British had a powerful navy, so they had the advantage in any battles that took place near water. George Washington had his hands full across Long Island, Manhattan, and New Jersey trying to keep the British armies there from carrying out their part of the plan. But since the British armies in the north were so far away from their navy—traveling through untamed wilderness— they were weaker. That's why they so desperately needed the help of the Iroquois. The British soldiers coming down from Canada did not fare so well—they lost important battles in 1777 near Saratoga, which spoiled the British plans to split the colonies.

"In 1778 the British and their allies decided to change their plan in the north. Small armies there would now focus on disrupting the American economy by destroying towns and farms. They wanted to take away the food supplies of their enemy. It was a time of horror for both the Iroquois and the colonists, as some awful events occurred that I'm not sure I should even tell you about, Little Butterfly."

"Please, Jan, I'm strong enough now. What happened?" I sat up.

"The Iroquois were bitterly angry about their own family members being lost in battle after the League divided and took sides. This was the first time that long-house brothers had fought against each other since the Six Nations was born—and each confrontation added steam to an iron kettle. The British, the colonists, and the Iroquois on both sides all behaved badly. On the wild frontier of Upstate New York, small raids, nighttime attacks, and terror ruled as each side sought revenge on the other. Finally, in a town called Cherry Valley in New York, the Iroquois on the side of the British did terrible things. They set fire to the village. They killed many innocent men, women, and children.

They took their scalps back home—a ritual that replaced their own lost family members. This was not something that was approved by Clan Mothers or chiefs of the villages. The warriors did it on their own.

"Word of these horrors spread throughout the colonies, and the talk went all the way to the ears of George Washington. He decided that in retaliation for attacks on women and children, all Iroquois villages and farms belonging to enemy tribes should be destroyed. In 1779 he sent General John Sullivan to lead an expedition of soldiers into Iroquois territory. He was to meet up with an army led by General James Clinton, and together they would journey northward into these ancient lands to carry out their orders. Washington believed that total destruction was the only way to quiet the northern frontier."

"Mr. Shepherd said the Iroquois and British set up a defense around the ridge right above my house," I told Jan. "They were going to ambush the Americans as they came up the river. So who won?"

"I think it would be best to ask Mr. Shepherd what happened at the Battle of Newtown."

"Oh, please, Jan, you tell stories much better than he does."

"I need to rest, Little Butterfly."

"Did the Iroquois really scalp children? That's so awful." I put my head on the soft rug and looked at Jan sideways. The ponytail rested uncomfortably in a big clump under my cheek. My eyes became watery.

"They feared for their homes and their loved ones. They thought the colonists would take their land. They were desperate and acting alone."

"Then why didn't they join the American side? Why did they go become our enemy?"

"Perhaps they didn't trust the colonists, who had

already taken a lot of land farther east from other tribes. They believed what the British had told them—that if the colonists won the war, all the Iroquois land would be stolen."

"Please, Jan, just a little more of the story?"

"Isn't your mother going to worry about you?"

*Mom.* I suddenly remembered that we were supposed to go to Elmira together and get clothes. That whole scene with her and Decto popped back into my head. She was going to lose confidence and quit being Robo-Mom unless I did something about it.

"Jan, I have to go. Thanks for the story and for fixing Decto."

I picked up Decto and his blanket and raced out the door.

# CHAPTER 20

Mr. Shepherd's green truck was parked on the gravel when I got home. There was a white truck parked next to it. I could barely see the house. Mom was sitting in her aluminum chair reading a book. A loud noise that sounded like a lawnmower came from behind the house. I rested Squeaky on his kickstand and put Decto down next to him.

"Mom, what is Mr. Shepherd doing?"

"Clearing the backyard with a weed cutter." She didn't look up from her book.

"Why'd you let him? We're supposed to go to Elmira." I peeked between the house and the barn. Little bits of weeds were flying into the air as Mr. Shepherd pushed a big machine with sharp blades on the front. He wore long blue socks that covered the bottoms of his pants, and something that looked like a space helmet over his whole head. The last row of weeds protecting us from the haunted forest was completely gone. My right arm went down and hit my leg with a tight fist. I couldn't tell Mom that she made a huge mistake because then she'd really lose confidence.

"I gave the money to Jill. She came over after you left to ask me what was wrong."

"But *we* were supposed to go. Me and you."

"She's good at picking out clothes for you. And she's my size."

"Mom, c'mon, get up." I pulled on her arm. She didn't budge. "I'm going to count to three. One . . . two . . ." I tried to tip the chair over so she'd fall onto her feet.

"Mr. Shepherd is here. We can't just leave."

"Why does Mr. Shepherd think he owns this place? He just barges in."

"He's always helped out when he comes to browse. When you were little he cleaned the rain gutters for us after they got clogged. Last year he chased away the rats in the attic. He fixed the mailbox when it fell over."

I thought about the quiet day that me and Mom were sitting around, and then Mr. Maybox suddenly said, "I say, old chap, *timberrrr!*" Clunk. He fell flat on his face.

"We don't have any rain gutters, Mr. Maybox is barely standing, and I hear rats in the attic all the time."

"It's not his fault a storm knocked the gutters off. He's a nice person for helping, and that's that."

"You always take his side." I sat on her lap and leaned back.

We were quiet for a while. The weed cutter wasn't growling anymore, and I heard Mr. Shepherd talking quietly to someone. I was out of ideas, so I just tilted my head back and pouted up at Mom.

"This is a nice touch." She played with the blue ribbon on my ponytail. I took it off, letting my hair fall back into place. I reached my hands around the back of her head and carefully gathered her hair. It was hard to do from my weird position, but I finally made a little ponytail. I tied the blue ribbon around it.

I got up and started walking toward the backyard.

"Cooper, one more thing."

I stopped and walked backwards toward her.

"You're going to be punished."

"I am? Why?" I spun around to face her.

"For running off in your pajamas without telling me where you were going. It's not even a garage sale day."

It was weird to hear Mom say the word *punished.* When I was little she once sent me to my room without supper for playing tag with the raccoon that lived in a hole behind the barn. Since then, the word had fallen out of her dictionary. It made me happy to hear it. Even though Robo-Mom had malfunctioned again, she seemed to be getting a little better.

"What's going to happen to me?"

"I haven't decided. Jill made some suggestions."

This was getting better all the time. I couldn't wait to find out what the punishment would be. It was something to look forward to. "I'm sorry. Jan fixed Decto."

"That's what I figured. Go put on your clothes. They're in the dryer."

When I walked into the backyard in my regular clothes, Mr. Shepherd was standing next to a tall, stern-looking man. He had a big shock of gray hair that pointed in different directions and a gray bushy beard. His arms were covered in curly gray hair—not just regular arm fuzz, but actual thickets big enough for endangered wildlife to nest in. The hair spread down his legs and even covered his kneecaps. If there's one guy in the world who actually needed a razor for his birthday, it was him. It made me want to puke. When a man's hair turns gray it's supposed to fall out, not get bigger. I didn't like the guy right away, but Mr. Shepherd kept whispering to him. They were staring down at the cannon. A little fence made out of sticks and red ribbons surrounded the ravine.

"Ah, here's the little man now," Mr. Shepherd said, clapping his hands. "Cooper, this is Richard Archer. He loves old things, just like we do. He got so excited about your finds that he wanted to see for himself."

"You live on a historic landmark, Cooper," the stern man said in a sterner voice. "It's a rare thing. I hope you realize that."

"Mr. Archer would like to follow us around while we

check the density of artifacts in the newly cleared land," Mr. Shepherd said. "Do you want to get your metal detector, Cooper?"

I looked at the stern man's feet. He had thick boots on that were made out of iron.

"Mr. Shepherd, can I talk to you for a second, privately?" I took his hand and pulled him over to the space behind the barn. I spoke softly and made super-sad eyes. "I liked it when it was just us yesterday. I don't want him to be here, too. Can't you get rid of him?"

"It is fun getting in a time machine, isn't it?" Mr. Shepherd whispered. "You want to hear more stories about my dad?"

I nodded. "So will you?"

"Cooper, do you even remember that you pitched rocks at my truck for ten minutes yesterday?"

I had forgotten about that. I drooped my head. "Sorry. I didn't get any sleep the night before."

"Did you get sleep last night?"

I thought about the full moon, the valley full of army ghosts heading this way, and talking to Tanner until dawn. "Not really, but it was still a good night."

"Stay here. I'll see what I can do."

Mr. Shepherd whispered to the stern-looking man for a while. Eventually the hairy guy walked toward me. I turned my back to him and stared into the little space between the bushes and the barn. Past the pile of cut weeds, on the far side of the barn, there's a vine-covered white archway hidden in the wall of pine trees that leads to my megasecret hideout. I thought about making a run for it, but the man tromped quickly onto the gravel. He said something to Mom, shattered some helpless rocks under his monstrous boots (I'm sure he has foot hair too), and sped off in his white truck. I turned around when the coast was clear.

"Better?" Mr. Shepherd said.

I nodded, wondering when to ask him about the Battle of Newtown.

"Do you want me to get Decto, or do you want to talk about stuff first?"

"Actually, I got you a present," Mr. Shepherd said. He pulled a narrow box out of a hidden pocket in his furry jacket and handed it to me.

"What is it?"

"Open it."

I opened the box. Inside was a white stick that looked like a magic wand. It had the words TREASURE SEEKER PROBE VERSION 1B on it.

"What is it?" I waved the wand, but it didn't do anything.

"It's a tiny metal detector. You know how sometimes it's hard to figure out exactly where to dig, and your first hole is a little off? This little detector probe will pinpoint the location for you if the object is shallow enough. Or if you've already dug a hole, you can just stick the mini-detector into it instead of picking up the big detector again. Keep it in your back pocket. It will help you pinpoint metal objects quicker."

"Thanks." I pressed the little switch on the back of the wand and waved the mini-detector over a tiny metal snap on my jeans.

"Beep beep," Mini-Decto said in a really high-pitched voice. I stuck it in my back pocket and felt like a real treasure hunter. Jan and Xavier would be proud.

I was just about to be happy when something popped into my head. Mr. Shepherd didn't like me at all. He was only using me to get closer to the historic stuff buried in my backyard. I stared into his eyes, waiting for him to admit that I was just some crazy kid who throws rocks and talks to metal detectors.

I thought of the story that Jan told me about the good

boy and the evil boy who looked alike. It was starting to become obvious that Tanner was the good boy and I was the evil one. That explained why Mom stopped being her old self after I grew up a little. One day she realized that the bad one survived. The good spirit is floating in heaven, holding up the blue sky. This morning is a perfect example— Robo-Mom was back, and we were going to Elmira. Now because of me she gave the money to Jill and she's sitting in her aluminum chair buried in a book again. Probably Jan doesn't really like me either—I just remind her of Xavier. Dad didn't want to stick around when it was just me. Jill might be the only person who really loves me—and that's only because we hardly ever see each other. That way she can't find out the truth.

My bottom lip started shaking.

"Cooper, if you want, I'd be willing to listen for a change. You can tell me what's bothering you."

I shook my head, but I couldn't talk because an explosion of tears would come out.

"Cooper, think of the one thing that you want most in the world. Close your eyes and imagine it."

Easy. I closed my eyes and thought about me and Mom out in the world going to garage sales again.

"You will never give up trying to make it come true. Nothing will ever stop you from trying. Right?"

I nodded.

"That's how I feel about a rare situation like this. In my life I will never have another opportunity to explore a fresh, undisturbed archaeological site like this one. The world is so busy and heavily explored. These types of finds are becoming rarer, and this one is right in our own backyard. Many battlefields are on preserved land—the government decides when and where to dig. We're in control here. They didn't make the park big enough. Do you understand that?"

I nodded. I felt my insides calming down.

"So whatever happens next, I want you to remember that it's just me going after my dream. I'll do anything for it, just like you would."

"What present are you going to get me next?" I wiped away a tear that almost escaped from my eye.

Mr. Shepherd laughed. "We'll see."

"I'm ready for the story of the battle."

"That's the last thing I thought you were going to say. Are you sure?"

I nodded and babbled out some of what Jan had already told me.

"Go sit down next to the cannon."

# CHAPTER 21

I stretched out on the grass next to the long hole. I put my arms behind my head and tilted my chin up, so the sun's rays could warm my face. Mr. Shepherd stood on the other side and flipped through a small notebook that he had pulled from a hidden pocket in his furry jacket. After a few minutes he shut the book and tucked it away. Then he began to tell his story:

"General Sullivan led his troops north through Pennsylvania. General Clinton led his troops west through New York. The two armies met up at Tioga, where the Susquehanna and Chemung Rivers join together. Between them they had over four thousand soldiers, nearly seven hundred officers, twelve hundred horses, and eight hundred cattle, along with medical staff, volunteers, and hundreds of supply boats. Nearly one-quarter of George Washington's entire army. Only a few Iroquois allies from the Oneida and Tuscarora—the tribes that had sided with the Americans—came along as scouts. On the twenty-ninth of August, 1779, there was a parade six miles long tromping up the Chemung River. Their mission was to destroy every village belonging to those Iroquois tribes that had sided with the British."

"Did the British have many troops here?" I asked.

"The British had only about two hundred soldiers and just under a thousand Iroquois allies from the four tribes loyal to them—the Onondaga, Mohawk, Seneca, and Cayuga. So the British were greatly outnumbered, even when you count their Iroquois allies, but they had two big advantages. The first was that they controlled the high ground up on that ridge, where they could see for miles and properly time their surprise attack. The other was that they were in a fixed location, with many hidden inside the breastworks. The Americans would be out in the open, making them easy targets as they marched along the river.

"Colonel John Butler, the British commander, did not like their chances for victory. He wanted to retreat and hide on the bigger mountain behind this one, then come out and fight in small groups. Even the Iroquois chief thought this was a better plan than a direct confrontation with an army four times the size of theirs. But the Iroquois warriors wouldn't hear of it. They were defending the doorway into their great longhouse—protecting their families, towns, and homeland."

"Iroquois warriors do what they want," I interrupted. "Just like in Cherry Valley."

"You're a genius, Cooper. It wasn't like the American army, where orders from commanders must be obeyed." Mr. Shepherd skipped around while he told his story, making big arm movements like he was in a play. He pointed up to Ghost Conductor's Bluff. "You see how that tree-lined ridge up there goes back to the north, like a—"

"Like a big train about to roar off the hill?"

"Yes, I suppose it does look like that. The British and Iroquois set up their breastworks below the peak, facing the meadow beyond that wall of trees and curving over your backyard. The structure went around the entire end of the mountain and concealed hundreds of men.

"In the meantime," he continued, "the Americans were having trouble keeping their troops moving. The heavy cannons kept getting bogged down in the mud, and many of their animals wandered off. The soldiers were running out of food. They were only allowed to eat seven ears of corn on the day of the battle. Small bands of Iroquois came out to taunt the Americans, hoping they could entice the whole army to follow them into the trap. Instead, General Sullivan sent a few riflemen ahead to scout the area. These men heard the sound of wood chopping. They climbed a tree to get a better look and saw men with painted faces hidden behind the breastworks. Imagine that, Cooper! Now we have global positioning systems and satellites that can spot a person from outer space—but those men saved themselves from a surprise attack by climbing a tree."

Mr. Shepherd paced in circles and pointed up at the sky, down toward the Chemung River, and over at the steep forest. He was moving so much that I was afraid he would fall into the hole with the cannon.

"General Sullivan came up with a plan. He positioned most of the soldiers in front of the breastworks—right here in this yard, your neighbors' yards, and the meadow beyond that wall of trees—under the command of General Edward Hand. This area was a big clearing back then, all the way down to the trail that followed the river. By putting the army here, they might convince the British and Iroquois that the main assault would come from the front. The cannons were also placed in this clearing under the command of Colonel Thomas Proctor.

"Another part of the army, led by General James Clinton and General Enoch Poor, was ordered to march into the forest behind this mountain. You can't see from here, but the next peak behind yours creates a hidden valley. There's a stream that meanders through there, and in colonial times it was shrouded in thick trees—they called it Hoffman Hollow. Their goal was to sneak behind enemy lines and surprise the British and Iroquois from the rear. It's called a flanking maneuver.

"Once the front brigades were in place, the riflemen were supposed to keep the enemy busy while the hidden army snuck into position. They looked up and saw the Iroquois warriors and British soldiers safely tucked away behind the breastworks. But could Hand's men convince them that this was the Americans' main attack? They fired their weapons. The British and Iroquois fired back. A volley of fire was traded back and forth for two hours—this was probably when those musket balls you found landed on the ground. The Fourth Pennsylvania Regiment was part of this strategy—maybe the button with the four on it was lost then.

"The cannoneers were supposed to wait long enough for the sneaking army to get into position. But the marshy ground slowed the progress of the soldiers between the hills, so they weren't in the correct place when the first cannons fired. Cannonballs, small pellets, and iron spikes rained down on the breastworks. Some cannonballs sailed over the ridge and exploded behind the Iroquois warriors— these were called 'bursting balls,' and they frightened the warriors into thinking that the entire hill was surrounded. Many of the Iroquois fled at that moment, leaving even fewer to face the American army.

"Finally, the armies of Clinton and Poor reached their position in Hoffman Hollow beyond the swamp. But they were spotted by Iroquois scouts, who shouted warnings to those on top of the mountain. With heavy packs on their backs and sharp bayonets attached to their muskets, the American soldiers struggled up toward the ridge in the summer heat. Some fainted from exhaustion. War cries and a volley of musket fire came from Iroquois defenders who charged down to meet them. One of General Poor's regiments became surrounded by Iroquois warriors, and many soldiers were killed or wounded. Nearby troops from Clinton's brigade scrambled across the steep hillside and counterattacked with a volley of musket fire, forcing the Iroquois back up the mountain. The American soldiers pressed on, driving their enemies from tree to tree with their bayonets. When they were near the top, they reformed battle lines and fired again, breaking through the British and Iroquois line that was protecting the rear of the breastworks.

"At this time, General Hand ordered the brigade in the meadow to attach bayonets and charge up the steep hillside toward the front of the breastworks. The remaining Iroquois within them, seeing the charging Americans and hearing the sounds of musket fire on top of the ridge, became certain they were surrounded and abandoned the fortifications. With the battle lost, all the Iroquois and British began retreating north along the ridge. The American army chased them for over a mile—through the land that makes up the Newtown Battlefield State Park today."

"So the Americans won? Then why did they leave the cannon here?" I sat up and peered down into the ravine.

"After the American army regrouped, General Sullivan decided that the heaviest iron cannons should be abandoned. It was too difficult to drag them across rivers, streams, and swamps. The army had a long journey ahead of them, and they were already low on food and supplies. They took the brass cannons with them and left the iron ones behind. A letter written to George Washington about the battle said that the cannons were sent back to the American fort at Tioga, but the Earth is telling a different story, isn't it? Maybe this cannon was damaged, so they buried it to avoid the hassle of transporting it down the river in a boat."

I looked at the rusty metal covered with blobs of dirt, wondering if anyone was hurt by this cannon. For once, I was glad that I didn't have Mom's power to see the history of an antique. I knew that whatever Mr. Shepherd was going to say next wasn't going to be pleasant.

"The Americans lost eleven men, and thirty-two were wounded. The British suffered five dead, seven wounded. The Iroquois may have lost twelve men or more—nobody is quite sure."

Mom's voice came from the front of the house. "Cooper, a customer would like to know how much we want for the button with the four on it, and the jar of musket balls."

I stood up. "Tell him they're not for sale!"

Mr. Shepherd smiled at me, but I didn't smile back. So that was the awful story that I would have to tell Jill sometime. I flopped on my back and looked up at the sun—the same star that had watched humans do horrible things to each other hundreds of years ago in this spot. One fluffy white cloud hovered right over our backyard, but the rest of the sky was perfectly blue.

# CHAPTER 22

"So now you know what happened in your own backyard," Mr. Shepherd said.

I nodded, then leaned over the ravine and threw up—a chunky green blob of vegetable parts. My stomach kept gurgling, so I got on all fours and puked over and over again. A long rope of spit stretched out of my mouth all the way to the cannon.

"I'm sorry," Mr. Shepherd said. "I forced you to hear the story."

"It's okay. I wanted to know." I broke the spit thread with my hand and shook it off.

"I misjudged you, Cooper. My son loves playing war. He runs around with his water gun and shoots me all the time."

"You have a son?" I wiped my mouth on my sleeve.

Mr. Shepherd grabbed the purple amulet around his neck. My heart skipped a beat. He pressed a hidden button and opened it into two halves. One side had a photo of a woman with orange hair, and the other had a picture of a boy and girl with orange hair. "John is six and Ashley is four."

"You never told me you had kids! If I had kids, I would talk about them all the time!"

"You're a tough grader, Cooper."

"Do you like them?"

"Love 'em. That's why this heart is on top of my heart." He snapped the pendant shut.

I squinted up at Mr. Shepherd and wondered what it would be like to live in his house.

"There's a creaky floorboard in my room," I said.

"That must be the secret entrance to the underground chamber," Mr. Shepherd replied. "I'll get the torch, you get our adventure journal. Draw a map as we explore. We have to be back by the time school starts."

Mr. Shepherd tilted open the floorboard, and we tiptoed down some creaky, cobwebby stairs.

"Coop, are you sure you're okay?" He waved his hand in front of my face.

"What should we do now?"

"Get your metal detector, and we'll try out the new probe."

Mini-Decto! I had already forgotten about him. He had fallen out of my pocket during the story and was hiding under some squashed weeds. I grabbed him and ran around to the front of the house.

"Mom, look. Mr. Shepherd got me a miniature metal detector." I put the tip of it against her aluminum chair, and it started beeping. Then I casually slid it into my back pocket.

"What an awful man. I never should have let him onto our property."

"Very funny." I picked up Decto. "So what's my punishment?"

"I'm not sure yet. Tell me which doll is eighteenth century and which is nineteenth century." She showed me two pages from a book.

"The wooden one is eighteenth and the bisque is nineteenth. Bye. Gotta detect. Keep thinking about it!"

When I got back to the clearing, Mr. Shepherd took Decto and hit the power button. "I'm going to show you a trick first," he said. "Those numbers that appear on the little TV screen tell you how conductive the metal object under the ground is—in other words, how quickly electricity passes through it. That can be used to identify the size of the object or the type of metal it's made out of—even before you dig it up. Eventually you'll memorize which numbers are bottle caps or musket balls or small rusty blobs. If you turn the discrimination knob, you can decide what types of metal objects you want the detector to find and what types you want it to ignore. Watch. I'll turn the knob all the way to the right and limit the signal to 1000, which is the highest it goes. This way the metal detector will ignore any buried metal with a conductivity of 999 or less. According to the history books, General Sullivan's army had two large iron cannons like the one we found. We're about to discover if they buried both." He handed Decto to me.

"Won't we miss everything else?"

"It should only take a minute. Run around. The detector will pick up a signal of 1000 only. What else could have that strong a signal other than a cannon?"

I ran all over the yard with Decto's face scraping against the cut weeds. Near the barn he started beeping, and the number 1000 appeared on the little screen. "Here it is! Cool trick."

"I'll flag it, and then head home to eat. Getting hungry. You must be too, since you just left your last meal in 1779. We'll dig it up next time."

My heart sank. The barn's shadow was hardly poking into the backyard, and Mr. Shepherd wanted to leave already.

"No, don't worry, I have food. Wait here." I ran inside and made my specialty—a plate of random stuff. When I kicked open the screen door, the last hinge broke and the whole door tilted down and crashed onto the gravel. My legs were definitely getting stronger.

"That's why I'm waiting," Mom said without looking up from her book. "I want the punishment to include everything."

I ran back and handed the plate to Mr. Shepherd.

"A chunk of bread in the shape of your hand. Looks appetizing. Okay, one second." He took that little electronic gizmo out of his pocket and pressed the glass screen a bunch of times. The device hissed at me.

"What did you write?"

"U 3 eat, with friend." Mr. Shepherd took a small green spray bottle out of a secret compartment in his furry jacket. He sprayed the whole plate with little squirts, and then he gobbled vegetables, cheese, and bread. Every few minutes he pulled a tiny blue spray bottle out of an even more secret pocket and squirted something on his face. He dabbed himself with a small yellow cloth. Lastly, he grabbed a tiny bottle of water out of the most super-secret pocket ever and took a bunch of miniature sips. I didn't eat much because it was more interesting to watch Mr. Shepherd do all those things.

"How long does it take you to get dressed in the morning?" I asked.

"'Bout an hour. If you count the shaving, face washing, and moisturizer. What about you?" He tossed the stalk of a pepper away.

"I usually sleep until the first customer, and then I can be dressed in ten seconds. Unless there's some hair sticking up weirdly. Then Mirror makes fun of me until I fix it."

"Mirror?"

"I have a grumpy old mirror that barely reflects."

"Is that like *Mirror, mirror on the wall, who's the fairest of them all?*"

"Sort of, only you'd never ask Mirror that question."

After eating, Mr. Shepherd pulled the white gloves and shower cap out of a regular pocket and put them on. We spent the rest of the day digging up whatever big thing Decto had found. Every few shovelfuls of dirt, I leaned into the hole and used Mini-Decto to see if we were getting close. Mr. Shepherd wanted to wait to tell me the rest of the story, now that I had new vegetables inside me, but I forced him to continue.

"The Americans didn't camp here. When the army was marching again, the next thing they did was destroy Newtown. The town was already abandoned when the Americans burned it to the ground. Then the expedition continued north. The Iroquois never wanted to fight a large battle again—they sent out only small raiding parties from then on. It wasn't enough. Over forty Iroquois villages were destroyed during the Sullivan-Clinton expedition. The last target might have been the British stronghold of Fort Niagara near the Canadian border, but with winter approaching and low supplies they decided to turn back."

"Do you think George Washington was right to send that whole big army up here because children had been scalped?"

"I don't judge, remember? I just seek the truth." Mr. Shepherd stopped digging. He looked tired. When he leaned down to examine the hole, his sneakers actually squished down a little. It gave me the courage to ask my next question.

"Does scalping hurt?" I ran my hands through my hair.

"I would imagine. They used a tomahawk to cut a slit from the back of the head to the front and then removed the entire scalp—skin, hair, and all. The British offered money for each scalp brought back to Fort Niagara. Or sometimes the scalps would be decorated and displayed in villages as a symbolic replacement for warriors lost in combat."

My stomach gurgled again. I held on to a big clump of my hair. It was horrible to think that part of me could be hanging on another person's wall like a trophy. It must have been scary for kids living in Upstate New York in 1779—

especially after people started telling stories about the horrible things that were happening. If you were Iroquois, you peered into the forest, wondering if every snapping twig was somebody coming to destroy your village. If you were American, you stayed awake at night, wondering if every creak and footstep was somebody coming to scalp you.

"Why did the Iroquois warriors have to do that?"

"They were afraid of being driven off their land by the Americans."

"They should have gone on the American side like two of their tribes did. The Six Nations should have stuck together. Those four tribes made a dumb decision to go on the British side. If you mess with George Washington, you'd better step back."

"Those enemy tribes eventually named George Washington 'Town Destroyer.' Even today some Iroquois use that term to refer to any president of the United States."

"Where did they go once their villages were destroyed?"

"Northwest to Fort Niagara. They gathered outside the fort, relying on British food and clothing to stay alive. But Sullivan's men discovered a very ancient Iroquois woman hiding in the rubble of an abandoned village. She was 120 years old, with long white hair and a wrinkled face. She was too frail to be moved, so the soldiers built a house for her and stocked it with food until her family could come back and take care of her."

When Mini-Decto finally beeped and Mr. Shepherd uncovered the top of a brown rusty cannon, I hardly even looked at it. I wished it was buried deeper so the warm sun could beam on my face while Mr. Shepherd told more stories. Well, there was that one fluffy white cloud that kept blocking the sun, but I knew Tanner was on top of it, peeking down to see what we were up to.

"Simply amazing," Mr. Shepherd said. "One cannon

was the find of a lifetime. A second one—almost too good to be true." He placed little sticks with blue flags all around the new ravine.

"Are you going to come back tomorrow?"

"Cooper, would you reconsider having an archaeological team excavate this yard? Not everything that was lost was metal. In a real dig they would remove all dirt and artifacts from the ground—pottery, ivory, wood, bones, stone, and whatever else. We're really spoiling this site by taking cores. We'll need financial backing—there's equipment and expenses—"

"I like it the way it is. I don't want strangers tromping through my yard."

"If I asked your mom, would you get mad?"

Somehow I had to make Mr. Shepherd happy before he ruined everything. I ran around to the front and got the button with the 4 on it and musket balls. After sprinting back I placed them in his hands. "You can put everything we find in the museum."

"Thanks, Cooper."

"Are you going to come back tomorrow?"

"Maybe. I'd like to take some pictures of the cannons in situ, and then we have to start thinking about how we'll get them up safely."

"What time will you come?"

"Not sure."

"Early?"

"Maybe."

"I think nine is a good time." I followed him around the front of the house, all the way to his truck.

# CHAPTER 23

After goodbyes and watching Mr. Shepherd's truck disappear at the bottom of the hill, I ran over to Mom and took that dumb book out of her hands. I plopped in her lap. We stayed quiet for a while as the crows cawed in the steep forest. Tanner's cloud had broken into a lot of little clouds, so it was just me and Mom.

"You're going to be grounded for three weeks," Mom finally said.

"What does that mean?"

"You can't go anywhere."

"Not even to garage sales?"

"Nowhere."

"Can I tell Jan?"

"No."

I wasn't mad, because really the punishment had backfired on Mom—Mr. Shepherd was going to come here each day, so I didn't need to go anywhere. But it was good that she was in the punishing mood. It made me think that she was getting closer to being Robo-Mom again, only for good.

"The mermaid has trapped me. Good job." I leaned back and put my arm around her neck. The aluminum chair groaned a little.

"That means you can't go out and steal the evil king's magical amulet."

"It doesn't matter. The amulet's not magical after all. I was going to call off the mission." I took the blue ribbon out of her hair.

"So are you going to tell me what happened on our property during the Revolutionary War?"

My stomach gave me a warning gurgle. "Later," I said. Mom tried to reach around me to grab the book, but I swatted her hand away. "You're not going to let Mr. Shepherd make an archaeological dig in the backyard, are you?"

"I think you'll be in charge of the excavation for now." She reached for the book again, but this time I let her pick it up.

I listened to the sound of Mom breathing and turning pages. I moved up and down with each breath, and a little to the left whenever she turned a page. This went on for hours, until a tiny car pulled onto the gravel. A small woman got out and browsed through the barn. I showed her all the little things for sale. Finally she bought a miniature grandfather clock built for a dollhouse. It wasn't even as big as the twenty-dollar bill she handed me.

There was enough stuff packed into the barn to outlast a three-week grounding, maybe a lot longer. Some antiques sit around for years before people buy them. Maybe the grounding would finally give me time to organize all the stuff and make it sell faster. And maybe Mr. Turner would come and bring me more things. I just wasn't sure about food. If Mr. Shepherd showed up each day with McDonald's, then it wouldn't be a problem—as long as I didn't put the fries anywhere near Decto.

That night, as the moon sent not-quite-maximum-power moonbeams through my cracked window, I heard a voice I didn't recognize. It wasn't Decto. He was snoring peacefully next to Mini-Decto on the floor near my bed. It wasn't Mirror. His reflection had turned off for the night. It wasn't Koala. He doesn't snore.

A big crack opened in the floor, and a beam of red light made my room glow an eerie color. A burst of heat filled the room, making me sweat big drops onto my pillow.

"Greetings, Cooper," a deep voice said from within the crack. "It is I, planet Earth."

"You can talk?"

"Yes, but only when my cousin the moon is done being full. I speak only to those who are worthy."

"I already have a lot of friends," I said.

A deep laugh came from under my floor. The whole room shook, causing Mini-Decto to wake up. He started crying. Decto comforted him.

"Dada!" Mini-Decto said. Decto's eyes opened really wide, and a big grin covered his whole plastic disc.

"I have so many secrets buried within my body," Earth said. "More than you can possibly imagine. Yet so few of the creatures that tickle my surface care anything about them. But you care, Cooper, and therefore you are among the worthy."

"Are you also friends with Mr. Shepherd?"

"Indeed," Earth said in that deep, booming voice. "We're pretty tight, actually. I gave him a pink scarf for his birthday. Do not take lightly being among the worthy. I care not for humans. Most litter my insides with tiny bits of junk, some bore through my skin until I bleed the black blood that runs their machines, and others steal my gold and diamonds for their own greedy pleasures. But you are unearthing my secrets and healing my flesh. Each tiny poisonous object that you remove from my skin brings me closer to being pure and perfect again."

"That's what Xavier believed," I said.

"Ah, Xavier, he was a good man."

"You knew him too?"

"Of course! Jan's husband of fifty-two years. He removed so many objects from me one year that it cured my chicken pox. Another time he removed a sharp bottle cap from me in Peru that caused a seventeen-thousand-nine-hundred-twenty-seven-step chain reaction that eventually formed an island in the South Pacific. Good times, good times."

"Jan thinks I'm Xavier reborn."

A fountain of lava spouted through the crack in the floor, waking up Mirror and Koala. They looked at the glowing, red-hot, gurgling room with scared faces.

"There is one more thing I must say," Earth bellowed. "*Beware the gifts of Mr. Shepherd.* I love that kooky human, but sometimes he cares about my hidden treasures a bit too much. Remember what happened to the Iroquois tribes that accepted the British gifts and went over to their side. Be strong, and don't let him inside your heart too quickly. Think about that time you had diarrhea and he bought that antique butter churner for a quarter before you could get to the garage sale. Now I must beg my leave. Some kid just built a sand castle next to one of my oceans, and I have to go wreck it."

There was a loud banging noise as the hole in my floor tried to close. It didn't sound like the type of banging the Earth would make.

I lifted my head from the pillow and noticed that it was daylight out. I rubbed my eyes. The hole in my floor was gone. Koala, Decto, Mini-Decto, Mirror—all of them were asleep. That banging and some low voices came from outside.

I jumped out of bed and put on my clothes in eight seconds. I ran to the front door. Mom was sitting outside, munching on something and talking to a dog-walking customer. Mr. Shepherd was putting the screen door back on with a big hammer.

"I brought you breakfast, Coop. I remember how you tore into those French fries." He put some oil on a brand-new shiny hinge.

"More fries?"

"No, your mom said you like cheese, so I got you some mozzarella sticks. Got your mom some too."

"Where are mine?"

"Over there by your bike." He pointed to Squeaky, who was standing up next to the green truck.

Strange. I remembered putting Squeaky inside the barn for the night. Mr. Shepherd opened the door for me. I walked slowly over to Squeaky. There was a bag on the gravel next to him. I could tell something was wrong right away. Squeaky's chain wasn't rusty anymore. His eyes were barely open! I fell to my knees and patted Squeaky's handlebars.

"Sorry . . . about . . . the mozzarella sticks," Squeaky sputtered. I looked down at the bag. There was a big hole in its side, and it was empty. I pushed him into the road and hopped on. When I pedaled, there was no noise at all!

Trying not to cry, I walked Squeaky gently back onto the gravel. I grabbed the ripped bag and tried to wipe the grease off the chain.

"Surprised?" Mr. Shepherd said. "Quiet, huh?"

Without saying anything, I walked over to the screen door, kicked it as hard as I could, and ran inside. The new hinges didn't even break. My legs weren't strong after all. Diving onto my bed, I buried my head under the pillow and cried for a long time.

# CHAPTER 24

Nobody cared that I didn't get out of bed the whole day. Decto and Mini-Decto did nothing but whisper to each other, never once asking me why I was upset. They had their own life now and didn't need me. There was no point in metal-detecting, anyway. Squeaky always thought I loved Decto more than him. How could I run around and have a good time digging up buried treasures now that he was dead?

I thought about some of the fun times that me and Squeaky had going to garage sales. One time we found a little old lady who had so many dolls for sale they didn't all fit in Squeaky's basket. I had to hold some under my shirt, and one was sticking out of my sock. We laughed so hard that his chain fell off. All the dolls watched from the curb while I put Squeaky back together. Some lady driving by told me that I had a nice doll collection, and she offered me a hundred bucks for them! After that, I washed Squeaky's basket and filled his tires with air.

If I had known he liked mozzarella sticks I would have gotten some for him with the next food delivery. The only comforting thing about his death was that now Tanner could ride him in heaven. It was like a hand-me-up. I assumed that somebody up there would lower the seat for him.

This is the part of the story where I sleep a lot because of missing Squeaky, and being grounded.

Grounded.

Nap.

Grounded.

Grounded.

Over the next few days I moped around and let Mom take care of all the customers. Sometimes I peeked out to see if Mr. Shepherd's green truck was there. Mostly it was quiet, except for the long churring of those summer insects. Having all that thinking time made me finally figure out what the bugs were saying to each other:

NOISY BUG 1: There's no way Mr. Shepherd's going to come back. He got Cooper fries, a milkshake, a miniature metal detector, and mozzarella sticks. And he tells stories in the sun.

NOISY BUG 2: Dude, I know, and Cooper is mean to him in return. Just let him into your heart already, kid, sheesh!

NOISY BUG 1: Now let's say that fifty thousand more times without taking a breath.

NOISY BUG 2: Good idea! And while we're doing that, let's shed our hard clear shells so Cooper gets grossed out by them.

NOISY BUG 1 (dropping gross shell): There's no way Mr. Shepherd's going to come back. He got Cooper fries, a milkshake, a miniature metal detector, and mozzarella sticks. And he tells stories in the sun.

NOISY BUG 2 (dropping gross shell): Dude, I know—

I couldn't listen to them anymore, so I jammed my head under the blankets and made humming noises.

"He thifn't mean to hurf Skweafy," Koala said.

Somehow I dozed off in all that chatter. When I woke up, the gravel lot was full of vehicles. There was Mr. Shepherd's green truck, a white truck, and a motorcycle.

I hopped out of bed, got dressed, and put Mini-Decto into my back pocket. Then I ran outside to check out all the action. It turned out that only the motorcycle was a customer.

A lady in a leather jacket was looking at our collection of beaded purses. The rest of the voices came from out back.

I ran back there and saw the man with the iron boots and mutant gray hair standing next to Mr. Shepherd. Iron Boots was pointing a tiny camera down at the cannon near the house, trying to press a button with a hairy-knuckled finger. He saw me stop in my tracks and whispered to Mr. Shepherd, "Shh, he's here."

They both turned and looked at me. I spun around and stared at the weed pile behind the barn.

"Well, I was just leaving, Shep. That's enough pictures," Iron Boots said in a cold, rusty voice. He stomped past my back without saying anything to me. I could hear him breathing heavily, as if his throat was clogged with hairballs. He said goodbye to Mom and drove away.

"You can turn around now, Cooper, and see the new present I got for you."

I turned around. Mr. Shepherd was holding a weird-looking belt with pouches in it.

"What is that?"

"It's your new pirate treasure gear." He pointed to a skull and crossbones printed on it next to the words CAPTAIN JACK. "It has a pouch to hold the small things you dig up. It even has a secret compartment for your best finds. This loop holds your miniature pinpointing probe, and here you can put a small trowel."

He tied it around my waist, and I slipped Mini-Decto into the loop. The little guy looked sad and scared, but he fit snugly against my hip. Mr. Shepherd put a small shovel with a black handle into the other slot.

"Thanks."

"Now you're all geared up for an adventure."

"You don't have to bring me something every time you come."

"I know—I'll slow down soon. Once you're properly equipped."

"Every third time would be fair. Except if it's food."

Mr. Shepherd took some big white pads out of a hidden pocket. He tied them around his pant legs so that the fluffy part covered his knees, like he was going to play football with me. Then he got down on his knees and clasped his hands together.

"Cooper, I'm begging you. Please let us invite archaeologists to excavate this yard. You can be the captain. We'll bring you French fries whenever you want."

I knew he was going to say something like that. Archaeologists probably all wear thick boots. No way was I going to let a bunch of tall, gray-noggined, arm-and-leg-hair-covered, smelly strangers ruin our fun.

"I like it when it's just us. I don't want a bunch of strangers tromping around."

"They won't be strangers for long."

It was time for my emergency backup plan. I took Mr. Shepherd's hand and led him into the little space behind the barn, past the pile of rotting weeds, and over to the line of tall trees with the white archway jammed into them. The super-secret entrance.

"I want to show you this," I said.

I led him through the hidden trail, where the wild bushes tried to claw our faces, strange flowers made funny smells, and bumpy roots tripped us. Mr. Shepherd put the doctor's mask over his face and made shrieking noises when any part of nature touched him. Swiping tree branches out of our way, I felt like a real pirate exploring the wilderness in my new gear.

Eventually we came out in a small clearing jammed right up against a clumpy, dirt-covered cliff. The ground was full of wild grasses and pretty flowers of all different colors, like a special balcony with a perfect view of the bigger mountain behind ours and a whole bunch of new valleys. A road came out from between the hills and curved all the way down to some houses near the highway. A dirt-covered farm with a lonely red barn took up most of the land below us. The tall line of pine trees kept our house and barn hidden, along with most of the Chemung River Valley.

It's such a special place that I wasn't planning to bring Mr. Shepherd back here, but then I thought it would make him realize that people in big boots don't belong on our property. The tiny little flowers are so delicate. Every Mother's Day I lead Mom back here and just point to the ones I would've picked for her. We stay here for a picnic and stare at the fresh view until we hear the popping noise of a customer driving onto the gravel.

"Amazing. You would never know this terrace was here behind those tall evergreens and the maze of bushes. That road is coming from Hoffman Hollow—the place that Clinton and Poor snuck through to flank the enemy. You can see the stream next to it!"

"This place is a secret—you can't tell anybody."

"This erosion is dramatic." He pointed to the steep hillside, where the reddish dirt was piled up in large mounds at the bottom. Far above us the dirt gave way to small trees near Ghost Conductor's Bluff. "Bet nobody's climbed up there for centuries."

"I think about doing it, but the ghosts would probably get mad."

If the ghostly train ever did roar to life, this little cliff would be the worst place to stand. The caboose would soar directly overhead, sending an avalanche of falling rocks and bits of mountainside into this little secret spot.

"Cooper, what is that thing sticking out of the cliff?" He pointed to a small, dark triangle.

# CHAPTER 25

The mysterious object was too high for me to reach, but Mr. Shepherd took a little white stick out of his furry coat and unfolded it a bunch of times until it transformed into a really long stick. He went on his tiptoes, reached up, and poked at the brown triangle. It came loose and slid down into a dirt pile.

I pulled Mini-Decto out of my belt and pressed his little face against the triangle. He started beeping. "It's metal," I said.

Mr. Shepherd carefully picked up the triangle. A wavy design was engraved near the edges, and it had a hollow circle attached to one corner.

"It's the head of a tomahawk," he said, blowing dirt off it. "A carved stick would be put through the hole to create the handle of an axe. Wood decays quickly, so only the metal survived."

"Have you found any before?"

That barely came out of my mouth before Mr. Shepherd sat down and tilted backwards onto an empty spot of ground. He moved his arms and legs quickly, like he was doing a doggy paddle.

"Yessss!" he said, punching and kicking the air.

Embarrassed, I looked out at the bigger mountain behind ours, hidden valleys with lonely houses, and oddly shaped farms rolling off toward a bend in the Chemung River. I don't visit this secret view too often, so it made me feel awkward and far away from home.

*"Who is this weirdo?" the beautiful landscape said.*

"Oh, that's Mr. Shepherd. He just likes your view so much he fell down," I lied.

"No, I wasn't born in the last thousand years, silly. Cooper, you should visit us more often back here. You would feel more comfortable if you did."

"Cooper, do you realize what a find this is? A brass tomahawk from the Battle of Newtown! Perhaps it belonged to an Iroquois warrior who had traded with the Europeans to replace his stone blade."

"Did it fall from where the breastworks were?" I asked, pointing to the bushes and small trees near the top of the steep hillside.

"Probably."

I grabbed the tomahawk from him and scraped it against the back of my head. It didn't hurt. "Doesn't seem like it could scalp someone."

"It's dull from weathering."

My plan of taking Mr. Shepherd onto the secret balcony was about to backfire. Now he would want to bring archaeologists onto our property more than ever. I looked at the big line of pine trees and wondered if being back here broke the rules of being grounded. After all, we were still on the edge of our property.

"For the museum, sir." I got down on one knee and made a bowl out of both hands with the tomahawk inside.

"Now don't you see why we need to carefully study this site, Cooper? Each find is a piece of a puzzle that will give us a whole picture when completed. That puzzle is part of a tapestry representing all of American history, and that in turn is part of a grand mosaic displaying the entire history of mankind. We would be contributing to the collective intelligence of humanity by studying this place. It's a miracle the land is so well preserved, unlike the spoiled areas down there." He pointed to the valleys, farms, and houses down below.

*"Hey!" the beautiful landscape said. "Next time you come back here, Cooper, don't bring that guy."*

I pictured our whole gravel lot full of big trucks. Mom wouldn't have any place to sit, and all of our customers would get scared away. Mr. Shepherd wouldn't even notice me.

"We can do the whole thing ourselves," I said softly. "We can map it and make drawings just like real archaeologists. We already learned a lot."

"Sit down, Cooper. I'm going to tell you a little story."

"Okay, hang on." I had to quickly decide where to sit. The sun wasn't high enough over the peak to make the whole flower patch sunny yet, so I plopped down at the edge in a bright spot. Then I spotted another sunny spot in a safer place that had a lonely drooping sunflower, so I scrambled there before Mr. Shepherd could start.

"When I was your age, my allergies were much, much worse. It wasn't just skin contact that irritated me, but airborne particles as well. Summer was the hardest. I hid in the library most of the time while the other kids were jumping in lakes. Dusty books didn't bother me. Sometimes I searched the shelves for the oldest book, or one that hadn't been checked out in a hundred years. Other days I time-traveled back to colonial times and daydreamed about the beginning of our country.

"The Declaration of Independence became my obsession. I wanted to know everything about it. I memorized the text of the entire document, including the names of all of the fifty-six people who signed it. I stood in front of the bathroom mirror and recited it exactly, pretending I was speaking directly to King George. I even traced John Hancock's signature in the very size it appeared in—almost five inches long—until I could draw it perfectly myself.

"Then I began reading about how the Declaration of Independence was written—that Thomas Jefferson composed a draft and showed it to a committee who told him to make changes. That made me wonder if the draft still existed—could I read and memorize that one, too? The librarian handed me a book with the text of the draft in it. I was thrilled. I gasped when I learned that Jefferson changed the phrase 'We hold these truths to be sacred and undeniable' to 'We hold these truths to be self-evident' for the final copy.

"Each time I learned a new fact, it was like going back to 1776. I read old letters, examined books full of old paintings, and visited museums to see important relics, such as Jefferson's portable writing desk and pen. I was a fly on the wall, witnessing one of the most important moments in American history. But it wasn't enough, Cooper. I got greedy. I wanted to know everything. How many times did Jefferson tap his foot while writing the draft, or chew on his knuckle? What did he mutter to himself? Did he take any naps to refresh his mind? Did he raise his left eyebrow or sneer while composing the part about all the bad things that King George did to the colonies? I couldn't sleep at night, imagining every last detail to be learned, if only my body could be transported back in a real time machine.

"One night while I was lying in bed, wondering if Jefferson had ever bitten his tongue while writing it, I remembered the rest of that phrase he had revised for the final copy: '. . . that all men are created equal, that they are endowed by their Creator with certain unalienable Rights, that among these are Life, Liberty, and the pursuit of Happiness.' I realized at that moment that my whole life could be one big time-traveling adventure if I worked in this field, just as my dad had suggested. I could be happy! So I attended Cornell University and studied history. I became interested in local history because around here we can still find artifacts from the American Revolution. When I got a job at the museum, I started filling it with historic treasures so anybody visiting could go on that time-traveling adventure with me.

"But I'm a glutton, Cooper, and I'll do anything to feed myself more history. There's always that secret longing to know how many times General Sullivan wiped the sweat off his face or what the soldiers said to each other around the campfires at night. I can taste those details—taste them! When I discovered that many soldiers on this expedition recorded their experiences in journals, I read every one of them, often skipping meals and staying until the library closed. But what about the other details, the ones nobody recorded? They happened, but now they're lost to time."

Mr. Shepherd hopped around while telling his story, making big arm movements and dancing. The whole flower patch became his stage, and suddenly the beautiful landscape wasn't complaining anymore.

"But every once in a while, a portal to those times opens up," he continued. "Not too long ago scientists looked at the draft of the Declaration of Independence with special high-tech equipment. They discovered that hidden under the word 'Citizens' was the word 'Subjects'—and a smudge the size of Jefferson's index finger. You see, before the ink from his feather pen dried, Jefferson got disgusted at the thought of having referred to the people of our new country as subjects—that was something you would call people who were ruled by a king, not those in a free country. Jefferson must have grunted, wiped the ink away with his finger, and written 'Citizens' on top of it. It took a powerful imaging device to spot the remnants of the original word left on the paper. For a brief moment I was a fly on the wall again, Cooper. I could see every pore on Jefferson's face.

"Then one day I met Cooper—the cleverest, most imaginative, gentlest boy in the known universe. Sure, we've had our little competitions to find rare items at garage sales—like the time he pretended to be sick and bought that eighteenth-century ceramic vase to throw up in while I waited at the curb. I had to buy it from him for fifty bucks. And wouldn't you know, that very same boy happens to have the greatest collection of hidden secrets still waiting to be discovered right here in his yard. Thank goodness he knows how important it is for trained archaeologists to study it—so we can *all* take one big trip back to the Battle of Newtown."

Mr. Shepherd stopped talking and sprayed himself from a little bottle. He dabbed himself with a cloth.

"The end," he said, bowing.

We were quiet for a while, listening to the chattering summer bugs and the twittering in the forest. Mr. Shepherd took small yellow binoculars out of a hidden pocket and peered up at Ghost Conductor's Bluff.

"That was a good story," I finally said. "There's only one thing you forgot. I like to time-travel too, and the Declaration of Independence says that I can have life, liberty, and the pursuit of happiness. I'm happy the way things are, with me and you digging stuff up."

"*Suh-weet argument!*" the beautiful landscape said. "*High five, Coop. Never mind, somebody might get hurt.*"

Mr. Shepherd looked like a ghost that just fell off the bluff. I grinned at him and shook the hair out of my eyes, even though I didn't really have much hair to clear away.

"Cooper, don't you see how selfish you're being?" Mr. Shepherd said. "There's only so many ways I can explain it."

"Why are you telling me Declaration of Independence stories, anyway? We're up to the part after the army left this area and went back home. I want to know what happened to the Iroquois after that. How did this battle change the whole war?"

"I'm not telling you—how's that?" Mr. Shepherd said,

crossing his arms. "That's exactly what it feels like to be cut off from time-traveling."

He was acting like a big baby.

"Fine, I'll just read about it at the library."

"You're grounded, and anyway, you're not allowed to ride your bike on the other side of the highway."

"You mean the bike you *killed*?"

"What do you mean?"

"Someone will tell me. I'll ask all the customers until someone knows." I realized that my hands were pulling long pieces of wild grass out of the ground.

"Look, Cooper," he began in a suddenly sweet voice. "If you want me to keep coming back and telling stories, you have to agree to this. I won't be able to come back otherwise—I'll have to start on a different project for the museum."

I knew he was lying because those big cannons were still in the ground. "Okay, I'm going to sell those cannons, then. I think five dollars each is a fair price."

"I can't talk to you when you get like this. Lead me back through the path, please."

Mr. Shepherd stomped over to the vine-covered, bushy opening and tapped his foot. I purposely took a long time to stand up, brush myself off, say goodbye to the sunflowers and the beautiful view, and perform a big arm-stretching yawn.

When we got back to the house, Mr. Shepherd didn't even say goodbye to Mom. He stomped all the way to his green truck, mumbling the whole time. When I asked him if he was coming back tomorrow, he didn't answer.

"Decto and I are going metal-detecting at nine A.M. sharp, if you want to come with us."

Mr. Shepherd didn't say goodbye to me either. The wheels on his truck squealed, sending gravel flying back at our house. He tore out of the parking lot and drove fast down the hill. I kept watching the truck until it disappeared completely around the turn at the bottom.

That's when I noticed an electric-company van parked in the street. A man came around the side of the house holding a clipboard.

"I was calling for you, Cooper," Mom said from her aluminum chair. "He wants to shut off the electricity."

I suddenly remembered that I had never mailed the electricity bill—it was back in my room with the coffee tin of money because Mom stopped paying attention to that stuff again.

"It comes to seventy-eight dollars," the man said. His arms and neck were bright red.

"Hold on," I said, running inside. I grabbed the money out of the tin and brought it to the electricity man. He handed me a receipt, which I jammed into one of the pockets of my pirate belt.

The van drove away, but I didn't bother watching it go down the hill.

"Jill brought our clothes," Mom said. She held up her feet to show off brand-new sneakers.

"Walk around."

Mom got up and took a few steps. The sneakers didn't squish down at all.

I flopped into her chair and slumped down.

"Don't they look good?"

"Whatever. Like anything on you looks bad."

"You're a grump-and-a-half." She sat down in my chair.

"When did Jill come by?"

"You just missed her. She went to work. Your sneakers and jeans are on your bed."

"Waste of money."

"And Captain John's pirate belt isn't?"

"Captain *Jack*. I didn't buy it. I'm grounded, remember?"

"Go try them on. I want to see how you look."

"Later." I kicked some gravel.

"What did you and Mr. Shepherd discover?"

"Nothing."

"When you're less than one grump you can tell me the story of what happened here."

"It's violent." I slumped down until only my back was on the chair. My hair got caught in one of the rusty hinges, and it hurt when I lost a few strands.

"Your metal detector was making noises. I think you left it on."

I shot to my feet and ran inside, pushing off the bedroom doorframe to launch into my room. Decto was crying! I hit the power button to quiet him down.

"What's wrong, Decto?" I was out of breath.

"Cooper, I want to make one thing perfectly clear. You are never to take my son away from me without asking first. Ever." He frowned at me. Mini-Decto was shivering inside my belt. I quickly handed him over to Decto, who wrapped him up with one of my dirty socks.

"I'm sorry, Decto. I forgot!"

"We'll be fine, but if you'll excuse us, we need some time alone."

"Okay."

I leapt onto my bed and landed right on top of my new jeans and sneakers. I kicked them out of the way and banged my head against the pillow over and over again until the room was spinning.

It doesn't take long for a day to go bad around here.

# CHAPTER 26

I couldn't get Mr. Shepherd's angry face out of my mind, so I used Mom's trick of thinking about sequences to see where things went wrong. I grabbed a pad and wrote out the whole chain reaction of my recent adventures. This time I began far back in the past.

STEP 1: The British King makes the colonies pay high taxes without their permission.

STEP 2: The colonies join together and declare independence from Great Britain.

STEP 3: The British send troops to get the colonies back under their control.

STEP 4: They offer gifts to the Iroquois to fight against the Americans, but only some tribes accept.

STEP 5: The tribes of the Six Nations fight against each other for the first time in centuries.

I wrote for a long time, scribbling down everything that Jan and Mr. Shepherd had taught me about what happened in my backyard during the Revolutionary War. I was up to step 25 when I ran into a problem: I couldn't go any farther into the future until Mr. Shepherd told me how the Battle of Newtown changed the war. I had to skip ahead and leave some blank spaces.

STEP 30: Cooper's ancestors settle on the spot where part of the Battle of Newtown happened. The ghosts from the battle still haunt the land.

STEP 31: Cooper and Tanner are born.

I put in all the steps I had worked out before the last full moon, like discovering Decto, making friends with Jan, and digging up battle relics in our yard. I went all the way to step 50, where Mr. Shepherd stormed off because I wouldn't let archaeologists dig on our land. By then I was in a little better mood because hundreds of years had gone by in my mind, enough time for things to calm down.

"Cooper, come out in the jeans and sneakers," Mom called to me.

The new sneakers hurt. A lot. My big toes had no way to peek out anymore. I used to be able to pick up a piece of gravel with my right big toe and toss it across the lot, if I concentrated enough. Now my foot was crammed and jammed inside. The sneakers were so bright it even hurt to look at them. The jean shorts were uncomfortable. The bottoms of the legs irritated the scrapes on my knees.

"Very handsome," Mom said when I trudged outside. One of her sneakers was off her foot and lying on the gravel.

"Very painful," I replied.

"They'll wear in." She brushed my hair with a pink hairbrush and held me away a little so she could get a better view.

"Why is your sneaker off?" I picked it up and jammed my nose into it—it smelled like new fabric. At least Jill remembered not to get leather.

"It was giving me a blister."

"See!" I sat on Mom's lap and leaned against her.

"Ow, stand up." She pushed me away. There was a red mark on her leg from my shorts.

"Mom, it was a good idea to get us new clothes, but we should save them for a special occasion."

"I guess you can wear them to school."

"Let's change back. I'll race you. Meet back here."

Giggling, we ran inside and got back into our comfortable old clothes, with all the holes, squishiness, and mom-smell that make clothes good. A lady customer pulled up just as we were bursting back out of the house. She must have thought we were crazy when Mom grabbed my shirt and pulled me back so she could sit down before me. I dove for her chair and made it fold up to foil that plan. I was being tickled very expertly when the lady walked up to us.

"Lively antique shop," she said. There was a lot of red makeup on her face, and she wore jingly costume jewelry.

"I win!" I leapt into my chair and crossed my legs. "Browse around, ma'am, the barn's packed."

"Do you have any old sheet music, antique mirrors, or cat figurines, and do you know why you're being surveyed?"

Mom got up and brushed herself off.

"What do you mean, surveyed?" I asked.

"There is a yellow truck down there, and next to it is a man dressed in yellow, and that man possesses a yellow tripod." She pointed a long red fingernail at the road.

I ran over to Mr. Maybox. At the bottom of our road was a strange man who looked just like the lady said. He was hunched over a three-legged device that looked like a telescope, minus the long lens. He was peering up this way.

The lady rummaged through our barn for a long time and only bought a sheet of yellow, crinkly piano music that teaches how to play "The Star-Spangled Banner." I was thinking about showing her Mirror, but I didn't want to lose him, even if he was an old grump.

"Smart prices," she said, handing a ten-dollar bill to Mom. "I'm a dealer myself, up in Horseheads, but I collect here and there. Normally I wouldn't comment, but you were a little low on this item. Old sheet music is rare because the paper is so perishable. Here, have this." She took off one of her costume jewelry pins—a rose with pink jewels—and pinned it on Mom's shirt. I scowled at the lady until she fled with the sheet music.

I held out my hand. Mom undid the pin and placed it gently on my palm. Jewelry is strictly forbidden because it's very painful for me, and then we'd be right back to where we were with the new clothes. I put a $10 sticker on it and tossed it into the barn, not caring where it landed.

Total boredom settled on the valley over the next week, swallowing everything in its path like a thick fog. Squeaky stood silently on the gravel near the road. Decto and Mini-Decto whispered to each other. Koala tried to help me fill in those missing steps in my sequence. Mirror reflected on all the weird events that had been going on lately. The man with the yellow tripod never returned. Mr. Shepherd stayed away, and I worried that he wouldn't ever come back.

I finally got the courage to go metal-detecting again. Squeaky would understand that we had to go on without him. Decto had forgotten that he was mad at me, and it was just like old times. Mini-Decto stayed in my belt, where he could easily be babysat.

"Let's find some treasure!" Decto said, sniffing the ground. "I feel so rested."

I dug a few holes between the cannons, but all I came up with was a new penny, a modern zipper, a ball of aluminum foil, and a non-antique spoon that was bent at a weird angle, besides some unidentifiable bits of wire and other trash. I turned the discrimination knob up to 200 so I wouldn't find any junky pieces of metal with low conductivity numbers—but then I didn't find anything at all. I got sick of that spot and took Decto through the hidden path to the secret flower patch. We started detecting right near the cliff, in those big reddish dirt piles.

"Beep beep!" Decto said right away.

I carefully pushed Mini-Decto's face into the dirt pile. He beeped at once. It was a musket ball that was completely squashed into an oddly shaped blob. At least we were finding old stuff again.

"Better mark that on the map," Decto said. "Mr. Shepherd will want to see it."

"Mr. Shepherd isn't coming back. Don't get your hopes up."

"Why not?"

"Because he doesn't really like me. He's just obsessed with going back in time."

"Don't be so sure. You remind him of himself when he was a kid."

"Great. Now Jan *and* Mr. Shepherd think I'm somebody else."

I moved Decto around to another part of the dirt pile. He started beeping and showed the number 500 on his little screen. Mini-Decto sniffed the pile and found something brown and round—the edge of it was poking out. I snatched it and wiped away the dirt with my finger. The year 1737 appeared. I felt dizzy and some strange noises came out of my mouth. Squeezing the treasure in my hand, I fell backwards and kicked and punched the air, just like Mr. Shepherd does when he gets excited.

I looked around to see if anyone was going to steal my treasure, and then I examined it some more while lying on my back. Over the date were three hammers wearing crowns. The words I Am Good Copper formed a circle around them. On the other side was a rough drawing of a deer. Value Me As You Please was written in a circle near the edge. I kissed the coin and then stashed it in the secret pocket inside Captain Jack's treasure belt.

"Decto, you are the most awesome metal detector in the world."

Mini-Decto squeaked.

"And you too, little guy."

"Let's find more!" Decto said.

"We shoulda checked these piles first. I thought the whole flower patch would be forbidden for treasure hunting. Gotta save the sunflowers!" The droopy sunflowers smiled at me and grunted, then went back to drooping.

I turned the discrimination knob all the way down to 50. I wanted to find every single scrap of metal in the secret flower patch, except for rusty nails and iron rocks. When Decto's head scraped against a different dirt pile, he beeped right away. Mini-Decto burrowed in and came back out quickly.

"Ow!" he squealed.

I carefully brushed the dirt away, revealing a long, sharp piece of metal. It looked old. Blobs of rust covered the whole thing.

"This is a hotspot," Decto said. "All this stuff probably eroded away higher up the mountain and collected down here."

"I'll mark them all on the map. This could be important."

The three of us made a great team. All day we huddled together on the little patch of ground overlooking the hidden valleys, sniffing every bit of metal out of those dirt piles—a crushed pewter flask, more musket balls, some round buttons with nothing written on them, the handle of a sword, the spout of a teapot, a cannonball, and a lot of random bits of metal that only Mr. Shepherd could identify. I lined everything up neatly near the sunflowers.

I dabbed the sweat off my face with a cloth that was from a different secret pouch. There was no way I would ever get as many hidden accessories as Mr. Shepherd, but at least it had taken me a grand total of three minutes to get ready for metal-detecting. For some reason that coin made me very happy. Xavier must have been looking down from heaven and talking about what a good treasure hunter I had become.

*"An eternity will go by, and zere will never be a better coin shooter," Xavier tells Tanner.*

*Tanner stares at him, squints because the sun is really close, and says, "Will you lower my bicycle seat?"*

I needed to tell somebody about these treasures soon, or I would just burst with joy.

*"Go for it," the beautiful landscape said.*

"Mr. Shepherd, come over!" I yelled down into the valley. "I want to show you what I found!" My voice echoed.

I wondered if any other kid ever had so much fun being grounded.

# CHAPTER 27

It was one of my greatest antiquing moments when I fought through the maze of bushes, thorns, and vines and came out in back of the barn, knowing that an old coin was safely tucked away in my hidden pouch and that I was the first human to touch it in hundreds of years. I shook the pine needles out of my hair when I was close enough for Mom to notice. Then I took out the cloth and slowly dabbed my dirty sweat away.

"Smart to wear your old clothes," Mom said.

"Do we have any books on old coins?"

"There's one up in the barn."

I placed Decto and son carefully on the ground, ran into the barn, and made my way up the creaky wooden staircase that leads to the loft. I hardly ever go up there. Books about antiques sit on broken shelves or in big piles on the floor. Some wrecked antiques wait patiently to be fixed—like the old clock with a pendulum that won't swing, or a metal wind-up car that doesn't run. I feel bad for them because they can't be with the healthy antiques and get a good home, but I'm no good at fixing things.

There's one cracked and foggy window that faces our house. At an angle I can spy on Mom, Mr. Maybox, and any customers that come by. One time I ran up here after yelling at Mom for giving a customer a super bargain for buying five things. I spied on her to see if she was sorry, but she just sat there and read a book about antique horse-and-buggy parts. So I watched her read for a while until my neck hurt.

I found a book about American coins and flopped down to read it, kicking some of the other books out of the way. I flipped through it, looking at all the pictures of old coins. Some had elephants on them, or trees, or a very blocky-looking George Washington, or that lady with the ribbon in her hair. It turned out that her name is Lady Liberty, and she was born at the same time as our country.

At the very beginning of the book was a picture of the coin in my hidden pouch. I had to rub my chest to slow my heart down. I put the coin right next to the picture in the book. I kept blinking my eyes—right, left, right, left—so each eyeball saw a different coin. When I did it fast enough, it was impossible to tell which was the picture and which was the real coin.

A gravelly popping noise came from out front. It sounded like a familiar car. A few seconds later there was Mr. Shepherd's voice.

I ran downstairs clutching the coin, but for some reason when I came out of the barn I sat in my chair without looking at him. I didn't say hello.

"How are you folks doing today?" He wore yellow pants that burned like the sun. His sparkling yellow sneakers had shoelaces of different colors now—one blue, one orange.

"Good," Mom said.

"So, Cooper, did you find anything interesting?"

I shrugged.

"Cooper, why don't you offer Mr. Shepherd a Coopcake. There are some on the table."

"Where did those come from?"

"Jill. She came by when you were metal-detecting. She brought groceries and took money from the can."

I missed Jill again! I ran inside and saw a platter of Coopcakes on the table. They're cupcakes that have faces drawn on them in colorful frosting—happy faces, sad faces, wavy mouths, a winking one. Jill has been bringing these since I was little, but usually for special occasions. She must have seen me moping around and felt guilty because the grounding was her idea. I stared at the weird faces and suddenly wondered why they're called Coopcakes. Does Jill think I'm moody?

I gave a frowny one to Mr. Shepherd and a smiley one to Mom.

"Thanks. I'd love to see what you found now."

"A coin," Mom said, biting the smiley face off in one gulp. "He's being secretive about it."

"Really? American?"

"Well, since everybody wants to know, ta-da!" I held out the coin. "It's a 1737 Higley copper coin. Samuel Higley made them in Connecticut, but he didn't put an exact value on them because people complained that his last coins were priced too high. That's why it says VALUE ME AS YOU PLEASE. He was just some guy that had his own copper mine and coin shop. Nobody said he was allowed to make them."

"Simply incredible," Mr. Shepherd said. "Your yard is a treasure trove." He and Mom gawked at the coin until I put it back in my secret pouch.

"I want to keep this one, but I found some stuff for the museum, too. Come see." I yanked Mr. Shepherd's hand and led him behind the barn, into the white archway, through the scraggly, grabby, protect-Mr.-Shepherd wild path, and into the secret flower patch, where all the treasures were lined up neatly next to the sunflowers.

In a comfortable spot I watched Mr. Shepherd do his thing. He examined each item with his giant magnifying glass and made all kinds of goofy noises. He told me what everything was, and whether it was British or American.

The sharp thing that hurt Mini-Decto was a bayonet—those big knives that attach to the end of muskets. The cannonball was a six-pounder that was fired into the top of the hill and then rolled down here as the mountain eroded.

"This could be the exact spot that Hand's men charged up after the artillery drove some of the British and Iroquois out from behind the breastworks," he explained. "And after Clinton and Poor flanked them by leading their men through that pass down there."

"I marked everything I found on the map." I showed him the clipboard with all the X's on the map. Maybe this would *finally* convince him that we could work this whole property by ourselves, forever.

"Good work. And here I thought you were mad at me for the way I behaved last time."

I shrugged.

"I, too, am a grump when I don't get enough sleep," he added.

"I thought *you* were mad at *me* when I saw that guy with the yellow telescope looking up here. I thought you sent him to scare us."

"Huh? What guy?" He placed the handle of the sword on the ground, put away the magnifying glass, and knelt down next to me.

I told him. It wasn't much, but it made him do a strange thing. He fell over and curled into a little ball, wrapping his hands around his legs and burying his face in his knees.

"What's wrong?"

"He's actually doing it. He's *actually* doing it. That backstabber."

"Whu-uht?"

Mr. Shepherd uncurled and then sat next to me.

"Do you remember Richard Archer, that guy with the big gray hair?"

"Iron Boots?"

"He and I had a bit of a falling-out on how to proceed on this property. If he comes back while I'm gone, tell him he's not allowed to step foot on your land. Can you do that, Cooper?"

I nodded. That wouldn't be hard.

"I can't explain now. I have to go, and I might not be back for a couple of days." He stood up, took a paintbrush with no handle out of a pants pocket, and brushed the dirt and plant particles off his backside.

"No. You're always leaving. Tell me." I pulled on his arm so that he sat down again, and the brush fell into the flower patch.

"Cooper, Mr. Archer works for the City Planning Department of Elmira. They have it in their heads down there that they can make your property part of the state park commemorating the Battle of Newtown. They have this elaborate plan to build a staircase up the hillside and connect it to the main park by a trail through the woods. They aren't interested in scientific inquiry—just preservation. They want to cover the cannon excavations with Lucite and make it part of the public tour."

"What do you mean? Me and Mom live here."

"There's something called eminent domain," Mr. Shepherd explained. "It's a law that allows a government to take over private property if it's for the public good. It's a very old law dating back to the time of kings in Europe. Basically, it means that nobody truly owns their property. It's part of the sovereign nation and can be taken at any time for a good enough reason."

My legs started shaking. I thought Mr. Shepherd might suddenly slap his knee and admit that he was just joking, but he didn't smile at all. He just scratched at a scabby red mark on the bald part of his head.

"But I don't want strangers coming here and visiting us at all hours of the night!"

"Cooper—you and your mom wouldn't be here. You'd have to move somewhere else."

I shot to my feet. A sudden dizziness swirled through my head, and I stumbled away from the edge of the flower patch so I wouldn't fall off. I imagined the sad look on Tanner's face after he discovered that he couldn't find me anymore by following the ray of moonlight that bounces off the gravel and leads to my bedroom.

"I never heard of any dumb law like that!"

"It hardly ever gets used. They do have to pay you for the property, but what makes this more complicated is that your house is in poor condition and the taxes haven't been paid on this land for twenty-two years."

I didn't remember ever getting a bill for taxes. My head was pounding. I could never, ever, ever explain this to Mom, if it really was true. "You're lying, I know it. This is just a way of sneaking into my yard and doing an archaeological dig. *You* brought him here."

"I know—huge mistake. I thought at first we would try to get support from the town for an archaeological dig, rather than from a university. That way the finds would make their way to our museum. But Mr. Archer has no interest in hiring archaeologists after all. He just wants the land. I found that out too late."

"Who else did you tell our secret to?"

"Cornell University's Archaeology Department. They showed some enthusiasm. I was keeping both options open."

I plopped down and buried my face in my lap.

"It could have been just us," I moaned between my knees. "I knew you were going to ruin everything."

"Cooper, I would never be involved in a plan like that against you or your mom. I promise on my locket." I heard the jingling of his purple amulet. "But now you realize how important this site is."

I rocked back and forth and promised myself that it was just Mr. Shepherd telling another story. He's always in these bedtime stories—the evil amulet, the castle, the valley with black clouds and the mermaid cave. All I really had to do was think and the whole story would change.

"I have to go talk to him," Mr. Shepherd said, walking toward the hidden path.

I unburied my face and stood up. "No, don't go. I want to show you something. Wait here." I tugged on his arm until he stopped.

# CHAPTER 28

I dashed out of the house with the report about my fifty-step sequence. When I came around the side, Mr. Shepherd was walking out from behind the barn. It was a little disappointing that he didn't need me anymore to get through the wild path. That would have been the perfect way of keeping him here as long as I wanted.

"Look." I handed him the paper.

He examined it for a while, giving it the same attention that he gave all those buried treasures. When he walked into a sunny spot to get more light, I knew he liked it. The paper crinkled slightly in his hands. I liked watching him read something that came from my mind.

"Impressive, Cooper. You're already a historian. I'm sorry about the blank spaces. Shame on me for withholding history from a curious boy."

"Who cares, just tell me now." I sat on the ground right there on the side of the house. That news he told me on the other side of the trees seemed like a distant dream. It was a whole different world over there, with a new view, exotic plants, unusual treasures, another part of the battle, and its own dumb laws. On this side of the trees everything was the same as always.

Mr. Shepherd plucked a fuzzy dandelion covered in cottony seeds out of the ground.

"It might help to think of a chain reaction as something other than a straight line," he began. "For example, let's pretend this dandelion is the Battle of Newtown." He blew on it, and all the little seeds leapt off the stalk, floated into the air, and scattered on a gentle breeze. "Each one of those seeds is a different result of the battle."

I fell over sideways and watched the seeds disappear into the sky. Mr. Shepherd's voice was starting to make my insides tickle, only it was different from when Jan talked— my ears twitched a little, and my nose felt itchy. It was kind of awkward lying near the house with my arms behind my head squinting up at Mr. Shepherd, but that's where we were, and it would be too hard to move to a more ordinary story spot.

"One of those seeds will land on the great Iroquois longhouse, the one they imagined spanning Upstate New York. That longhouse had split in half when the League of the Iroquois divided over whether to join the American side or the British. Now it would crumble completely, and the people who had watched over these lands for a thousand years would lose their home. The four nations that went on the British side—the Onondaga, Cayuga, Mohawk, and Seneca—thought about nothing but seeking revenge on the American people for destroying their villages. From Fort Niagara they continued to send out raiding parties and terrorized towns on the frontier. In turn the American people sought their own revenge and did terrible things back to them. There were no more major battles, but the horror, bloodshed, and fear remained strong in the north—and with no end in sight.

"Then by chance one dandelion seed floated all the way to the humid swamps of the southern colonies. There it joined together with seeds from many other battles, the spores parachuting down onto the heads of George Washington's army that had surrounded the British in Yorktown, Virginia. With their northern strategy foiled, the British had looked to the South for victory—hoping to find support from colonists who were loyal to King George.

But they ran into the same problems far away from their strong fleet. British General Charles Cornwallis, waiting for reinforcements and supplies from those very same ships, put up a strong fight as the Americans lay siege to Yorktown. Many of the same regiments, soldiers, and officers that had participated up here in the Sullivan-Clinton Campaign, including James Clinton himself, fought under Washington in the last major battle of the Revolution. At the start of the war in 1775, the United States had no real army—just ordinary citizens holding muskets. By the siege of Yorktown they were a genuine army, highly trained and experienced in combat. With the help of the French fleet, the American army prevented the British from resupplying Cornwallis, and he surrendered to George Washington in 1781. Who's to say that the war would not have dragged on longer if seeds from all the battles of the Revolution, including Newtown, had not journeyed there." He dropped the stalk on the ground and handed the paper back to me.

"Where did the rest of the seeds from this dandelion go?" I said, picking up the stalk. "What *aren't* you telling me?" I blew on it to free one last stubborn seed that refused to go. It wouldn't cooperate, so I tossed the stalk away and tried to push myself back into a sitting position.

"Another seed floated all the way to Paris, France, where the peace treaty between the British and Americans was signed in 1783, officially ending the war. Unfortunately, the British did not even mention the Iroquois in the treaty. Perhaps they were bitter that the Iroquois allies hadn't provided the strength they needed in the north, and the homeless tribes had become a burden to them. The Iroquois had put their trust in King George, and he betrayed them in return by giving away all their land to the United States. The U.S. government entered into its own treaty with the Iroquois that preserved a large part of the ancient lands occupied by the Six Nations, but many members of the tribes fled to Canada, where they tried to survive in small tracts of wilderness."

"If I could go back in time, I would tell those four Iroquois tribes not to join the British," I said. "I would show them history books. Maybe that would convince the Six Nations to stick together and join the Americans."

"Time-travel changes are another exciting thing to dream about. I've spent a lot of nights speculating on what I would change. It's hard to decide. Remember that every spore that lands will grow a new dandelion, which will release its own spores into the sky. That creates an intricate web of sequences from the past to the future. You would need the greatest computer in the universe to track it all, yet historians have been brave enough to attempt it for thousands of years."

"You're probably changing something in the future right now by standing there and telling me this," I said.

"True."

"So don't stop."

"I really have to go."

"I know you're not telling me something. You never mention the two tribes that were loyal to the United States."

"The Oneida and Tuscarora. That's a sad, sad seed, Cooper. It floated down into the ancestral homeland of those tribes, which our young government promised would remain in their hands. But the rest of the dandelion's spores had scattered across the country, landing in people's ears and telling them what a beautiful region this was, with mountains and valleys, streams, and fertile ground for farming. The soldiers who had marched up here spread the word of its beauty, and soon people flocked to the area to start a new life. More and more land was needed for houses, and nobody remembered that the Oneida and Tuscarora had helped the United States in the Revolutionary War. They were poor and hungry, with little game left to hunt in the wilderness, so they had no choice but to sell their land for very little money. Some of their forests were stolen, and other areas were given away for small gifts in tricky land treaties with New York State. They moved onto reservations, or left the area to make new settlements in other states. The League of the Iroquois, which had dominated these lands for hundreds of years, became just a shadow of what it once was. The tribes are scattered in different places, keeping their ancient traditions alive."

I closed my eyes and rested my head on the dirt. Ever since Jan started singing that sad song, I was afraid of hearing something like that.

"Cooper, I really, really have to go now. I told you everything." He tried to walk past me.

"No, please." I grabbed his leg so he couldn't move. "It's not true. George Washington wouldn't betray his allies."

"It's more complicated than that. Over the years the U.S. government's treaty with the Iroquois was ignored, and the lands of all six tribes dwindled away. But during Washington's time as president, the Iroquois felt that *he* treated them fairly. Many forgave him for what had happened in the past. In fact, according to Iroquois legend, he's the only white man to be allowed to enter Iroquois heaven." Mr. Shepherd tried to take a few steps, but I hung on and forced him to drag me.

"Please, just tell me what the League of the Iroquois should have done."

"Nobody knows. We can't replay it."

I hopped up and raced in front of Mr. Shepherd to block his path. He tried to go around me, but I did a pretty good job of straddling left and right, trying to figure out which way he would go next. I accidentally stepped on the purple flower where I had found my first musket ball. He finally faked me out and darted past me. I raced after him all the way to the green truck.

"Five more minutes."

He patted my cheek and said, "I'll be back tomorrow with French fries, I promise."

I grabbed the wall of the truck and pulled myself up, stepping onto the tire to help me get into the back. "So where are we going?"

Mr. Shepherd unlatched the little door in the back and climbed up. He put his hands under my arms and lifted me up. He placed me on the gravel. "Cooper, please stop. I have to go take care of that thing we discussed."

"One more time. Then I'll stop."

"Fine."

I climbed up the side of his truck again. This time I put my feet under a ladder in the back so he couldn't lift me up. It didn't work. My foot slipped, and he picked me up just the same and put me on the gravel.

"That one didn't count." For some reason I couldn't control myself. I was breathing really fast. I climbed into the back of his truck again.

"Hang on, I have something for you," he said. "I know you said a gift every third time, but I already had this." He opened a box and pulled out a wooden square covered with glass. Black velvet lined the inside. "It's for the coin you found. A display case." He handed it to me.

"Thanks." I climbed down, rubbing my oily finger on the glass.

"I'll be back tomorrow. Now stand away from the truck when I start it." He waved goodbye to Mom and then hopped into the driver's seat.

"Fine. I'll be in this same spot."

When the truck roared to life, I fell backwards dramatically and flopped onto the painful gravel. After he drove away I stayed in that spot without moving and held my breath as long as I could. Eventually I gasped for air. I fiddled with the glass case, trying to figure out how to open it.

It was back to just me and Mom. The loneliness crawled out of the gravel and seeped into my body. I probably should have been sad about Squeaky's lifeless body standing over me, or that Mr. Shepherd mentioned the horrible thing on *this* side of the trees, or that everybody betrayed the Iroquois, or that I once made Jan stop singing that sad song, but all I could think about were the old times, when I wished for it to be me and Mom, and nobody else.

We used to play catch over the whole house. I would stand in the backyard and throw the ball over the roof. Mom would catch it near Mr. Maybox and throw it back. Once I got stronger the ball would sometimes land in the road and roll all the way down the street until it disappeared at the bottom. Years later I found one of them on the way to a garage sale.

It was probably a dumb idea to let other people into my heart. Other people betray you. They give you nice gifts, and you want them to protect you, and eventually you need them there, and then they steal your land. Even after all that you let them into heaven because you're so gentle and nice. I peeked at Mom through an opening in my hair and let the sharp gravel dig into my ear.

# CHAPTER 29

The grounding ended nine days later. Mr. Shepherd didn't come back with French fries like he promised. I spent my time collecting the biggest pieces of gravel and piling them in a mound next to Squeaky, in case Iron Boots came by. It didn't even matter whether I was grounded or not—Mom couldn't be left alone for one second. If anything happened without me there, I would never forgive myself.

Sometimes Decto and I went metal-detecting, but not in the secret flower patch. It was too far away for me to protect Mom. We poked around near the steep forest and looked for hotspots in the dirt mounds, but these piles were smaller and didn't have good stuff. Each time a customer pulled up, I placed Decto and Mini-Decto on the ground and ran to the front. No Mr. Shepherd, no Iron Boots, but at least we made more sales.

"Isn't the coin beautiful?" I asked Decto.

"Yes, but do you need to bring it everywhere?"

The Higley copper coin was inside the small glass case, and the whole thing sat on a patch of flattened weeds. I really loved the picture of the deer on the front because it looked like it was made by a kid. Maybe Tanner's drawings would be like that.

"Too bad the coin book didn't say how much it was worth." I turned the discrimination knob up to 150 because Decto was chirping a lot on little bits of iron junk.

"Xavier never cared about the money. He just loved every coin."

"I don't remember seeing this one in Jan's basement."

"Beep beep!" Decto said. I dug softly with the shovel. Out of the dirt came a faded and crushed Pepsi can that somebody threw into the forest long ago. I jammed it in my treasure pouch. All the trash we find goes into a big pile in the corner of my room, so I can give it to Jan sometime for her sculptures.

"Do you think Mr. Shepherd will come back soon?" I asked Decto.

"I don't know." He sniffed the air. "I don't smell French fries. You two sure have been spending a lot of time together."

"Yeah, remember when it was just us, Decto? You gave me detector face."

A butterfly with black and gold wings fluttered over to me and danced around my head. I was sure it was delivering a message from Jan.

*"Little Butterfly, come back when the time is right."*

"Beep beep!" I dug up the little metal tab that once opened the Pepsi can and dropped it in my treasure pouch. The butterfly darted away.

A popping and crunching sound came from the gravel lot. I ran to the front. Iron Boots was stepping out of his white pickup truck. The thick clumps of hair on his arms and legs were wet and flattened against his skin. Gray hair sprouted from places that I hadn't noticed before—like his nose and ears and elbows. It was a virus spreading across his whole body. Sunglasses were jammed into the forest on his head. He walked toward Mom holding a yellow envelope.

My breathing got heavy. My stomach gurgled.

Everything was happening fast.

I didn't know what to do. My rock pile was all the way over by Squeaky. I tried to breathe calmly. My heart pounded.

Mr. Shepherd had told me what to say. "You're not allowed on our property," I told him.

He took a few steps closer. I ran between him and Mom. I still had no rocks. Dumb, Cooper, dumb. I should have put the pile near Mom.

"I came to talk to the land owner, not a minor."

Mom put down her book. She stood up.

More heart pounding. "Get out, don't you understand?" I picked up a handful of gravel.

The hand went above my head.

He took a step back. "Better think carefully about what to do with those rocks, son."

Mom yelled, "Cooper, put down those rocks this second!"

An insect that sounded like electricity screeched in the trees.

The rocks fell to the ground. My lips started shaking. Both feet took me inside.

I ran into Moppy's closet and slammed the door.

I curled up in the corner and covered my ears. Tears flowed down my cheeks, and small hiccup-like gasps made my chest bounce up and down. Mom was out there all alone with *him*. Abandoned. My body rocked back and forth, rolling my head against both walls. My crying echoed in the bare closet—only Moppy was there to help.

"Hey, kid." She has thick strands of white hair that hang down in messy clumps. Huge sunglasses cover her eyes. She's even skinnier than me—her body is just one long stick.

"Hi, Moppy," I blubbered.

"Why all the tears, kid?"

"Iron Boots." I tried to breathe, but it just came out as one long siren sound.

"Creatures with feet think they're so superior," Moppy said. "Except you, kid. You're the best, for real. How long have I been telling you that?"

"Long time."

"And who taught you how to shake the hair out of your eyes like you own the world?" Moppy shook thick strands away from her sunglasses.

"You did, Moppy."

"And who showed you the technique for pushing out your bottom lip and blowing air up at your hair? It doesn't really do anything, except give you a small feeling of accomplishment." Moppy blew air up and barely moved one strand.

"You did, Moppy."

"Remember the first time ghosts came on that full-moon night, and you hid in here with me? I told you to be strong and go out there, in case they got too close to Mom."

I nodded.

"Good, then we have some trust, you and I. You don't visit me often, so it's easy to forget. I could use a little shaky shaky squeezy squeezy every once in a while to clean out the dirt. How's my breath?" Moppy shook off some flakes of dirt and breathed in my face.

"Smells like dead rat."

"That was breakfast, kid. It's an eat-or-be-eaten world in here." She motioned with her head to a small hole in the wall by my feet.

"Okay, Moppy." I wiped tears off my cheeks.

"So let me tell you how to solve your little problem. Go outside and find the sharpest piece of gravel in the lot. Jump on Iron Boots's back, and cut all that ugly gray hair right off his head. Then jam those sunglasses down his throat. They're not a name brand anyway, just cheap knock-offs." Moppy showed me the price tag hanging off the side of her sunglasses.

"Okay, Moppy."

"Now get out there and make me proud."

My crying stopped, and all that was left inside me was

a bubbling, gurgling, boiling anger that wanted to come out. I creaked open the closet door and took small steps toward the front. My hands made tight fists.

When I got outside, Iron Boots was still talking to Mom. She was holding the envelope. My heart wasn't pounding, and all the summer sounds had disappeared. Clouds with gray bottoms filled the sky.

I walked over to my rock pile and picked up the sharpest one. Creeping slowly toward Iron Boots and facing the ground, I carefully stepped on the quietest gravel patches. He was really tall, and the closer I snuck, the taller he got. I didn't know if I would be able to jump on his back and hold the rock at the same time. There was sweaty hair on the back of his neck. It made me gag.

Just then he turned around to leave. I dropped the rock and ran back inside, all the way into the same spot in the dark closet. Another failure. I covered my eyes with my hands so Moppy wouldn't see my new tears.

"Hey, kid, you haven't gotten up yet. You got the legs, I got the plan. Let's go!"

Had I been in the closet that whole time?

I felt Mom's gentle hand on my cheek. I moved my hands away and saw her hovering over me.

"Mom, I'm having violent thoughts."

She picked me up and carried me to my bed. There wasn't any talking for a long time after that—just Mom's soft hand rubbing my forehead and moving the hair out of my eyes. When the tears came this time, she caught each one with her finger. That went on until dusk made the room gloomy, but she never missed a tear.

I don't know if I dozed off, or made a really long blink, but time zoomed ahead. Mom was still there when it was night out. My desk lamp was on. Her head was resting next to me, and she was staring at me really close up. The weird thing is that I can close my eyes and actually *hear* her staring at me. I've never figured out how.

"What are your thoughts like now?"

"Back to beautiful mermaids and moonlit caverns."

"You're supposed to cheer up after the grounding's over. Not the other way around." She held my hand and smiled.

"It's him. Iron Boots."

"He just wanted to buy the house, that's all. The envelope has an appraisal and an offer letter."

"No, you don't understand, it's way worse."

"Let me take care of it and stop worrying about every little thing."

I stared over at the tin of money and unpaid bills on my desk. There was nothing to say that wouldn't hurt Mom's feelings.

"It's been forever since I had a bedtime story, so start thinking."

I kissed Mom on the cheek and went outside to lock the barn and get my metal-detecting stuff. The moon was starting to get full again. The night smelled like distant skunk mixed with truck exhaust.

# CHAPTER 30

Cannon fire woke me up the next morning. I groggily thought that the army was coming to drive me and Mom off our land. Only none of the cannonballs were making any crashing noises. Mirror is usually the first to panic when the room shakes. For some reason he was smiling. I hopped out of bed and stood in front of him, trying to figure out what was going on.

"What are you smiling at?"

"Not your hopelessly hopeless hair." His laughter caused a little more of his reflection to chip off.

"Very funny." I patted my head with both hands.

"If you must know, I'm smiling at your heart. You didn't sell me to that lady with the costume jewelry, even though I'm a grump-and-three-quarters most of the time. I respect you for that."

"So you'll be nice to me now?" Another cannon went off in the distance.

"I will say that you have only five ribs showing now. Keep eating those Coopcakes." I flexed my not-as-puny muscles in the mirror.

"It must be August twenty-ninth," Decto said. "They're honoring the battle up in the state park." Mini-Decto yawned and snuggled up next to him.

"Then today's the perfect day to go metal-detecting. I have a plan."

I ran into Mom's room and tiptoed over to her bed. She was reenacting Sleeping Beauty, and I didn't want to mess up that performance. I reached under her bed and found the envelope that Iron Boots had brought over. I grabbed it and tiptoed backwards out of the room.

The papers covered my whole desk. They were filled with gibberish—like "Assignee of rights to waive future claims to equity" and "Offer of fair market value minus outstanding liens of category 1a, 2a, and 3b." Like that means something in any Earth language.

The papers got scarier toward the bottom. There were math formulas, pictures of our house taken from space satellites, and tax papers from the U.S. government. Mom was silly to believe this was just an offer to buy our house. Mr. Shepherd was right—he was trying to steal our land using some dumb law, so it could become part of the state park.

I got dressed and went outside. There wasn't anybody around. I didn't even know what day of the week it was. The whole sky was filled with those clouds with dark bottoms. A few drops were coming down, but I decided to open the barn anyway, even though Mom might have to wait inside for customers.

Our rotting barn has survived thunderstorms, wind, lightning, termites, mice, raccoons, ghosts, and old age. I wasn't going to let some stranger take away everything me and Mom had. Every antique in there has a story about who once used it and how it ended up in our barn. Sometimes me and Mom talk about them on lazy days.

This was my plan: The next time Iron Boots showed up, I wasn't going to hide in the closet. I was going to take him into the backyard and show him a big, teetering mound of rusty metal—all the stuff still buried underground that me and Decto were going to dig up. That way he would realize there was nothing left to preserve.

We got started right away in the backyard by the far corner of the house, near Jill's yard. That spot hadn't been metal-detected at all yet.

"Okay, Decto, discrimination to zero. We're digging it all," I said, turning the knob all the way to the left. The sky was drizzling more, but that didn't stop us. Anyway, the water would make the stuff rustier.

"Are you sure you want to dig everything? Discrimination of zero means even iron rocks made by the Earth will make me beep."

"Everything, Decto. It's the plan."

After only a few seconds Decto beeped and flashed the number 3 on his screen. Soon I placed the first rusty blob on the ground. Now I just had to do that a thousand more times. I dug and dug and dug and sweated and grunted all day while the sky cried on me and dirt got under my fingernails and in my sneakers. My hands turned reddish brown. The pile got almost as tall as my foot by lunchtime. Mr. Shepherd probably wouldn't be able to identify any of those things. Some of them looked like meteorites.

When it really started to pour, Decto flashed the number 600 on his screen. That number didn't seem like rusty metal, so I dug more carefully. I found something in the hole that taught me why the sky was crying all day. It was the brass mouthpiece to a musical instrument.

Like a fife.

My hands were shaking when I put it back in the hole and covered it with dirt. The rain came down stronger. It was hard to tell if it was tears or raindrops dripping down the side of my nose. I brought Decto back to my room and flopped into bed in my wet clothes. I curled up with Koala.

"Decto, we're not digging anymore here."

"Okay."

"Aren't you going to ask why?"

"Because there are spirits here, Cooper."

"You knew that? Why didn't you stop me before?"

"Mr. Shepherd tried."

"*You* didn't! I would have listened to you."

I buried my head under the pillow and got very mad at Mr. Shepherd for not coming back. There were more questions to ask him—like *who* exactly died in this battle, and how old they were.

I got sick. Really sick.

The next day my face was sweating, and Mom took my temperature. 102. My body ached, and my clothes were still wet because of all the fevery sweat. Mom helped me change into old pajamas that I never wear anymore, the ones with fire trucks and ladders on them. My body was shaking so much that it made my teeth chatter. I kept rubbing my stomach to make some heat, which didn't really make sense because my body had fever.

"If Mr. Shepherd comes back, don't send him away."

"I don't think we'll be letting him in the house." She put a wet cloth on my forehead.

"Why?"

"He brought that man here."

"So now you hate Mr. Shepherd? You were the one that said he fixed the gutters and stuff."

"We don't bother others, Cooper, but we don't let people take advantage of us, either."

I looked over at my desk. The envelope, bills, and coffee can were missing. "It wasn't him. He's trying to help. The hairy guy betrayed him."

"He might have told you that."

"He's my friend."

"No, he's not."

Maybe it was the fever, but I didn't even recognize Mom. She never talked like that. It made me so mad when she said that Mr. Shepherd wasn't my friend. I was old enough to pick my friends. A friend is somebody who makes your insides tickle when they talk, and your arm fuzz stand on end. There were only four people that did that—Mom, Jill, Jan, and Mr. Shepherd.

"Did you read those papers or something, Mom? What's wrong with you?"

"Jill and I sorted through them."

"So now what? Are you just going to do nothing, like how you didn't pay the taxes for twenty years?" *Like how you probably just sat there when Dad told you he was leaving us. Like how you won't ever tell me what happened to Tanner because it probably had something to do with you.*

"This is for me to worry about, not you, especially with a fever." She made me take a sip of disgusting-tasting purple liquid.

"Can I talk to Jill, please? Or do you hate her now, too!"

"Be angry if you want. I let you take on too many responsibilities."

"You're going Robo on me now? Now? Let me talk to Mr. Shepherd. It's not him. He just wants to make an archaeological dig."

"You're always doing a million things. Rest and don't think so much." She covered me with the blanket, but it didn't make me any warmer. I was shaking really bad.

"P-p-please, I n-n-need to know who died here. It's imp-p-ortant."

"Sleep." She kissed me on the cheek and stood up.

"Wait, don't go." I reached out for her arm but missed. "Please. Everybody's always leaving me."

Mom stared at me for a little while, and then she climbed up the ladder. She went into Tanner's bed. It was almost impossible to get her to do that anymore. The mattress sagged a little. She took a deep breath, like she was going to dive underwater for a long time. That's her trying to smell Tanner in the old bedsheets up there.

Tears flowed down my cheeks and made two puddles on the pillow. It was going to be a full moon soon, and I wouldn't know how to tell Tanner that we might have to move. A wave of guilt washed over me from the direction of Decto. If I hadn't dug up that stuff, then Mr. Shepherd would never have cared about our property, and he would never have invited Iron Boots over. The whole chain reaction was starting to crumble. If I hadn't gone to Jan's, then I would never have gotten Decto in the first place, and if Mom had cut my hair this summer, maybe I wouldn't look so much like Xavier.

The fever made everything run through my head in random order, along with shapes and strange noises and twisty, loopy feelings, like the whole room was a roller-coaster ride that was going to launch me onto another property, one where nobody fought a battle and died—land that nobody would ever want to steal.

Decto started packing his things and explaining to Mini-Decto why the human didn't want the two of them anymore. The guilty wave finally hit me and soaked through my pajamas. I was too tired to change again. I squeezed Koala and tried to stop thinking.

# CHAPTER 31

A bright light woke me up. I opened my eyes and saw an angel's face hovering above mine. There was a halo over her head. Giant wings came off the sides of her body and got crammed and jammed in the corners of the ceiling. It looked uncomfortable, but she was smiling.

"Hi, Cooper."

"Hi."

"Feel any better today?" A small fly foolishly landed on her halo, making a zapping noise and a little spark.

"Are you here to take me to heaven?"

"No, silly, I'm here to see how you're doing." She put a thermometer in my mouth, and when that was done she tied something around my arm that squeezed it tight. Then she put a cold metal circle on my chest and listened to it with a rubber thing in her ear. She was so gentle that it made me glad to be sick. "Looks like a summer flu, kiddo. Lots of rest and only liquids and soft foods for a few days."

"Do you want to see the coin I found?" I reached out toward my desk, even though there was no hope of stretching that far. The angel picked up the coin case and handed it to me.

"It's beautiful. Where did you find it?"

"Right here. Our yard is a battlefield from the Revolutionary War." I told her all about the coin and battle. She packed up her little black bag (it also had wings), but I kept talking and didn't take a breath so there was no chance for her to leave. I talked, talked, talked, but the story of the battle didn't come out right.

"You've been busy. Maybe you want to metal-detect my yard when you're on your feet again."

"I don't know if it's okay to metal-detect in heaven."

She laughed and said, "The ground's too fluffy, like marshmallows."

"Can you lower Tanner's bicycle seat when you go back? I sent my bike up to him, but he's not tall enough to ride it."

"I did already." She put her hand under my sweaty hair and lifted my head off the pillow. Her long ivory fingers held a tiny paper cup to my mouth. Gross liquid flowed onto my tongue and burned my throat. "He rides it everywhere and goes off ramps that launch him through the air and into the clouds. The tricks he does with that bike—the other kids admire him."

"That sounds dangerous. Does he wear a helmet?"

"No, because you don't wear one, and he copies you."

"Will you take money from the can and buy me one?"

"Of course." She spread out her monstrous wings. They slammed into the wall and made Mirror sway back and forth.

"Those other kids—are any of them wearing triangular hats and holding a fife?"

"Not that I remember. I have to go to work, but I'll be back tomorrow to check up on you. I want to know more about that battle, and *you* are so smart." She gently poked my nose.

"Jill, wait." I squeezed the angel's hand. "Don't let them take our house. Please."

"You and your mom live such a beautiful, peaceful life here. Nothing's going to change that. Let us take care of it. You sleep."

"Can you tell Mom that Mr. Shepherd is on our side?"

"Of course."

That made me feel so good that I got the courage to ask her a personal question. "How do you clean your rug?"

"Shampoo."

"That's it?" I slammed my hands against the covers.

She nodded. "You really think about a lot, Cooper. Try to rest and not worry so much."

The angel kissed me on the cheek, flapped her wings, and burst through the roof, making a big hole and causing bits of the ceiling to crumble around me. The sun beamed on my face. The bright light made the stains in the yellow rug seem bigger and uglier. I wondered how much shampoo it would take to clean the rug in the whole house.

It made my body feel stronger to know that people were out there doing things for me. I pictured Mr. Shepherd, Mom, the angel, and Jan sitting in aluminum chairs on the gravel, saying adult things to each other, using grownup powers. I could just lie here covered with sweet-smelling angel dust, putting my hands behind my head, crossing my legs, looking up at Tanner's bed, and things would still happen.

That's when I decided that I was never going to leave home again. Just like Mom, I would never even step into the street. To check the mail I would have to tilt Mr. Maybox all the way back and pluck envelopes from his open mouth. All our antiques would come from Mr. Turner and other people who travel here to sell to us. Word would spread quickly— Cooper is buying stuff.

Everything would be perfect. I would never start another sequence that could ruin our lives. My whole life would be like this:

STEP 1: Cooper stays home.
STEP 2: Cooper and Mom hang out together and run the antique store.

I squeezed the blanket and wished hard for the grown-ups to win, just this one time. After that, I'm grounding myself forever. When it's just me and Mom, things are perfect. Maybe we could play hide-and-seek again. I hide in the flower patch, asking the sunflowers to disguise me. When she finds me she shrieks and tells me to stay right there— *"Gotta run and get the camera to take a picture of your face inside all the smiling sunflowers."* She giggles all the way back to the house.

I drifted off to sleep thinking about all the fun we would have. When I woke up, Tanner was standing next to me playing with a yo-yo.

"Finally," he said. He put the yo-yo in a ghostly pocket.

"It's a full moon already?"

"No, I got leave to visit you. We get three family sick days a year." He gave me a hug. His hair smelled like sweaty Tanner. I moved over and patted the bed, and he climbed up next to me.

"Did you get Squeaky?"

"You mean the bike that never stops talking? Yes, thanks. I jumped the ramp to the Optimus cloud. They gave me a prize."

"So the angel lowered the seat for you?"

"No, George Washington did it."

"George Washington lowered your bicycle seat? He's supposed to be in Iroquois heaven."

"Sometimes he visits." He took my forehead towel and wet it in the bowl of water on the floor. Then he put it back on my face.

"Are there any kids there with a triangular hat and a fife?"

He shrugged. "I was on top of those crying clouds when you dug up the mouth part to that musical instrument. It has lines, Mom showed you."

"Huh?"

"Lines."

Sometimes Tanner didn't make any sense at all. I stared into his zillion freckles, which came alive and jumped around to form different symbols. They started out as simple shapes and then got more complicated, until I couldn't tell what they were. When one of the freckles touched his bright red lips, they all jumped back into their original positions.

"You should wear a helmet," I said.

"Watch what I've been practicing." Tanner pouted his lips and said, "Have you seen my lost cat named Fluffy?" He laughed.

"You're making fun of me!" I tickled him, and the covers shook. His leg kicked the wall.

"Cooper, are you okay in there?" Mom said from her room.

I covered Tanner's mouth, but he wouldn't stop laughing. My palms got wet, and I could feel his teeth. His body was shaking.

*"Don't make me come down there!"*

He pushed my hand away. "I know they want to steal our house. You don't have to hide it from me. I'm smart."

"How'd you find out?"

"George Washington. He tells me everything."

"Try to keep him as your friend. Don't play any practical jokes on him." I poked him on the nose, just like the angel did to me. He poked my nose even harder.

"I won't if you give me a Coopcake."

"Okay, take the one with the blue smiley face. I was saving it for last."

Tanner tiptoed out of the room and came back a few minutes later with blue frosting on his lips. "It was good." He licked his finger. "Are you and Mom going to move?"

"No way. Don't worry, everybody's helping. People really like us."

"It would be cool if they made a park here. There could be ramps and stuff, and a big candy machine."

"Not that kind of park, silly. Anyway, how would you find me on full-moon nights? The moonlight bounces off the gravel and points to my window."

"I got this now." He lifted up his arm and showed me a big watch with glowing green numbers on it. "It has a Global Positron System that uses satellites in space to tell me where I am. I can set it to your new house and follow the arrows."

"Where'd you get that?"

"That was the prize for jumping Squeaky to the Optimus cloud. George Washington programmed it for me."

"George Washington programmed your GPS watch? Now I *know* I have a fever."

"Don't I look like a robot?" He pulled the covers over us and moved his arms and head at strange angles. Our whole little cavern glowed green.

It really bugs me sometimes how little kids learn new technology so fast. My eyelids felt heavy, so I just said, "Cool watch."

"I need to take a nap. Don't go anywhere." I squeezed him tight.

# CHAPTER 32

When I opened my eyes, I didn't feel so sick. Tanner wasn't in my arms anymore, but it wouldn't be long before the next full moon. I had gotten a bonus visit just for having a fever.

Mr. Shepherd was tapping on my window.

I rolled out of bed and opened it. The window slammed against the top of the wooden frame.

"Take this. I can't stay." He handed me a folded up newspaper through a rip in the screen. "Page three."

"Wait, don't go. You were gone so long."

"I think your mom is mad at me."

"So, you can still stay."

"I have to go before she wakes up."

"No, please." I stepped on Decto's head as I ran over to my desk. I grabbed the treasure map of our yard and jumped back to Mr. Shepherd. "Go to the yard and find this musical instrument part. I put it back in the hole."

"Cooper, I really shouldn't."

"Please?" I coughed extra-loud and banged on my chest, and then I pretended to nearly fall over.

Mr. Shepherd covered his mouth with a fuzzy scarf and disappeared from the window. He didn't go back to his truck, so that meant he was following my orders.

I dove back into bed and looked at the newspaper. It was Saturday. I turned to the garage sale ads in the back—even though I wasn't going to any of them, I just had to see what was out there. One read, "Old books, postcards, maps, and other antique paper items." That sounded good. Paper stuff sells quickly. Another said, "Vintage carnival miscellanea: buttons, prizes, costumes, vending machines." That sounded good too. I like it best when people have old things that I've never seen before, even if I'm not going to buy them.

I didn't want to think about what I was missing at those garage sales, so I turned to page three like Mr. Shepherd said.

## New Struggle Looms Over Newtown Battle Site

**Chemung Valley, New York.** The year 1779 brought everlasting fame to our valley when George Washington ordered nearly one-quarter of his army to march up here and squelch the terror unleashed by British and Iroquois raids on frontier towns. Determined and meticulous, Generals John Sullivan and James Clinton combined their forces and marched north along the Chemung River, destroying enemy villages along the way. The largest battle of the Sullivan-Clinton Campaign took place on August 29 on a hillside overlooking the Chemung River and its tributary valleys. Named the Battle of Newtown for a nearby Iroquois village of that same name, the American forces emerged victorious and promptly destroyed the namesake village. They subsequently continued northward, laying waste to over forty Iroquois villages across Upstate New York.

A state park was created in 1912 to commemorate the battle. However, unbeknownst to many of its visitors, most of the battle did not take place on park grounds. The parkland overlooks the five-square-mile battlefield, as well as the approach route of the American soldiers. Today, a new battle is brewing over the location of at least part of the battle, where many Revolutionary-era artifacts have recently been unearthed. Two iron cannons, abandoned by General Sullivan after the battle, are among dozens of artifacts found there, which have been authenticated as relics from the 1779 altercation. A mother-son team of antiquities dealers currently owns the property, running a year-round antique store on the site. However, the city of Elmira has other plans for the land—namely, annexing it to the state park and allowing guests to follow a planned trail down to the battle site, where they will see the cannons perfectly preserved in their original locations.

To acquire the private land, town officials are working closely with the New York State Office of Parks, Recreation, and Historic Preservation. They are exercising the legal right known as eminent domain, which allows a governing body to acquire privately owned land without the owner's consent. The statute is often used for the purchase of acreage for highways and other public works, and rarely used for historic conservation.

Richard Archer, the gray-maned spokesperson for the Elmira City Planning Department, says, "This is a unique opportunity to reclaim land that should have been part of the state park in the first place. Larger, more famous battlefields enjoy such preservation, so why shouldn't this one? Our ancestors fought and died for our freedom here. It's a sacred site."

Not everyone agrees. Elias Shepherd, the flamboyantly dressed director of the Elmira Museum, adds, "Certain freedoms exist in this country—they are inherent in our founding documents. Namely, citizens should be free of tyranny and able to exercise the same liberties that we gained from being an independent nation. Ample opportunity exists to perform an archaeological dig on privately held land and use the knowledge gained there to inform the historical record. Furthermore, there are many historic sites nationwide that exist on private land— we assume that state and national parks have covered them all, but that's far from the case. Should we clear out whole neighborhoods because of this? Should we let history cripple our right to live in the present day?"

The thick-booted Archer responds, "Although it sounds tyrannical, eminent domain is hardly that at all. As a first step, a fair offer has been made on the property, which, I should add, is in a state of distress and in tax arrears. If the offer is accepted, there won't be any contention at all."

Indeed, that is the first of many steps. The eminent domain procedure can take months, even years, to complete, depending on the level of legal opposition involved. Although the landowner declined to comment, it appears that the current residents have no desire to cooperate with the town's wishes. Simply put, they want to live on the land that has been in their family, and covered in history-masking weeds, for nearly two hundred years.

The new battle has begun.

Weird. The words made everything seem so real. It wasn't some feverish, sweaty, out-of-control, crazy dream. It was actually happening.

I put my hands behind my head and crossed my legs. The whole world was topsy-turvy because of me. And I couldn't do anything but lie here and have visitors.

Mr. Shepherd showed up at the window. He poked his hand through and held out the brass mouthpiece in a white-gloved hand.

"You found it!" I said, scrambling over and snatching it.

"Don't worry, Cooper. It's modern. You can see the seam that the machine left on it."

I spotted a thin raised line going around the outside. So that's what Tanner was talking about! It amazed me that he could spot that from all the way up on a cloud.

"I didn't see it before."

"It's not even from a fife. It looks like it belonged to a French horn. Colonial fifes were mostly wood, and the mouth opening was just a small hole in the tube. There's nothing in the history books about a drummer or fifer getting injured in this battle. You got scared, that's all."

"I'm still not digging here anymore. It's wrong."

"Did you read the article?"

I nodded. "Are we going to win?"

"Cooper, I'm trying to make things right. People might read this article and come to your defense."

"But there's nothing about me in there. There should have been a picture of me like this." I showed him my deluxe pouty face. "That works. Guaranteed."

"There will be more articles. I've been feeding the reporter information. I'll tell her about the pouty face."

"Don't go so long without coming back. It got me sick." I waved a finger like he was being naughty.

"My not coming here made you sick?"

"That, and metal-detecting in the rain."

"Go rest. We need you to be healthy."

"Stay five more minutes." I tried to grab his arm through the screen door, but he ducked and rolled out of the way. History and germs make Mr. Shepherd a good athlete.

"If I do, you'll beg for five more." He crawled back to the window.

"Seven total, and that's it. I'll keep the germs inside." I put my hands behind my back.

"Fine."

Mr. Shepherd talked at my window for fourteen more minutes. He finally figured out what he would do if he could go back in time—he would warp to 1802 and tell George Washington's wife not to burn all their private letters before she died. Hundreds of papers went up in smoke, all about the Revolution and him being our first president. Poof. Gone. Just like that. By luck two letters had fallen into a little nook at the back of his writing desk, where they were discovered years later by the desk's new owner. Then not long ago someone found a third letter—that one fell out of an old book in a library. That's it, though. Only three letters from George to his wife survived.

It bugged me that Mr. Shepherd didn't want to go back in time and *not* tell Iron Boots about the cannons that we found in the backyard. That's what he should do first. Then yell at Martha.

# CHAPTER 33

Every time I woke up, my pajamas were drenched in sweat. I didn't have anything good to think about, except when Mom or the angel visited me, and my weird dreams were torturing me—like the one about the roll of sticky tape that I could never get started. So a few days later I rolled out of bed and crawled outside. The gravel dug into my knees, but I went past Mom's feet and pulled myself into the small aluminum chair. The sun started drying my pajamas right away.

There was hardly any noise from the steep forest—it was mostly a smell day. My nose was getting unstuffed, so it sniffed out the hot pavement, sweet dandelions, musty paper in the antique shop, dewy wood from the shady part of the barn, Mom's skin, and my own baking sweat. I closed each nostril to see which one worked better. Trucks roared by in the distance. On smell days the highway comes back to life.

"Anything happen?" I asked.

"One customer." She turned a page.

"My fever melted."

"Don't go anywhere until it's normal."

"I'm never leaving again. Not even into the street or to Jill's house. Like you."

"School starts soon."

I fell out of my chair and flopped onto my back. My arms and legs went limp. "Not going."

"The truant officer will come again."

"She'll have to carry me." I pulled myself over to Mom

by her leg. I struggled up with my arms, until I was sitting on her lap for a backwards hug. Only the hug never came—Mom pushed me off.

"Double hugs when you're better."

I flopped back onto the ground, purposely letting the gravel hurt me so maybe she would see me bleed. When I was little, nothing could stop Mom from hugging me—not even cooties or the plague. She would make vanilla pudding and let me sleep in her bed. It was starting to become obvious that Mom didn't want it to be just us anymore. She wanted to be alone with her dumb book while I went off to horrible school, or garage sales, or my new friends.

"Want to play catch over the house?" I asked.

"You're sick." Her voice made it seem like I was dumb for asking.

"When I'm better."

"We'll see." She turned the book around and showed me a colorful page. "Tell me which of these clocks is made in Germany."

"No. And don't say I'm a grump-and-a-half, or bigger."

Mom didn't say anything. I stayed on the ground smelling the dusty gravel with each nostril. I made a little hole with my finger that must have tickled the Earth. The underground was warm. It made me realize that Mom and I could survive together for years here without leaving or paying our bills. In the winter my friend the Earth could keep us warm by making a big crack and sending steam up. Mom could read by the lava flames. If I made a garden next to the flower patch, maybe I could grow enough vegetables to last the winter. Nature could help us survive.

That's when I remembered how everyone was supposed to come to our rescue because of that newspaper article. They didn't come, just like I figured. Trucks roar down the highway, and tree branches grow over the Revolutionary

War signs, and nobody cares about us or this battle. That's probably why the forest was quiet—even the bugs and animals knew that evil was coming our way, and they packed their things and bought tickets out of here. Whatever I dug up in the backyard had disturbed the old spirits, and the Ghost Conductor would be up on his bluff during the next full moon, calling "All aboard!" The whole mountain would chug to life, creaking and groaning and crumbling, bursting off the tracks, the lumpy train zipping under the full moon and onto the ridge of a distant peak. We would be very alone after that.

Even our best customers didn't come to say how sorry they were that bad people were going to take our land. I guess that's a thank-you-very-much for spending years going out at dawn to buy things for a quarter that I'm going to sell to them for fifty bucks. I always knew everybody was jealous of my lips. Those people can't be early birds. If you don't know how to pout, then you might as well get an extra hour of sleep on Saturday morning, and don't hate me for it.

A sound finally broke the hot, smelly stillness—some cars coming up the road. They didn't sound like customers. Customers have quiet cars that creep up the street. These cars raced quickly. I sat up and saw Mr. Archer's white pickup truck and a black car with dark windows pulling onto our gravel lot. My heart started pounding.

"Go inside," Mom said.

"Should I lock the barn?"

"No. Inside. Now." We ran for the front door. Mom dropped her book as Mr. Archer's hairy leg came out of the truck. An iron boot hit the ground. We slammed the door behind us and sat with our backs against it. I reached up to turn the lock. Outside, the gravel crunched. The screen door opened, followed by a loud knock. We held on to each other as the person banged and banged and banged. I looked at the closet door and thought about taking Mom in there, but it would've made too much noise. We stayed put and just breathed.

Low voices came from outside, and then the knocking started up again. I didn't know if Iron Boots would kick down the door. I held on to Mom, and she held on to me, and we just huddled there, like the time a spring storm swept through and blasted bolts of lightning at the barn's roof. I leaned my head on Mom's shoulder.

"Ma'am, it's Richard Archer. I brought a lawyer. We're only here to deliver some information. It's nothing to worry about. We just need your signature."

The voice of Iron Boots made my stomach gurgle, and I imagined slimy gray hairs slithering through the door cracks and wrapping around me and Mom.

"Mom, c'mon, the closet." I stood up and pulled her arm. She didn't want to go. She thinks Moppy is a bad influence on me. I pulled harder. We ran into her room and leaned against the wall under the window. That way we could hear what was happening outside. I didn't like it because we were in a bad spot if someone tossed a brick through the window. But I couldn't get Mom to change our hiding place, so we stayed there while they pounded on the door. The vibrations made a little sailboat painting on Mom's wall tilt at a strange angle.

Eventually it got quiet. The screen door closed, gravel crunched, car doors slammed, and Iron Boots and his lawyer drove away.

We didn't move in case it was a trick. I leaned back and did an upside-down peek through the window, hoping Jill would come home soon. Our hands were sweaty.

"I'm sorry I brought this to us," I said.

"You dug a hole, Cooper."

"But that was part of the sequence."

"Don't be afraid to do things."

"Are you afraid?" I put one hand on her cheek.

"When you were two you used to sit on your dad's shoulder, and he would give you rides. Wherever you pointed, he would run there—behind the barn, through the hidden path to the flower patch, around the outside of the house, down the road, inside the house, up the steep forest a little. There was no spot too dangerous for his little guide. When you told him to run, or crawl, he obeyed. This went on for hours until you fell asleep right on his shoulders."

"I don't remember." I wanted that memory very badly, so I told my mind to turn it into a fake memory.

"That's the real Cooper. You run around and explore everywhere—even inside the Earth."

"Jan calls me Little Butterfly. It stands for Little Butterfly That Flapped Its Wings and Never Stopped Flapping."

"And a beautiful one. You look like your dad."

"I wish my hair was yellow like yours."

"You're part Iroquois. From him." She untangled my hair and stroked it gently.

If someone had thrown a brick through the window right then, or a big crack opened in the Earth, or the ghost train roared to life, I probably wouldn't have noticed it. I stared into her eyes to see if she was joking.

"Are you serious?"

She nodded.

I stood up and put a hand on each of her cheeks. "Are you seriously serious?"

She nodded.

"I mean you swear on your pile of antique books serious?"

"Yes."

"Why didn't you ever tell me this?" I squeezed her cheeks so that her lips puckered.

"I wuth waithin untith you whuf olth enuth to untherthan."

I gave her a little peck on the lips. Then I remembered that I was sick, so I tried to wipe it away. Then I remembered that my hands were covered in germs, so I scrubbed her mouth with my pajama sleeve. There were so many people I could tell this good news to. There was Koala, Moppy, Mirror, Decto, Mini-Decto, Jill, Jan, Mr. Shepherd, Earth, the beautiful view, the sunflowers, the Ghost Conductor, Tanner, the sun, the moon, Mr. Maybox, the noisy bugs when they woke up again, the rest of the ghosts, George Washington (Tanner would tell him), Squeaky (Tanner again), and anybody else I forgot. Somehow I would have to do all that without leaving home.

A customer pulled up. I made sure it was really a customer, and then we strolled outside. The evil visitors seemed like just a really bad daydream because a few minutes later we sold the wooden rocking horse that had been in the barn forever. Sometimes, on smell days, it seems like the birds aren't chirping just for me.

We were still in business. And I was Iroquois.

# CHAPTER 34

I wouldn't let Mom tell me any more of the story just yet because I didn't want her to say anything that was going to ruin it. It was hard to talk about Dad and have only good things come out. This was big. Really big. When I went back to rest, I cuddled with Koala and didn't think fever thoughts anymore.

"Whut duth Iroquoith mean?" he asked.

"It means that part of me is descended from Ji-Gon-Sa-Seh, an ancient lady with white hair who watches over this land. I'm one of the original people who lived here."

"Could this news, in any small way, convince you not to get rid of us?" Decto said.

"I'm not getting rid of you!"

Decto gave Mini-Decto a hug, and they both smiled.

"I knew all along that I was reflecting someone special," Mirror said. "Your freckles move around and form symbols that tell the ancient story of this valley. I've flaked off half my reflection squinting to read them."

That night a jagged crack opened in my floor, sending up a burst of heat and fountains of lava. There was still a big hole in my ceiling from where the angel busted out, so the lava went above the house, lighting up the treetops and clouds in an eerie orange glow. The full moon sprinkled some of her gentle white light on top of everything.

"So now you know why you are so beautiful and gentle of soul," the Earth said. "And why you can speak to spirits, the heavens, the sky, the moon, the sun, and the forest creatures, and how you can live off my surface with so few possessions, but with so much love in your heart."

"I understand now."

"Now listen carefully. You are still a child, so I will forgive you for continually forgetting that your peaceful valley has once again been filled with sadness. My land, which you so gently tend, is threatened. You must feel it in your heart, like an ancient boulder lodged there, one that will not shake free until the threat is lifted. So heed my words! You are not to smile or rejoice again until you see the valley itself casting forth from its depths the sadness that has polluted this region for so long. Only then may you continue shining the light of your happiness on our hillsides."

"How will I know when that happens?"

"You will know. Tomorrow you must go to Jan and tell her all that is happening. She will know what to do—bring the newspaper article, for the answer itself lies hidden between its lines."

"I will do what you say, Earth."

The bubbling lava erupted into a sky-high fountain that burst into outer space and scorched the full moon. A moonbeam escaped and dashed down the starlit sky like a comet, until it struck our gravel lot. The glowing ray bounced through my window and lit up my bunk bed. Moments later Tanner slid down the moonbeam, dove through the hole in the ceiling, and crash-landed on the top bunk with a loud thud.

"What happened to finding me with your GPS watch?" I asked.

"It broke." He climbed down the ladder and crawled next to me. His freckles were clumped together into the symbols on the Iroquois flag.

"You talk first," I said.

"Yesterday I jumped Squeaky to the Dragon Delta cloud. Nobody ever did that before. They gave me a superadvanced dirt bike. Now I have sponsors." He showed me some patches on his sleeve.

"Cool."

"Next I'm going to jump over the moon. It's going to be a whole show. All these kids are going to do acts, and then I'm going to go last."

I never knew that Tanner would become a biker kid in heaven. It made me worry that he wouldn't look up to me anymore, now that he's pro and everybody admires him.

"That's silly," he said. "You'll always be pro at being big bro." He tugged the blanket so that he had more of it.

"Let me guess. You learned how to read minds in school." I pulled the covers back.

"Yep, and for homework I'm supposed to practice mind-reading and write a poem. Now I'm done with both."

"Don't you get summers off?"

"No, winters. That's when we're supposed to go haunt people. On those cold, blustery days when it gets dark early and the floor creaks." With one big yank he stole the whole blanket. "Your turn."

"Did you know about Dad and how he's part Iroquois?"

He shook his head. "But I know about the freckle symbols. I see them on you all the time."

"I'm going back to Jan tomorrow. Earth told me she'll know what to do." The crack in the floor closed, and the room cooled off a little.

"Don't tell her about being Iroquois. She thinks you're Xavier, and he was French."

"Good point."

A cloud covered the moon. Howling wind blew through the valley, creating a whirlwind that knocked the newspaper off my desk. Decto and Mini-Decto were huddled together on the floor, their teeth chattering. That's when I realized that the night forest had seeped into the room through the hole in the ceiling. Fireflies and moths danced around the moonlit bunk bed. Pine needles, dried leaves, and clumps of rotting plants covered the rug. Crickets chirped from dark corners. Stardust sprinkled down from the sky, tickling my eyes and making my vision blurry. Tanner and I hid under the covers and peeked out.

Ghostly deer galloped through the wall and fled through my door. Men dressed in deerskin and holding bows and arrows crept through the room and followed their trail. Twin boys fell from the sky and smashed into the floor, where they began fighting. They chased each other around the room, climbing the bunk bed and leaping off, hanging from walls, and screaming. They called on birds, squirrels, gophers, and bears to help them, until the whole room was filled with ghostly confusion. Soon Ji-Gon-Sa-Seh arrived and swung her long hair at them, knocking them out of the room and into the forest, where they fled.

Songs and chanting came from the direction of Newtown Village. The sweet music filled the night sky with millions of dandelion seeds, which poured through the broken ceiling and choked us in a fluffy, tickly cloud. They squeezed under the covers and surrounded my whole body, turning me over onto my back. The spores carved a little wooden door in the center of my chest, just above my heart. Forest fairies rode in on dragonflies and blew the spores away with gentle breaths. They crowded around the door and unlocked it with a little rusty key. The creaky door opened.

Drumbeats and fife music came from the direction of the Chemung River. The soldiers were on the march again! The valley rumbled from their footsteps. Terrified screams of men, women, and children came from the village. They fled before the army could reach them, but this time they came toward me—through my walls in a long, ghostly parade. They turned into wisps and flew into the little door-way on my chest. Their shouting turned to calm whispers as they plunged into the depths of my heart. My body vibrated, and the rest of my fever escaped, leaving a thousand years' worth of sweet and salty tastes in my mouths.

I held the spirits of a doomed people. Whichever path they chose would lead to their destruction, but somehow they would manage to survive.

So they could create me.

Tanner closed the tiny door just as the cannon fire woke the sleeping mountain. We covered our ears and bur-ied ourselves under pillows as the battle raged around us. When it was over, the steep hillside was quiet, except for the faint whispers of ghosts.

"That awful business is over, so now where should we haunt?" one ghost asked.

"The tall weeds are gone," another said.

"No ticks for us," a third ghost added.

"The Ghost Conductor will tell us where to go," a deep voice cried. "Make way for the Ghost Conductor!"

Rustlings and animal sounds and scraping tree branches came from the woods. I hopped out of bed and peered up at the steep forest. I couldn't see Ghost Conductor's Bluff, not even when I squeezed myself against the wall and stood on my desk chair. It didn't help much when the moon came out from behind the clouds. The hole in the ceiling just wasn't big enough. I would have to go outside to see up there, and that would be way too scary. I only go outside on full-moon nights in serious emergencies.

"Have you ever seen the Ghost Conductor?" I asked Tanner.

He shook his head. I jumped up on my desk to try to get a peek at him.

"Get your tickets ready!" a gruff voice said.

"Tickets! Tickets! The Ghost Conductor is coming!" all the voices sang at once. "Ghost Conductor! Ghost Conductor! Ghost Conductor!" Their voices sounded like a train chugging along the tracks. The ground rumbled as the mountain awoke from an ancient sleep. I dove back into bed and held on to Tanner. Mirror fell off the wall and shattered.

"The Ghost Conductor is on his bluff!" all the voices yelled.

"Hooray!"

# CHAPTER 35

I woke up to the sound of a faint truck horn on the highway. It was morning. My ceiling was still there, Mirror was up on the wall, and the newspaper was back on my desk. My fever was gone.

I leapt out of bed and got dressed in only a few seconds. I chugged down breakfast and wrote a note to Mom about where I was going. My promise never to leave our land lasted only a few days. Earth was right, though—I had to tell Jan what was happening here. She would know what to do.

My heart felt heavy, and I had to struggle to walk straight. I threw the folded-up newspaper into Squeaky's basket and rolled him into the street. Jill's car was out front, which made me feel better about leaving Mom home alone.

"Hello, old friend," Squeaky said in a weak voice.

"Hi, Squeaky." My feet pedaled down the street.

"You don't sound excited to see me, Cooper."

"I am, Squeaky, but things got bad while you were with Tanner. I can't feel good again until this valley is free of sadness." I remembered Earth's warning not to smile until then, so I just petted Squeaky and told him that the rain must have washed away the oil.

We whizzed around corners. It was good to have my hair trailing behind me again, the fever gone from my body, Squeaky alive and well, and two Tanner visits in one week—but that wasn't enough to make me happy anymore. Things wouldn't be right until Mom could sit outside without worrying that evil cars were going to drive up and scare her. I don't know why it took so long for that idea to sink deep inside me.

When Jan opened the door, the hundreds of wrinkles surrounding her mouth became puppet strings that lifted her lips into a smile. It collapsed after only a few seconds because she peered into my eyes and saw the sadness in my heart.

"Little Butterfly, what's wrong?"

I held out the newspaper. She unwrapped my fingers to get it free. Her bony hand gently led me inside. We went into the room that had the high ceiling with windows in it. She sat in her chair next to the small table and read the article while I wandered around and looked at her beautiful sculptures.

There was a new one on a small shelf near the kitchen. It showed a boy holding a metal detector. He had ripped jeans, green eyes, and black hair down to his shoulders. His body was made from thousands of tiny slivers of bottle caps—blue pieces for the pants, green shards for the shirt. His sneakers had holes in them, with a big toe sticking out made from the metal end of a pencil, with a little bit of the rubber still attached. The boy's hair was made from thin black wires, and the red lips were tiny bits of a Coca-Cola can. The eyes were green metal buttons held in place by tiny silver grabbers.

The metal detector's neck was made from a hollow pipe, and the disc at the end was a silver dollar with scratches in the shape of a face. I moved close to the sculpture and then back away from it. When I was far, the sculpture looked exactly like me and Decto. Close, it looked like thousands of metal bits. I peeked at Jan's chair, with the long white mane dangling off the back, and wondered if she was thinking about me a lot while I was gone.

"Do you like it?" she asked without turning around.

"It's beautiful."

"It's for you to keep."

My heart jiggled a little, but I held in the smile. Nobody had ever made such a complicated present for me.

"I thought you would be mad that I didn't come back for so long."

"I knew you were fluttering somewhere, and that eventually you'd flit this way. Come sit by me and listen to a story. Bring the sculpture." She placed the newspaper on the small table.

"Thanks for making it." I picked the boy up carefully by the metal base, which was made from hundreds of small circles with holes in them. It was heavy. I carried it with both hands and placed it on the floor by Jan's feet. Then I sat down and waited for her story.

"There's an old Iroquois legend that I want you to hear. It might lift the spirits in your heart."

I wondered if she already knew about my being part Iroquois, and that there really were spirits in my heart, along with Mom, Tanner, Mr. Shepherd, Jan, and the rest. It was getting crowded in there, but there always seemed to be room for more.

Here's the story Jan told:

## The Friend of an Abandoned Boy

One day a group of hunters in the forest discovered a lonely boy who did not have a father or a mother. He wasn't very tall, so he could not hunt for food. The hunters had too many things on their backs and would not carry the boy back to their village, even though he begged to be taken with them.

They left him in a small house by a stream, leaving plenty of deer meat and corn for him to eat. They promised to send help as soon as they returned to their village. The boy cried, and his wails could be heard for days as the hunters journeyed homeward. The boy ate the corn and meat, but before long it was all gone. He sat by the edge of the stream and watched the fish swim by, but he did not know how to pluck them from the water.

The hunters returned to their village and told the chief about the lonely boy. At once the chief sent a swift messenger to rescue him. However, when the messenger entered the forest he transformed into a furry bear with sharp claws and fierce teeth. The bear leapt high above the trees and landed deep in the forest, creating a big crater in the ground. He leapt again, and in this way did he journey to the little lost boy, thinking of nothing other than eating him.

One night the boy was shivering by the fire, and there was a knock on the door. A sound like a snowy blizzard swirled outside.

"Who's there?" the boy said, his little legs shaking.

"Young one, I am here to take care of you. You are not going to die because I will help you. Whenever you need a friend, think of me and I will come." The swirling noise went away, and the boy was alone again.

The next morning there was fresh deer meat hanging from a tree, and a pile of firewood on the ground. The boy smiled and made a fire to cook the meat. Suddenly he did not feel so lonely. He wanted to meet his new friend.

That night there was another knock on the door, along with the sound of snow swirling outside.

"Is that you, friend?" the boy asked.

"There is no time to waste," the voice said. "The chief sent a swift messenger to rescue you, but it has transformed into a bear and now plans to eat you. I will leave a club under the old hemlock tree on the far side of the stream. When the bear comes, look at his furry, clawed feet and see which one has thicker padding. Hit him in that foot with the club."

"I will do as you say, friend," the boy said.

The next morning the boy waded across the stream and found a club leaning against the ancient hemlock tree. He took the club and climbed the tree. When the bear landed nearby and made a big crater, the boy gasped in fear. The bear spotted him and leapt into the tree. With one mighty swing the boy landed the club on the bear's thicker foot. The bear screamed and fell to the ground. He scrambled into the forest, unable to leap over trees with his injured foot.

That night the sound of snow swirling returned to the boy's house.

"The chief has sent more men for you," the voice said. "Soon you will leave here, but do not forget to call on me if you need help. You will never see me, but I am called Géha, which means Wind. You will grow tall and strong. One day you will become the swiftest runner in the land, but you must never brag about your speed."

The next day men arrived to take the boy back to the village. He was adopted by the chief, and he spent his days running through the woods practicing his speed. Before long he hunted deer by running after them and bopping them on the head with his club. He watched other boys run and noticed how slow they were, but he never bragged about his own swiftness.

Then one night there was a scratching at the boy's door. The furry bear had returned!

"I tried to eat you," the bear said, "because Creator had vowed that you would be swifter than I. Now I challenge you to a race. Meet me at the top of the second mountain at dawn. We will race across the hills and valleys until sunset. The winner gets to eat the loser."

The boy was scared, but he packed his best moccasins and dried corn to eat. The chief tried to stop him from going, but he was determined. He climbed to the top of the second mountain. At dawn the fierce bear landed nearby, making a big shaking that woke the valley. The bear's foot had healed, and he growled at the boy with sharp teeth.

"Start running!" the bear said.

The boy ran down the mountain, but the bear leapt into the air, sailed across the valley, and landed on the next mountain over. The boy thought it was unfair that the bear could leap across the whole valley while he had to run through it. He knew he was going to lose and be eaten, and so he called on his friend Géha to help him. At once the swirling wind came and carried the boy into the air, across the valley, over the far mountain, and into the next valley. He flew past the bear and gained the lead in the race. By sunset the bear had run out of energy. He declared that the boy had won and was indeed the fastest creature in the land.

The boy did not eat the bear. Instead, he removed the bear's thick padding from his feet so that he could never cheat in a race again. He ran all the way home to tell the chief and villagers what had happened. All the children admired him, and one day he grew up to be their chief.

Jan took a sip from a mug on her little table. I almost smiled at her, but I stopped it just in time. I couldn't move from the spot where my head had leaned over onto the rug. Her voice had seeped inside my body and shut off every muscle.

"That was a good story."

"Do you understand its meaning?"

I tried to shake my head, but my right cheek was already jammed up against the carpet.

"You've told me that nature is alive inside your mind—the sun, moon, heavens, forest creatures, spirits on the mountain, flowers and insects, the beautiful landscape, the Earth, and even your toys. But you never mentioned the one element of nature that can help out a little butterfly the most—the wind. Now let's wait and see what our friend the wind blows into the valley, shall we?"

I nodded, which I could still do with my head on the carpet. It made my right cheek burn. Jan picked up her little electronic device and began pressing things on the glass screen. She hummed quietly while she did it.

# CHAPTER 36

I pushed Squeaky on the way home so Jan's statue wouldn't fall out of his basket and break. Also, I was thinking hard about Jan's story. For some reason I had never talked to the wind before, probably because it makes such scary noises and rattles the windows at night. It tears the pinecones off the trees so they crash against the forest floor, and sends Swiss-cheese clouds to smother the sun, speckling the distant forest with sunny pieces and gloomy parts. On some mornings it refuses to blow the fog away, until I get lost on the way to garage sales.

"I also make your face feel cool when you ride downhill, and I twist your mom's hair into an impossible mystery of beautiful twirls and knots."

"Oh, hello, Wind," I said. A small leaf blew across the road and stuck to the curb.

"I blow storms away from your house but leave a single cloud so Tanner can watch," she continued. "I make pine trees creak and sway so there's something to see while waiting for customers."

"But you scare me at night."

"I help little butterflies in flight."

"You make whirlwinds that mess up my room."

"I scatter pollen so flowers can bloom."

"You once sent Jill my aluminum chair."

"That gave you an excuse to go over there."

"You howl, whistle, and brag."

"It's to show off the American flag."

"You blow my hair into my face."

"I slow down meteors from outer space."

"You tear branches off trees."

"Only when I sneeze."

"You knocked over Mr. Maybox."

"But you have to admit that was funny," Wind said, giggling.

I almost smiled, but then I remembered that Mom was home alone and it was taking a long time to get there. I pushed Squeaky faster. The wind became silent, and the heat made my face sweat.

"Okay, Wind, you can be my friend. I'm sorry I never talked to you before."

"You've made me so happy, Cooper."

I pushed Squeaky up my steep street, relieved to see that Mom was sitting safely in her chair reading a book. No cars were there. A squirrel stood on the roof of the house, nibbling a nut quickly and staring all around, as if somebody might steal its food. Little pieces of shell rolled down until they got stuck. At any moment our peaceful afternoon could go bad. I didn't forget that, just like Earth told me. My heart felt like a lump of solid iron, and it didn't seem like even the wind would be able to budge it.

As the days and nights went by I listened closely for every whisper, groan, and howl of the wind. If a big breeze rattled the windows at night, I peered into the darkness to see if anything was coming. During the day I curled up on the gravel at Mom's feet and watched the tippy-tops of the pine trees sway back and forth. Most of the time gentle breezes darted around, tickling my feet or scraping a branch against the barn's metal roof. If anything was coming to save us, the wind kept it hidden.

On a Friday before garage sale day, a thick fog blew in and choked the whole valley. Our house was lost in a cozy cloud, and I couldn't see past Mr. Maybox. I knew the wind was trying to tell me something, so I crawled back into bed and listened for what she would do next. Jan's statue stayed perfectly quiet, watching me from an antique shelf next to Mirror.

When my eyelids were half-closed, a noise came from outside. I hopped out of bed, nearly banging my head against the top bunk. A beat-up car drove out of the fog and stopped in front of our house. It had an Ohio license plate. A plump man with a white beard got out and stretched his arms and legs. Then he opened the trunk and pulled out a sign. After jamming its pole into the ground next to Mr. Maybox, he pushed and leaned until it stood on its own. The words were facing the road and stayed secret. The man gazed around our property for a while, then got back into the car. It disappeared into the fog.

"Decto, wake up. Someone just put a sign up out there."

Decto muttered groggily, curled up next to his son. I tried to wake Mirror and Koala, but it was no use. I dove back into bed and tried to guess what the sign said.

I couldn't wait to read it, so I put on my bathrobe and went outside in my bare feet. The misty air tickled my nose. I tiptoed across the gravel, trying not to cut my feet. When the sign got close, I took a deep breath, closed my eyes, and jumped into the street. I spun around and read it. Here's what it said:

> Antique Dealers:
> **DON'T LOOT OUR BATTLEFIELD!**
> From Concerned Citizens.

My heart sank. The white-bearded guy wasn't on our side at all! Somehow, the message about what was happening got all the way to Ohio, and people decided not to like us. I knew deep down that without a picture of Mom's beauty and me pouting, that newspaper article was going to make things worse.

Mr. Shepherd kept ruining things for me and Mom. I was beginning to think that Mom was right. His stories in the sun were lost in the thick fog and the soggy, are-those-tears-in-your-eyes-again morning. The wind had betrayed me already. Maybe Mr. Shepherd did too. It's not like there's a long list of men around here who have loved me enough to care what happens to my life.

I yanked the sign out of the ground. It had to go away before Mom woke up. There's a dark lonely space between the far side of the barn and the wall of pine trees, so I tiptoed back there and leaned it against the wooden shingles, next to an old aluminum chair with no fabric. My feet sank into the mud, and sharp weeds poked my toes. Even though that part of the yard is so forgotten and lost, it made my stomach tighten to think that I would never see it again if me and Mom had to move. I put my finger into a little knot in the siding, and then I slogged through the muck and gravel and went back inside.

I flopped onto the lumpy couch, letting the springs dig into my ribs. Mom was sleeping peacefully on her bed and had no clue that the whole world was against us. It made me mad when her blanket went slowly up and down, because the only reason she breathed so calmly was that her slumbering mind knew Cooper took care of things around here. I was the man of the house. And the best idea the man could come up with was to talk to the wind.

Dumb, Cooper, dumb.

There were going to be some big changes around here. Huge changes. Things that were going to make Mom proud of me and make me less of a little kid. First, I was going to start taking showers instead of baths. That was going to start right away because my feet were muddy. I sprang up and walked on my heels into the bathroom, leaving little brown circles in the yellow rug.

Showers are dangerous around here because the water comes out of the big brass spout with so much power that it could knock you against the wall. Even Mom doesn't take showers. In the distant past the showerhead must have wrecked the whole bathroom—it has flower-covered wallpaper that's peeling, a squishy floor that's lifting up near the walls, a sink with big craters in it, and a tub with black spots. Dad was probably strong enough to take showers.

The shower roared when I turned the handle.

"Muahaha," it said. "Come let me scrape off your skin like I scraped off the skin of the tub."

No, actually the shower didn't say anything because I'm done talking to things, too. Mom never liked that. I jumped in the shower and winced in pain when spray needles hit my stomach. I turned my back to the water and stared down at the brown, blotchy tub. Moppy—I mean my regular mop that doesn't talk—can never get rid of those spots because they're a permanent part of the tub.

I made a whole list of Cooper's new life in that shower. Here it is:

1. Showers only, and no rubber duckies even when the water builds up at your feet.
2. No talking to Koala, Mirror, Decto, Squeaky, Mini-Decto, Wind, Earth, and anything else that's not human.
3. No sitting in Mom's lap.
4. No more bedtime stories from Mom. Read a book like a real man.
5. No hugs from Mom. Shake hands only.
6. Stop saying no when friends at school ask to hang out because you have to go home to Mom.

7. No pretending you have a lost kitten. Just ask if you can go into the garage sale early, starting tomorrow.
8. You will tell Jan that you are not Xavier reborn. It's wrong to let her think you are. Tell her the truth about being part Iroquois.
9. You will tell Jill that she's a beautiful angel instead of just playing it in a game.
10. You will ask Mom more about what happened when you were little, instead of being so afraid all the time.

I turned off the shower when it hurt too much to stay in there anymore. The water had filled up the whole tub, so it was more like a standing bath. At least my feet were clean. The bathrobe felt good against my red, bruised skin. As I brushed my hair back into a slick, wet streak, it occurred to me that maybe we really should move, just like Iron Boots and everybody else wanted. We were living in a graveyard, with lots of sad memories in the far and near past, and maybe it would be good for Mom to start a new life somewhere else. Tanner's GPS watch could be fixed so he could always find me wherever we went.

I slumped my head. Tanner.

Rule 11 had to be no more visits from Tanner. I was almost crying when I walked out of the bathroom and saw Mom sitting at the table eating an egg. Rule 12 had to be less crying.

"I took a shower." I wiped away the tear and pretended it was regular water.

"I would have to be in another state not to know that."

Ohio. It reminded me of the sign. I sat down and ate the egg that Mom made for me. My hand went across the table and stayed there until Mom figured out that she should shake it. She smiled in a confused way.

"Jill told me the Associated Press picked up our story,"

Mom said. "It might even be in the *New York Times*."

I didn't want to tell her that it wouldn't help. The world was just going to think that we were here to steal treasures from the battlefield and sell them. There were just going to be more people out there not to trust.

"Should we move?" I said. "We can use the money to buy a house with a bigger barn."

Mom chewed for a while.

"Those sunflowers were in the flower patch when I was a little girl," she said in a quivery voice. "I used to believe they could grant me wishes, but only one wish for each sunflower."

"What did you wish for?"

Mom couldn't say anything after that. I dropped the fork and ran around the table to bury myself in her warm arms. Rule 5 was so getting crossed off. I inhaled Mom's sweet smell and wondered what I was thinking.

# CHAPTER 37

> ## GARAGE SALE
> Saturday 9 A.M. to 4 P.M.
> 13 Old New York Road
> (Just off Route 17, southeast of Elmira)
> Clothes, Furniture, Baseball Cards,
> Wind-up Toy Collection,
> Dollhouse Accessories, Pewter, Tablecloths,
> Power Tools, Knickknacks, Curios, Baubles,
> Gewgaws, Ephemera, Miscellany, and more!

Getting ready on garage sale morning was a quiet, lonely way to spend the last weekend before school started. Nobody made a sound in my room. Not a peep about my hair, or whether we were going metal-detecting, or the muffled gibberish of speaking without a mouth. Decto's lifeless disc was covered in a glob of scratches and hardly looked like a face anymore.

It didn't help much when I found a bag of school supplies outside on my aluminum chair. At least there was a brand-new bicycle helmet hanging from Squeaky's handlebar—only it wouldn't be as much fun to wear without a comment about how it looked on me. It didn't seem fair to make that rule so soon after Squeaky came back to me, but I couldn't cross it off just for that reason.

My bike soared through the thick fog that still choked our valley. The slimy air filled my lungs and made me feel lightheaded. My brain was half-asleep. My head felt like it was getting softer, and the bicycle helmet dug into my skin. Within the mist I saw visions of people metal-detecting in murky backyards. Around every corner there were more of them—shadowy figures pulling things out of the ground. I was the only person on the road, but they completely ignored me and kept swinging their detectors, like robots. Rule 13: No more crazy daydreams!

I knocked on the door of a small house with two chimneys. I had no idea what half the things in their garage sale ad meant, but they couldn't be that good because nobody else was waiting at the curb for it to start. The door swung open, and a stern-looking lady with glasses on the end of her nose frowned at me.

"Ma'am, can I come into your garage sale early? I have no reason for it, I just like to be first."

"And do people normally let you in?"

"I'm afraid so. I used to pout a lot and talk about my lost kitten named Fluffy."

"You lost your kitten?"

"No, ma'am."

She stared at me, confused.

"Are your parents with you?" She looked behind me, toward the road.

"No, my mom waits back home. We run an antique store out of our barn."

"Oh, you must be the family from that article—the Newtown Battle piece. I've been following it in the paper. It's so interesting that we all live on a battlefield. That's why I joined the project."

"What project?"

"The museum project." She pointed to the side of her house. A tall lady swinging a metal detector walked around the corner. She wore a blue shirt with the words FINGER LAKES METAL DETECTING CLUB. IN MEMORY OF OUR FOUNDER, XAVIER.

I rubbed my eyes and pinched myself to see if this was one of those crazy Cooper dreams. That's when I saw more of those shadowy figures metal-detecting in other yards, all wearing the same blue shirts. It wasn't a dream or a misty vision. The grownups had gotten together and used their adult superpowers, and something was actually happening! Something big was going on! A burst of energy raced through my body.

"Did you find anything?" I asked the tall lady.

"A few musket balls, a belt buckle, and a brass button." She came over and showed me the things in her treasure pouch. "Find Harry across the street. He found a silver lieutenant's button. Lisa found a musket by the river."

Mr. Shepherd's truck drove out of the fog and stopped in front of the house.

"That's Cooper," he shouted out the window.

"You're the famous Cooper?" the tall lady said. "So you're the one with the enchanted metal detector. I saw your amazing finds at the museum. I'm Emily." She held out her hand for an adult-style handshake.

"Nice to meet you," I said, shaking her hand as strongly as I could. A gust of wind blew through the valley, blowing big clouds of fog down the street.

I also shook the garage sale lady's hand because I didn't want her to feel left out. Then when Mr. Shepherd walked up to us, I reached out and shook his hand, too. Seeing him in a blue raincoat that covered his whole body, including a little helmet with a pop-up window for his face, purple gloves, and blue puffy boots made me feel guilty for ever thinking that he should be kicked out of my heart. He's probably the only person on the planet that needs full-body protection from fog, and I was ready to betray him because he wasn't around for my mind to remember those little things. Earth was right—I was a child for being so forgetful. I stared at the ground, ashamed of myself. I had to do something to stop those dumb tears from coming yet again.

So I gave Mr. Shepherd a hug right in front of everybody. It was uncomfortable because of the crunchy plastic raincoat, but I didn't care. The ladies probably felt left out that they weren't getting hugs, but there are limits. I can't just let everybody into the little door in my chest. That's why it has a key guarded by fairies riding dragonflies. (Note: I am not making a grow-up rule about that. It's cool.)

"I guess you like the project," he said when I uncrunched away from his raincoat.

I nodded.

Mr. Shepherd told me that Xavier's metal-detecting club and the museum had a big secret meeting and had planned a project to metal-detect this whole neighborhood. They knocked on people's doors and got permission to dig on private property. It would be impossible to do an archaeological dig on a whole housing development, so why not find everything they could before it was all lost from yard work and building pools and making houses bigger? They're going to make a big map of the battlefield that takes up one whole room of the museum, and display all the relics exactly where they were dug up.

"But I thought you hated metal-detecting."

"The museum is popping with visitors since I put up the relics from your yard, and also because of the newspaper articles. The *New York Times* ran a piece about this battle, and suddenly people care again. We've teamed up with Cornell University to do three archaeological digs in spots that have a high density of artifacts."

"Will my yard be one of them?" I suddenly realized that some other kid could get Mr. Shepherd in his backyard, telling stories in the sun and eating plates of vegetables and bread. That would make me so jealous I would just scream. Then wouldn't I feel dumb for not wanting the archaeologists there?

"A time machine is still waiting to be dug up," he said.

I smiled. Then I put my hands over my mouth because

it was breaking Earth's rule. Another wind whipped down the street, clearing away more of the fog. The sun peeked out, and that's when I noticed just how many people were metal-detecting on the hillside. I ran over to a high spot and tried to count them all—but it was impossible. A bubble of happiness gurgled inside of me, but I wouldn't let it out until the prophecy came true. I remembered Earth's words exactly:

*"You are not to smile or rejoice again until you see the valley itself casting forth from its depths the sadness that has polluted this region for so long. Only then may you continue shining the light of your happiness on our hillsides."*

"Take that back," Earth said, grunting. A musket ball popped out of the ground and landed in the hand of one guy who was digging. Artifacts were launching out of the ground all over the place, and I could hear Earth breathing a sigh of relief. My heart felt lighter as all the ancient souls inside me learned that their valley was becoming pure again. I wanted to open the little door and free them all, but it wasn't the right time. Instead, I smiled and shouted as loudly as I could, putting my arms in the air.

"You can't make us all move, Iron Boots!" My words echoed in the valley. I couldn't stop laughing, and my breathing was fast. A truck whizzed by on the highway and honked. Even the driver understood what was happening here.

I hopped on Squeaky and rode him back to my steep street. I didn't remember if I had even said goodbye to Mr. Shepherd. I waved and smiled at everybody who was metal-detecting.

"I bet you're thinking that this is the best day ever," Squeaky said.

"It's good to have you back, Squeaky." I petted his handlebars.

"You just never know what's going to blow into this valley," Wind said.

"Oh, hello, Wind. I'm sorry I didn't trust you."

"It'll take patience to make this valley like new."

"Now I'm giving you a permanent place in my heart."

"Then our friendship is off to a wonderful start."

"So you won't scare me anymore at night?"

"Oh, but young boys can use a good fright."

"Then maybe you can whip up a storm and cancel school?"

"Something tells me you've broken your second rule."

"I'd really like the power to make you start and stop."

"I'm not a tool to be used, like a mop."

"Did you know that my favorite color is orange?"

The wind went quiet. The fog was completely gone, and our whole valley was coated in a dewy, shimmering glaze. There wasn't a rainbow, but I made one in my mind—it went across the whole valley from the top of our mountain to the one on the far side. I giggled, wondering how many other boys at school knew how to silence the wind.

# CHAPTER 38

I dragged Mom out of bed and made her walk all the way into the backyard in her nightgown. We went behind the barn, through the hidden path, to the secret flower patch. There was a better view of the people metal-detecting from back there, at least the ones on that side of the wall of pine trees. It took a long time to explain everything to Mom, and she didn't see how this would make Iron Boots go away—but I begged her, please please please, with fifty-seven more pleases, if I could spend the weekend helping out Mr. Shepherd on the hillside.

She said yes, and then it took forever to get her to walk back to the house. The sticks and shrubs kept getting stuck on her nightgown. I put my treasure-hunting belt on and grabbed Decto and Mini-Decto, and we hopped onto Squeaky and whizzed down the road. My bicycle helmet wasn't even uncomfortable anymore.

"This is the big world out there," Decto said to Mini-Decto. "You were too young to remember."

"World!" Mini-Decto said.

Strangely, I didn't metal-detect too much in the beginning. My job was to run around crazily to all the diggers and help put blue numbered flags in the spots where they uncovered relics. Mr. Shepherd marked them down on a sheet of paper. We were a team. I followed his truck as he drove two miles an hour to each new spot. He never once said that he had to leave and go do something better. We only stopped to have lunch—there were hundreds of metal detectors and people eating in a big field. A truck came with mounds of McDonald's bags.

"This is a French fry," Decto said to Mini-Decto. He put one long French fry in the little guy's mouth, and it slowly disappeared as he chewed it. Then his eyes opened wide, and he started panting for more.

It didn't even bother me that Decto and Mini-Decto mostly kept to themselves, like always. I met a lot of new people who had the same hobby as me. Most of them had much better gear. They wore headphones and used special tools to cut different kinds of ground. One shovel had a jagged side for cutting plant roots that get in the way. There were special tweezers with rubber tips for pulling delicate items out of the ground, small magnets for poking through dirt piles, and deluxe carrying cases for the metal detectors.

Everybody was extra-nice to me because I was Cooper, the kid who started this all—but they also liked that I could tell them almost anything about the battle, and about the whole Revolutionary War. It felt safe to be near all those people, like when we have a lot of customers in the barn at the same time. For some reason Iron Boots didn't have any power when everybody else was around. Sometimes everybody was talking at once, and only the metal detectors were listening.

After lunch my job was to knock on people's doors and ask them if they had found any old stuff over the years while gardening or doing other yard work. Amazingly, a lot of people had stuff—most of them didn't know what it was but kept it around anyway. One guy had a jar of musket balls over his fireplace. They all donated their stuff to the museum project. Hardly anybody slammed the door in my face. I only had to pout once and speak in an extra-innocent, batting-my-eyelashes, puppy voice.

I followed Mr. Shepherd's orders the whole weekend. He never ran out of stuff for me to do, and everybody gave him respect. He was the boss of a lot of people, which made me even more proud that he was my actual friend—the guy who didn't give up on me even after I threw rocks at his truck for ten minutes. I thought back to the bad old days, when I used to think that his purple amulet was evil, and that he was a goofy guy with weird clothes who just wanted to steal my garage sale treasures.

Dumb, Cooper, dumb.

That weekend seemed to last forever, but then the wind blew something awful into our valley to punish me for my dumbness. It was . . .

School!

Actually, the first month of school wasn't that bad because our assignment was to write a report about what we did over our summer vacation. I used the long sequence that I had been working on, about the history of this valley and my adventures—only I made it start with twin boys battling each other for control of Earth. It was one hundred steps, and it ended with the museum project. My teacher gave me an A and put it up on the bulletin board. Maybe she just felt bad that me and Mom were in the newspaper a lot lately.

Reporters often came and took pictures of me and Mom. One picture showed me with my best pouty face. Another showed me holding on to Mom's leg. Soon, more signs started appearing in front of our house, only the new signs weren't angry at us. They were nice. One said, PRIVATE PROPERTY—DON'T STEAL THIS LAND. Another read, COOPER AND HIS MOM CAN STAY. There were lots of them. I didn't put these signs on the lonely side of the barn. I arranged them so that they weren't blocking each other, and all the customers could read them.

One day Mr. Shepherd came by and told us that Iron Boots had abandoned his plans to steal our house because too many people were against it. He said nobody wanted to extend the park down the mountain and into our backyard anymore. Artifacts were popping up all over the place, so they would have to kick a hundred families out of their homes to get all that land. The museum project won out.

Mr. Shepherd, Jill, me, and Mom traded hugs back and forth until there was nobody left to hug. A tear nearly fell out of my eye, but then it remembered my grow-up rule about no more crying, and jammed itself back inside. But then the sneaky little thing trickled down the inside of my left nostril and came out above my lip. It squeezed into the crease between my lips and traveled sideways until it left my mouth. Then it dropped off my chin and splattered onto a piece of gravel, turning it shiny.

I visited Jan to tell her the good news and to thank her for helping me and Mom. Even though our adventure was over, the whole experience had given me a tiny wrinkle in my face. I pointed to it and told her that it would always contain the story of how she helped me rid this valley of sadness. After explaining how she was permanently locked away in my heart, I brought in a huge bag of metal trash from my backyard and dumped it on the pile in the basement so it could mingle with the metal scraps that she and Xavier found over half a century.

"You took flight as an Early Bird and transformed into my Little Butterfly," Jan said, giving me a hug.

The next day I rode Squeaky back over to Jan's house to show her the Higley copper coin. She had never seen it, due to all that drama with me being grounded and Iron Boots trying to take our land. She sat down in her chair and examined it for a long time. She hummed a sweet melody, so I knew it was a special coin.

"This coin is worth over ten thousand dollars," she finally said.

It's a good thing the floor has a soft rug because I collapsed right there in front of her.

I crawled over to her and reached for the display case. "Will somebody really pay that much for one coin?"

"Oh, sure. If you want to sell it, I can help you have it authenticated and put in an auction." She handed it back to me.

"But you and Xavier never sold your coins."

"It's for you to decide. Your heart will guide you."

I didn't sell the coin even though it would have been enough to pay off our taxes. The little deer on the front looked sad, like he knew that he might be separated from the rest of the artifacts. All those things were part of our history and belonged together in the museum display. You should have seen the look on Mr. Shepherd's face when I gave him the coin. He told me I can take it back from the museum if I ever change my mind. It was nice of him to say it, but I'm just going to go to twice as many garage sales to pay off our taxes.

When I came off the school bus one windy day, red vans were parked on the gravel lot. My heart beat fast until I saw the name CORNELL UNIVERSITY on the side of them. People were in the backyard putting sticks in the ground connected by string. They set up tents and carried supplies inside. They were all wearing boots, but they were really nice to me. I already added to my grow-up rules that it doesn't matter if somebody wears non-squishy boots or really soft sneakers. They could be nice either way.

At first I was a little shy around everybody, but Mr. Shepherd kept including me in the conversation, and all the archaeologists talked to me so much that eventually I forgot to be afraid. My best friend out of the whole group is Pix. He doesn't have any hair at all, and his whole body is covered with tattoos. One of them shows a creepy castle, and it covers his entire back. He's really friendly, but he calls me Coopy, which I don't really like. But just one of his arms is bigger than my body, so he can call me whatever he wants.

Mr. Shepherd comes by a lot to check up on how things are going and to see if there are any artifacts that Cornell doesn't want, so they can go in the museum. Pix gave him an ivory powder horn that was found in the first hole. It's some poor cow's horn that was made into a holder for gunpowder. It has a map carved into its side that was done by one of the American soldiers, showing the path the army followed while marching up here.

The agreement is that Mr. Shepherd has to tell me stories for at least a half hour in the secret flower patch before he leaves—but usually I can get him to stay for an hour if I ask enough questions. We talk about everything now, even Tanner. I also get to help him work on the museum display on Saturdays, after we're both done going to garage sales. We haven't started yet, but we will soon. He's going to drive me in his truck, and Mom said it was okay.

# CHAPTER 39

One day I was hanging out in the backyard with everybody when Mr. Shepherd showed up with a new present for me. It was a book, but all the pages were blank. That gift was a little disappointing.

"It's for you to fill up with your stories," Mr. Shepherd said.

"That sounds like a lot of work."

"I started it for you. It's part of a bedtime tale I've been working on for my kids."

The first page had tiny writing that was hard to read:

Once upon a time there were two civilizations that flourished on different parts of the Earth. After thousands of years they collided, and from the impact a child was born—one who would grow up to heal the land where the wound occurred. There he would dig, until he pieced together the whole story of what happened, including how he came to be.

"It's a little wordy," I said, closing the book.

Mr. Shepherd laughed. "Fill the book, Cooper. We're counting on you." He handed me a pink pen with a mane of purple threads flowing off the back.

"Pix, do I have to?" I looked at him in desperation. He was much bigger than Mr. Shepherd.

"Afraid so, Coopy. I want to be the first to read it."

"Oh. Then can I make my own beginning and use your paragraph later in the story?" It was obvious that the book should start, *My name is Cooper, and when I turned nine I started going to garage sales on my bike.*

"Sure," Mr. Shepherd said.

Ideas started jumping into my brain. The beginning was done, the middle would be easy, but I didn't know how the story should end. I brought the book to school every day and worked on it during free writing time, tickling my forehead with the hairy pink pen until ideas popped out.

After a few weeks I *finally* came up with an ending—I was staring out the bus window and smiling the whole ride home. When the bus stopped at the bottom of my street, Hunter Dodson said for the millionth time that the Battle of Newtown wasn't important because fewer than fifty people were killed. He's jealous that there's an archaeological dig in my backyard and not his, and that Mr. Shepherd spends time with me and not him. I actually said something instead of just walking off the bus. I asked him if he even knew one person who was ever killed. When he said no, I slung the backpack over my shoulder and hopped onto the road.

When I got home, Mom was reading a newspaper in her aluminum chair. She tried to hide it, but I could see that she had circled a few garage sale ads. I pretended not to notice and gave her a kneeling hug. The archaeologists were busy in the backyard, so I ran inside and got the silver dime that Decto and Mini-Decto had helped me find down by the river a few days earlier. I casually walked out back.

"Hey, Cooper," Hannah said. "Whatcha got there?"

"What's up, Coopy? You found a seated liberty dime? Nice going."

"Yo, Coop, you're the man." Jack gave me a high five.

"Coop's the champ!"

Dropping the dime in my pocket, I walked to the edge of the steep forest and took a few steps onto the hillside. I stumbled backwards after it quickly got steep. When Dad carried me back here on his shoulders, he couldn't have gone any farther than that. It would have been too dangerous for me.

I spun around to see if anybody would tell me to stop. They were all back in their square holes with little brushes and tiny shovels. I leaned back—only the bottom trees were visible from so close, plus a few higher branches that poked into the sunlight. I took a few steps in reverse, until the steep hill tried to make me run forward. Then I spun around and grabbed a twisty, bumpy root sticking out the side. I pulled myself up and grabbed onto the skinny trunk of a baby tree. Nobody seemed to be stopping me, so I pulled myself from tree to tree until the backyard got smaller beneath me.

I forget how long I monkey-climbed, but one time I wanted to see how high my body was, so I hugged a rough, prickly tree trunk and twisted my neck around. Down below were the tippy-tops of our house and Jill's house. The archaeologists looked like little dolls, except for Pix, who looked like a regular-sized human. A cool breeze filled my nose with sweet-smelling sap. A pinecone fell off the rustling branches and tumbled down until it disappeared into a thicket.

Every clump of dirt, rock, leaf, and pinecone on the forest floor was special up there because nobody had seen them for hundreds of years, except for the ghosts and the forest creatures. My arms were tired of pulling me, but I had to keep going because there was something I wanted to do—so I pulled harder and didn't look back anymore. My lungs let out a squeal when a snake wrapped around my leg, but it was really just a vine. Some crows cawed in the distance to answer whatever I had said in their language.

I gorilla-climbed by grunting and clutching a tree trunk, then rolling my body around it until sharp bark was digging into my back. Then I monster-climbed by letting out a roar and bursting up to another tree. I robot-climbed when I was too tired to think anymore—I just let my body do what it wanted. Some trees had turned red, yellow, or orange, and their soft colors made the forest seem warm and cozy. I got tired and sleepy.

Eventually I saw sunlight above me. The trees gave way to a steep part of the hill that was covered in dirt and small bushes. Above it sat a little private clearing that was probably Ghost Conductor's Bluff—only it looked different up close. I pulled on roots and thick clumps of grass until dirt covered my clothes and the sunlight dried the sweat on my face. When I made it to the top, I flopped onto my back, waiting for my heart to slow down and my breath to go back to normal. A little white cloud hovered in the sky, looking exactly like it always did.

I hopped to my feet. A cold wind made me shiver. In front of me was the most spectacular view—Route 17 filled with tiny toy trucks, the shiny green river that twisted next to the highway like a slithering serpent, hazy valleys jumbled together near the horizon. The jammed-together buildings of Elmira looked tired and dirty off to my right. I finally figured out why some of the distant forests have gaps that go up the mountain in a straight line—they're paths for electricity poles to climb one mountain and connect to the next.

From my spot I could see the secret flower patch on the other side of the wall of pine trees, the pointy treetops, the reflective roof of the barn, and Mom reading. Mom and the sunflowers were so close together that it made my journeys through the hidden path seem not so daring. I still couldn't figure out why that long line of trees went down our side of the valley, but at least there's one mystery left around here.

A little way north along the peak of the mountain was a white stone monument pointing skyward—part of Newtown Battlefield State Park. It finally made sense why they put the park there. The battle took place all over this mountain, so why not pick the spot with the coolest view? Mr. Shepherd told me that people were trying to get the park promoted to a national park, and our whole adventure could help make that happen.

With my arms out I spun around and around, making the endless valleys blur together. From my secret spot I could go any which way and find a good journey, and have something to tell Pix and Mr. Shepherd, in a keep-my-special-secret kind of way. I stopped spinning when a control panel covered with buttons and flashing lights lifted out of the ground.

It was time.

I pressed a red button and at once the mountain began rumbling. Little metal barriers came up around me. The ground shook like an earthquake, sending owls, chipmunks, rabbits, gophers, butterflies, caterpillars, snakes, foxes, squirrels, and deer fleeing the forest. A million pinecones rushed down the hill in an avalanche, but got all jammed up before they could spoil the archaeological dig. Nobody down below seemed to notice that the slumbering hilltop was waking up.

Dirt fell away from the front of the bluff, revealing the steel nose of a giant train and a track that tilted upwards but ended suddenly in midair. Below, tree trunks crackled as roots tore from the ground. Out came gargantuan wheels, ten times taller than me and sparkling in the sunlight. When I pressed a blue button a cloud of steam erupted from a vent, creating puffs of smoke that drifted away. A maze of poles and levers chugged to life, spinning on oily hinges.

"All aboard!" I yelled. My voice echoed in the valley.

Mom kept reading her book in the tiny aluminum chair, like she didn't even notice that a sky-high train clanked and whistled behind the house. Some archaeologists looked up for a moment but quickly went back to work. I pressed a yellow button and the train inched forward, sending a thousand years' worth of dirt draining out of hidden crevices. When I pushed a lever the train zoomed ahead, off the end of the track, and into the sky. We soared away from the mountain as the wind made my eyes tingly. I pulled a lever and the train tilted back, heading straight for the sun.

We passed the puffy cloud. Tanner sat on his shiny new bike wearing sunglasses, kneepads, and a silver helmet. He waved to me as the train picked up speed and headed for the edge of the sky. Below, bits of the mountain rained down into my backyard and clattered on the roof of the barn. Everybody down there would have to go on without me for a while.

The air got thin and hard to breathe. My lungs felt ticklish, and the clouds warned me to turn back. But I had to go a little farther, just a bit more, until I could finish what I wanted to do. When the train slammed into the Earth's outer atmosphere, little fires sprouted up around the wheels. I pressed a green button and fountains of water put them out and drenched me with cool spray.

Angels with gigantic wings appeared in the distance. I pressed the white button. Thousands of fairies riding dragonflies appeared, swarming around my chest until they inserted their little key into the wooden door. It opened on creaky hinges. The spirits burst out and flew in a long line of dark shadows. After every last spirit was free, I slammed the door and pulled a lever that made the train go in reverse. My stomach felt queasy as we plunged back toward Earth. The parade of spirits became tiny specks against the fiery sun.

The moon gave me a sliver of a smile because it knew that I would be making this trip again when it was full.

I wasn't afraid of the haunted forest anymore.

—THE END—

# AUTHOR'S NOTE

The Sullivan-Clinton Campaign of 1779 is considered by many historians to be the first U.S. government response to an act of terror committed on American soil. The Battle of Newtown, on August 29, was its largest conflict. Today, part of the battlefield sits under a housing development. Residents occasionally dig up musket balls, buttons, belt buckles, and other artifacts during gardening and yard work.

I gathered the historical information regarding the Sullivan-Clinton Campaign, the Battle of Newtown, the League of the Iroquois, the Declaration of Independence, and various colonial facts from the latest secondary sources dedicated to these subjects, primary sources where available, Internet research, and visits to the Chemung Valley History Museum, Chemung County Historical Society, Newtown Battlefield State Park, and local neighborhoods sitting on the battle site. I would like to thank the many people who assisted me, either in person or by e-mail and phone, during the time I spent on this project.

For the sake of Cooper's adventure, I've placed a number of relics on his property—the cannons, the Higley copper coin, the button with the 4 on it, and the brass tomahawk—that were not actually found there. In reality, the Americans did abandon some of their heavier artillery after the Newtown battle, including two six-pound cannons. A letter written to George Washington explains that they were sent back to Fort Sullivan at Tioga by boat, but they disappeared from the historical record after that. In Cooper's story the cannons reemerge, but I have added the fictitious twist that they were buried on the land where Cooper now lives rather than being carried downriver. Higley copper coins, brass tomahawks, and numbered regiment buttons are the types of items that might have been lost on that eighteenth-century battlefield, but these specific metal objects were included for the sake of the plot.

The ivory powder horn discovered by the archaeologists is inspired by similar horns that have survived from this campaign, on which soldiers sometimes carved maps as a record of their journey. Additional metal finds uncovered by Cooper and Decto were inspired by items—such as bayonets, drinking flasks, eyeglasses, sword handles, and teapots—that were found on other Revolutionary War–era battlefields and military campsites and which are housed in various museums around the country. All together, these relics buried in Cooper's backyard created an untouched battlefield for him to make archaeological discoveries and go on a historical adventure.

# FURTHER READING

*A Guide to the Battles of the American Revolution,* by Theodore P. Savas and J. David Dameron (New York: Savas Beatie, 2006).

*The Iroquois in the American Revolution,* by Barbara Graymont (Syracuse, NY: Syracuse University Press, 1975).

*The Sullivan-Clinton Campaign, Parts 1–5* (Elmira, NY: Chemung County Historical Society, 2004–2005).

*The Wilderness War,* by Allan W. Eckert (Ashland, KY: Jesse Stuart Foundation, 2003).

*Year of the Hangman: George Washington's Campaign Against the Iroquois,* by Glenn F. Williams (Yardley, PA: Westholme Publishing, 2005).

CPSIA information can be obtained at www.ICGtesting.com
Printed in the USA
LVOW13s1445130414

381505LV00006B/703/P

9 781608 981502